W9-CLQ-234

MOTOR CITY BLUE

LOREN D. ESTLEMAN is a graduate of Eastern Michigan University and a veteran police-beat journalist. Since the publication of his first novel in 1976, he has established himself as a leading writer of both mystery and western fiction. His western novels include Golden Spur Award winner *Aces and Eights*, *Mister St. John*, *The Stranglers*, and *Gun Man*. His Amos Walker, Private Eye series includes *Motor City Blue*, *Angel Eyes*, *The Midnight Man*, *The Glass Highway*, Shamus Award winner *Sugartown*, *Every Brilliant Eye*, *Lady Yesterday*, and *Downriver*; the most recent Walker mystery, *The Hours of the Virgin*, was published in August 1999. Estleman lives in Michigan with his wife, Deborah, who writes under the name Deborah Morgan.

"This is one genre author who follows the procedures [of detective fiction] without debasing the language or insulting the intelligence."

— Marilyn Stasio
New York Times Book Review

"Mystery aficionados compare [Estleman's] prose to Ross Macdonald's and Raymond Chandler's. As a Macdonald fan, I can testify this writer does that master one better."

— *Forbes*

MOTOR CITY BLUE

LOREN D. ESTLEMAN

ibooks
new york
www.ibooksinc.com

DISTRIBUTED BY SIMON & SCHUSTER, INC

An Original Publication of ibooks, inc.

Pocket Books, a division of Simon & Schuster, Inc.
1230 Avenue of the Americas, New York, NY 10020

An ibooks, inc. Book

ibooks, inc.
24 West 25th Street
New York, NY 10010

The ibooks World Wide Web Site Address is:
http://www.ibooksinc.com

You can visit the ibooks website for a free read and
download of the first chapter of each of the ibooks titles:
www.ibooksinc.com

ISBN 0-671-03898-2
First Pocket Books printing January 2000
10 9 8 7 6 5 4 3 2 1

Cover design by Jason Vita
Interior design by Michael Mendelsohn at MM Design 2000, Inc.

In memoriam
JOHN BRANCH
for kindnesses unforgotten

Share your thoughts about these and other ibooks titles
in the new ibooks virtual reading group at
http://www.ibooksinc.com

MOTOR
CITY BLUE

1

FACES FROM THE PAST are best left there. If, two hundred odd pages from now, you agree with me, this will all be worthwhile.

My lesson began while I was setting fire, or rather trying to set fire, to a Winston in just about the only place where it's still legal to do so, a public street corner. Specifically, it was the corner of Watson and Woodward, and a November gale was whistling toward Lake St. Clair that was just a couple of knots shy of the one that washed Superior over the *Edmund Fitzgerald* four years ago. I tugged down my hat to keep it from bouncing clear to Grosse Pointe, where it had no business being, swung my back into the wind, and was coaxing a steady flame out of my third match when the man to whom the aforementioned face belonged stepped out through the doorway in which I was huddled, bumped into me, and knocked the match out of my hand into the slush at my feet.

Back some more. For three weeks now I had been an employee of the Midwest Confidential Life, Automobile & Casualty Company in the capacity of investigator, which is my life's calling. Off and on for that same period I had been watching the man who lived on the second floor of the establishment on the opposite corner. This was a homely, soot-darkened building erected about the time Detroit was beginning to make something out of an adolescent auto industry, a crumbling structure that had somehow managed to retain its dignity in spite of the deterioration of the surrounding neighborhood and the garish legend on the marquee of the five-year-old movie theater on its ground floor: 24-HOUR ALL-MALE SEX SHOW. UNDER 18 NOT ADMITTED. Before that it had been a massage parlor and before that a flophouse, the natural fate in this town for a hotel that had begun its existence catering to the millionaires of another era. The gentleman in the apartment above the theater had filed suit against a client of Midwest Confidential's for injuries sustained in a fall which, he claimed, left him unable to walk without the aid of canes and a pair of steel braces on his calves. Medical tests having proved inconclusive, and it being company policy to investigate all claims, it fell to me to get the goods on the plaintiff, assuming that there were goods to be got.

The brand name was patience. Sometimes on foot, sometimes parked across the street in my heap, I had shot most of November keeping an eye on George Gibson's comings and goings in the hopes of catching him without those canes. In my pocket was a Kodak Instamatic 20, the best thing modern technology has come up with since the telephone tap, to record the event when and if it occurred. The Nikon in my car was a more reliable piece of equipment, but it wasn't as easy to conceal on my person, and I'll sacrifice quality any time if reaching for it might cost my cover.

Dry, grainy snow—the kind that usually falls in the city— heaped the sills of unused doorways and lined the gutters in narrow ribbons, where the wind caught and swept it winding like white snakes across the pavement, picking up crumples of muddy newspaper and old election campaign leaflets and empty condom wrappers and broken Styrofoam cups as it went, rattling them against the pitted sides of abandoned cars shunted up to the curb; weathering the corners off ancient buildings with bright-colored signs advertising various hetero-and homosexual entertainments; banging loose boards nailed over the windows of gutted stores defiled with skulls and crossbones and spray-painted graffiti identifying them as street-gang hangouts, Keep Out; buckling a billboard atop a brownstone two blocks south upon which a gaggle of grinning citizens gathered at the base of the Renaissance Center, near where its first suicide landed, urged me in letters a foot high to Take Another Look at Detroit. The air was as bitter as a stiffed hooker and smelled of auto exhaust.

I was prepared, when the match was jostled from my grip, to defend myself against the usual cluster of lean young blacks policing their turf, but was surprised when I swung around to find myself facing a well-fed Nordic type with gray eyes and blond hair wisping out from beneath the fake fur rim of an astrakhan-style hat. I was doubly surprised when, half a beat later, I recognized him.

It wasn't mutual. Scarcely glancing at me, he muttered a terse apology and pushed past, heading south in stiff, hurried strides. I watched his retreating back for a long moment, then, decisively, snapped away my cigarette, which I had nearly bitten through upon collision, and began following him. It didn't look as if Gibson was coming out again today, and the coincidence of literally bumping into someone I had last seen seven years ago in another hemisphere set my curiosity ticking.

Wherever he was going, he was either already late or didn't want to be. Twice more he came close to running into pedestrians as he threaded his way through the sidewalk traffic, eyes skimming the street in search of a cab, and once he was forced to do a wild Charleston to keep from falling when he slipped on an icy patch. Not that the narrow escapes made him any more cautious. If anything, he stepped up his pace as if to make up for the lost time. I followed at what the spy novelists call a discreet distance, which means I almost broke my own neck trying to keep him in sight.

I'd be younger now if he'd caught that cab. Then I would have lost him and gone home and maybe read about him in the papers later and sat there reminiscing for a few minutes, and that would have been the end of it. I was to wish that he had, before much more time had passed. But there were no cabs in sight, and I'll always blame Checker for everything that happened afterward.

I tailed him to Adelaide—scene of crusading reporter Jerry Buckley's gangland-style execution in 1930—where he finally spotted one of the yellow cabs and was stepping out to flag it down when a blue Nova that I hadn't noticed pulled over from Woodward's outside lane to box him in between two parked cars. He hesitated a moment, then, cursing, reversed directions and started to hasten around one of the cars when a man on the passenger's side of the offending vehicle climbed out and called his name. The nasal voice was pure Rhett Butler.

At the sound of his name, my quarry stopped and turned. This gave the man who had been driving the Nova time to circle the parked car and approach him from behind. This one and his companion looked enough alike to be brothers. Beefy and nose-heavy, they both wore dark suits beneath gray topcoats with black ties and slicked their longish, dirty blond hair back greaser-style, the way a lot of them still do down south. The driver was larger and older, but aside from that they could have been twins.

A low conversation ensued, during which I stepped into

a doorway—force of habit—and pretended to be using its shelter to fire up a fresh fag while I watched. As I did so, a young, well-dressed woman who happened to be passing turned to give me the evil eye. I got it going and grinned at her through the smoke.

"Don't get the wrong impression," I said brightly. "It's marijuana." That didn't set any better with her. She kept moving.

I wasn't able to hear what the three were saying, but it was pretty obvious by their tones and gestures that my old acquaintance was burned about something and the others were trying to mollify him. After a few seconds of this the younger of the two rednecks placed a hand on the third man's arm as if to escort him to the car. The latter appeared to go along willingly. That's how it appeared. I'd been an MP for three years and I knew better. I recognized a no-resistance hold when I saw one; with that grip on his elbow it was either move or learn to get along with a stiff arm the rest of his life. The driver had an identical grasp on its mate. Together they led him to the car like a whipped spaniel.

At the last moment, when the back door was open and they were putting him inside, the younger of the abductors let slide his grip and their prisoner started to struggle, but the former put a stop to that in a hurry with a short, well-aimed jab just below the ribcage. It was an immobilizing blow. The captive stiffened and the two folded him into the seat and the younger man climbed in beside him and pulled shut the door in less time than it takes to tell it. Then his companion walked back around to the driver's side, slid in behind the wheel, and drove off south without so much as a chirp of rubber on the windswept asphalt.

It was a honey of a snatch. If you weren't watching closely it was just another car pool picking up a passenger on the way home from work. I probably drew more attention standing there in the middle of the sidewalk scribbling down the license plate number in my dog-eared pocket notebook than did the incident itself, which may or may not be a commentary on the attitude Detroiters have toward crime, depending upon whether you're working for the newspapers or the mayor.

I looked around for a cab, but I needn't mention what came of that. Then I made my way to the nearest public telephone, which wasn't near enough, and punched the right sequence of buttons to connect me with police headquarters. That beat hell out of the physical labor involved in spinning an old-fashioned dial. I asked for Lieutenant John Alderdyce, and after I had repeated the request for the benefit of a pair of hollow-voiced female receptionists, the lieutenant's deep tones came onto the line.

"Alderdyce."

"John, this is Amos Walker. I need a license plate number traced in a hurry."

"Call the Secretary of State's office."

"I don't know anyone there. That's why I called you."

"What's the beef?"

"A snatch."

"Call the Feds."

"Quit screwing around, John. I'm talking about life or death." That sounded like the set-up line to an old joke. I tried again. No, there was only one way to say it. I sketched out what I had seen. There was a pause before he spoke. Talking to him on the telephone, you'd never guess he was black. He grew up on the middle-class West Side and was educated at the University of Michigan, where competition with white students left him with little of the relaxed drawl his parents' generation brought north during World War II.

"Can you describe the victim?" he asked.

"Better than that. I can give you his name."

"Damned thoughtful of him to introduce himself." There was an edge to his tone.

"The guy was my company commander in Nam. That's why I was following him. Captain Francis Kramer, age forty, give or take a year, five-ten, five-eleven, a hundred and ninety pounds, blond hair, gray eyes—you getting all this?"

"Wouldn't miss it."

I described the abductors and the car they were driving, finishing with the license plate number. "Look," I said, "if you won't trace it for me you can at least put it through regular channels. I'm not after any favors."

"How many saw this besides you?"

"Nobody."

"Nobody?" Disbelief coupled with anger. "On Woodward at five-thirty in the afternoon? Who the hell are you trying to kid? The last time that happened was during the riots."

"I didn't say there was nobody else there. They just didn't see it."

"And you did."

"I was looking for it. I'm telling you, these guys were pros."

"I'll give it to the boys in General Service."

"Why can't you handle it?"

"I'm Homicide. I've got my hands full with the Freeman Shanks killing. Don't worry, I'll ask them to take special care with this one, seeing as how you and Kramer were friends. I wouldn't do it if our fathers hadn't been partners. I don't hate you yet, Walker, but give me time."

I let that slide. "We weren't friends. I just don't like to see people snatched on public streets in broad daylight. It makes me wonder who's next."

"Stay available. General Service will want to talk to you."

"I've an answering service and a beeper, if the batteries are still good," I assured him. "Any leads in the Shanks thing?"

"Several hundred. Which is why I'll be a member in good standing of the Detroit Yacht Club before it's solved. Unless you know something about that too?" It was sarcasm, but backed with desperation. The investigation into the August shooting of the popular black labor leader was in its third month and both the *News* and the *Free Press* were screaming for action or certain officials' scalps.

"Who killed Jimmy Hoffa?" I said.

"Go to hell, Walker." The line went dead.

2

C OME AND VISIT ME sometime in my little shack just
west of Hamtramck, but don't bring too many Poles
with you; the neighborhood is predominantly
Ukrainian and ancient antagonisms die hard. It's a one-story
frame dwelling, built during the great European famine in
the 1920s, when refugees came here in droves, and boasts
a bath, a bedroom, a combined living room and dining area
big enough for one or the other but not both, and a full
kitchen, currently an endangered species. It's not the lobby
of the Detroit Plaza, but it's still more space than one person
needs. Maybe when we know each other better I'll tell you
about the person who used to share it with me. In any case,
it will suit me until the taxes eat me alive.

I got home just in time to catch the meat of the six
o'clock news on Channel 4, the part that comes after the
first commercial when the sweetness and light they like to
lead off with these days is over. There was nothing about
Francis Kramer. Channels 2 and 7 had just as much to say
on the subject, but then unlike 4 they generally line up the
hard stuff for their first pitch and I might have missed it.
I'd bought the evening editions of the *News* and *Free Press*,
but I didn't expect to find him there. They had hit the street
about the time he was taking that jab in the liver.

Dinner was with Mrs. Paul, or maybe it was Birds-eye;
once the label's off they all defrost the same. Not that I can't

cook, but every now and then it's nice to see that somewhere someone's following a set pattern. Peas in one place,
meat in another, little round potatoes all lined up like lead
soldiers in neat rows. I broke them up with one deft stab of
my fork.

My digestive juices were massing for the kill when I returned to the television set. The Canadian station carried
hockey and I watched a couple of minutes of that, but they
staged one fight too many and I switched it off. If I wanted
to see human nature at its worst I'd go back to the news.
I'm talking about the fans, not the players.

I considered putting a 78 on the J. C. Penney stereo but
vetoed it. My collection of jazz and early rock had been a
source of some pride before the divorce settlement left me
with just a bunch of records. I could do without the depression playing one would bring on.

Out of sheer boredom I consulted the listing and struck
paydirt. Bogart was on Channel 50's Eight O'Clock Movie.
The Barefoot Contessa, not one of his best. But what the
hell, it was Bogart. I had an hour and a half to kill before
it came on. I settled into my only easy chair for a systematic
and intelligent reading of the *Free Press*, starting with
"Beetle Bailey."

The telephone hollered just as Rossano Brazzi stepped
out of the bushes with Ava Gardner's corpse in his arms. I
gave it its head until the credits flashed on the screen, by
which time it was winding up for its seventh ring.

"Amos Walker?" A nothing voice, not young, not old.
But definitely male. I confirmed his suspicion.

"Ben Morningstar wishes to speak with you."

My grip didn't crack the receiver; that would be an ex-
aggeration. But it came close. Ben Morningstar wasn't
someone you spoke with on the telephone. He was a name

in *Newsweek*, a photograph taken at a funeral by a G-man with a telephoto lens across the street, a pair of nervous hands fiddling with a package of Lucky Strikes in a Congressional hearing room on television in the early fifties. He was Anthony Quinn in a thinly veiled role that had never hit the theaters because the lawyers had it all tied up. He was the brass ring for every government prosecutor with his eye on the Attorney General's office. To Hymie "the Lip" Lipschitz, a smalltime bootlegger and numbers book forgotten except in an old Warner Brothers whitewash they keep bringing back on the late show, he was eighty pounds of cement and a lungful of Detroit River. After a couple of seconds, disguised as an hour, I found voice enough to say, "I'm listening."

"Mr. Morningstar doesn't use the telephone," explained the voice. "We'll send a car for you."

"From Phoenix?" That's were *Newsweek* had him living these days.

"From Grosse Pointe. Look for it in about an hour."

"No good. I'm out early. He can reach me at the office tomorrow afternoon." Tomorrow morning Gibson went out to collect his unemployment check, and while he wasn't dull enough to go on that errand without his canes, there was no telling what he might do in a hurry.

"We'll send a car." The line clicked and buzzed.

I stood there listening to the dial tone until the recording cut in to tell me to hang up. I cradled the instrument before the automatic warning system could start bleating. That's one more thing technology has taken from us lately, the right to leave the telephone off the hook. My only consolation was that this was one time I hadn't gotten myself into whatever it was I was in. So far as I knew.

At five minutes to eleven the doorbell clanged. For cross-town it was good time, but not spectacular. The 1967 riots having dealt a crippling blow to whatever nightlife the city had left, streets generally shut down around ten-thirty on a weeknight. From then until two, when the blind pigs started doing business, you could score a direct hit with a mortar shell on Cobo Hall from the upper end of Woodward without fear of striking anything in between.

When I opened the door I half expected a pair of plug-uglies poured into loud suits tailored to make room for their shoulder rigs, noses folded to the side and at least one cauliflower ear between them. I was disappointed to find a tall young black man standing on the stoop, the kind you see in the United Negro College Fund ads, all earnest and serious-looking in a blue Hughes & Hatcher under a light gray topcoat and black-rimmed glasses. If I'd wanted to see that I'd have gone down to Wayne State.

"Mr. Walker?" A bold voice, with just a hint of Alabama around the r's, once removed. It wasn't the voice I'd heard on the telephone. He had prominent teeth that flashed white and straight against his coffee-colored skin when he spoke. With the glasses, he reminded me of Little Stevie Wonder, another Detroit product.

"Where's your friend?" I asked him.

"Friend?"

"Don't you usually travel in pairs?" I struggled into my coat and screwed on my hat, smoothing the brim between thumb and forefinger.

He killed a moment studying that from both sides. Then his expression cleared and he smiled, blinding me with his eighty-eights. "You've been watching too many old movies. I'm too dark for George Raft and too skinny for Barton MacLane." He stood aside while I came out and closed the door behind me, locking it.

"A black man who knows old movies," I said, shaking my head as we made our way down the walk toward the street. I turned up my coat collar. The storm had blown over. The sky was as clear as Lake Michigan used to be and the cold was straight from outer space. Breathing it was like snorting ground glass. "I didn't know you partook."

"We don't spend all our time sticking up liquor stores and raping white women." The way he said it brought the temperature down another notch. Suddenly he sensed that I was kidding. The grin flashed. "I try to avoid Stepin Fetchit."

I laughed. "I had to know who I was dealing with."

"Did I pass?"

"Poor choice of words."

He gave that one all the mirth it deserved, and opened the passenger door of a yellow Pinto for me. There went another illusion. Next he'd be telling me they'd traded in their tommy guns on Daisy air rifles.

As a driver he was no great shakes, but at least he knew who has the right of way at stop streets—a dying art—and had the presence of mind to fry the eyeballs of a couple of jokers who refused to dim their lights as they approached from the other direction. After a dozen blocks I asked him how long he'd driven cabs.

His grin reflected the lights of an oncoming semi an instant before they reached the rest of his face. "How'd you know that?"

"You know the shortcut from Hamtramck to Grosse Pointe, but I'd bet my next retainer you're not from this part of town. The rest was guesswork."

"Sherlock Holmes, yet!" He let the tires slue their way through a slick spot without a qualm.

"It works one time out of six."

"I'm beginning to think the boss didn't make such a bad choice after all."

"Choice for what?"

He changed the subject. "A white man who wears a felt hat," he mused, eyes on the street ahead. "I didn't know *you* partook."

"Ninety percent of human body heat escapes through the head and feet," I said. "Want to see my socks?"

He chuckled but didn't say anything. The lines were drawn. I didn't ask him about his mission and he kept his nose out of my wardrobe. That left the weather, which was obvious. We made the rest of the trip in silence.

Whoever said all men are created equal must have had his eye on a home in Grosse Pointe. In this democracy, any boy can hope to grow up and live in the riverfront suburb, provided his credit rating is A-1 and he's prepared to mortgage himself to the eyes. Something over a hundred years ago, a healthy chunk of the area to the west was under the control of Billy Boushaw, boss of the First Precinct of the First Ward, whose old saloon and sailors' flophouse stood at the northwest corner of Beaubien and Atwater streets, but that's a slice of history they don't serve in the local schools. Now it's rich town, and the best-patroled square mile in the city. On maps it usually appears in green.

The house was a letdown. It didn't have more than forty rooms and the Austrian cavalry would have had to settle for column of sixes to get through the front door. An eight-foot stone wall surrounded five acres of yard over which kliegs mounted in trees near the house slung hot yellow light, which must have raised hell with the grass in summer. Here was where we crossed the line from public image into private necessity.

The man who appeared on the other side of the steel

picket gate as we pulled up to it had collar-length blond hair bare to the elements and crisp Teutonic features, the kind that look the same year after year until they finally fall apart overnight. He hadn't anything to worry about for a while. He was young and tan and healthy and wore a navy blue peacoat over a white turtleneck shirt. I satisfied myself that he wasn't the one I'd spoken with on the telephone either, when my companion climbed out to speak with him and he answered with a German accent straight out of *Stalag 17*. Ben Morningstar was an equal opportunity employer.

After a moment of conversation, during which he turned to squint at me through the windshield, the kraut nodded and unlocked the gate. He had it open by the time the black returned to the car and we drove through. A hairpin drive of freshly scraped asphalt swung past a skimpily modern front porch and broadened for the turnaround in front of an attached garage you wouldn't call skimpy unless the Pontiac Silverdome had spoiled you. We parked in front of the porch and got out.

The door was opened by a man in a red and black checked shirt fastened at the neck with a string tie and a Hopi totem of turquoise and silver. He was about my height, which made him less than six-four and more than five-ten, and wore a broad smile that went all the way up to his eyes, brilliants mounted in a setting of deep crow's-feet. Naturally lean, he had developed a slight paunch in recent years that he tried to keep cinched in with a belt with a rodeo buckle around Levi's so new they rustled when he moved. His face was full of tiny cracks and creases and burned by a kind of sun Michigan never saw. He looked fifty. He might have been forty or sixty. He had a full head of crisp black hair that swept down in a natural break over his right eyebrow.

It was a big head, much too big for the rest of him except for his hands, one of which enveloped mine in a grip like a third rail.

"You'd be Amos Walker," he observed, straining the smile a notch farther as he stepped aside to admit us. His drawl was pure El Paso.

"And you'd be Paul Cooke." I pried my hand loose and kneaded the bones back into place.

The twinkle in his eyes deadened. "We met?"

"You're famous. Ever since 'Sixty Minutes' aired that exposé last year about your hotel in Tucson. What did they call it? 'Little Caesar's Palace.' "

The grin was gone. He said something that was as much Detroit as it was wide open spaces, then, "You'll hear more of it before I'm through. Do you know I had to close down after that ran? No more convention business. Guests were scared they'd be machine-gunned in their beds. Nothing bad ever happened in that place, not in the six years I owned it. Okay, one rape, eighteen months ago, and they threw that suit out of court. Turned out she was a hooker. Those New York bastards are going to learn something about the penalties for libel."

"Slander."

"Huh?"

I said it again. "In print it's libel, spoken it's slander. Common mistake. TV newscasters make it all the time."

His face now was a desert. Nothing like a smile had ever grown there or ever would. He glanced at the black man, who took a step in my direction. I read his intent behind the glasses.

"I'm heeled," I said. "On my belt, a thirty-eight, left side." I unbuttoned my coat one-handed and spread my arms.

Without taking his eyes off mine, the younger man

reached under my jacket, groped around, and drew the blue steel Smith & Wesson from the snap-on holster inside the waistband of my pants. He handed it to Cooke, who accepted it by the butt between thumb and forefinger and watched as the other lifted my wallet and went on to pat all my pockets and run an expert hand around the inside of my thighs down to my ankles. Then he rose and, almost as an afterthought, removed my hat and subjected it to the same thorough analysis. By the time he was finished he knew how much change I was carrying without having seen it. Finally he stepped back with a nod and turned the wallet over to the Texan. Cooke opened it, glanced at the photostat license and the buzzer I had obtained from the Wayne County Sheriff's Department during my process-serving days and never given back, and returned it to the other, who handed it back to me. My faith in the conventions was restored.

"Not smart," said Cooke, still holding the revolver as if it were a dead rat. There were a few in his occupation who had no taste for iron. They paid others to carry it for them.

"I don't usually play in this yard," I replied.

There was nothing for him in that, so he let it float. "You'll get it back later," he snarled, thrusting the gun toward the black, who grasped it less gingerly and dropped it into his topcoat pocket. Then Stevie Wonder and the Midnight Cowboy ushered me without further preamble across a quietly carpeted foyer and into the Presence.

3

THEY GOT THE BODYGUARD from central casting. On the short side, with bowed arms and a chest you couldn't measure with an umpire's chain, he was doing a fair imitation of Gibraltar in the space between the two sliding library doors as we approached. His black suit was painted on and he wore his striped necktie in a knot you couldn't undo with a screwdriver and a pair of pliers. He had no neck, or maybe he did have and someone had accidentally chopped off his head and pasted a brown, gray-streaked wig on the stump and penciled on features to make it do for a substitute. Certainly they could have been penciled on, flat and lifeless as they looked, with bladderlike scar tissue over the eyes and a crescent of dead white skin on each cheek. Either he had Roderick Usher's ears or he had been watching through the crack between the doors, because we were still coming when he slid them open noiselessly on rollers and struck an *Arabian Nights* pose with one refinement, his thumb hooked in his lapel near where something spoiled the line of his suit beneath his left arm. I'd have laughed at him in the theater. Not here.

"It's all right, Merle," Cooke told him. "This is the guy."

Merle looked doubtful. "He carrying?"

Bingo. Smooth and moderately pitched, his voice was in such contrast to his bouncer build that I'd ruled him out as the man on the telephone before he'd opened his mouth. I was wrong. What's more, seeing him and hearing him at the same time, I suddenly knew who he was.

"Not now. Wiley frisked him."

"Check his socks?"

Cooke nodded, and favored me with a wry look. "He always asks that," he explained. "Ever since someone slipped past him two years ago with a baby Remington in his argyles."

I remembered the incident. Two bullets from a .32, one in the ribcage, the second describing a path beneath the scalp from a point just above the right temple around the skull to the nape of the neck. Morningstar was released from the hospital two weeks later, straight into a nest of popping flash-bulbs. His assailant was scooped up from the floor of the victim's living room by a couple of morgue attendants the afternoon of the shooting. There was the usual political circus afterward, the usual Grand Jury investigation, the usual congressional re-elections the following year to show for it. The unwanted publicity forced Morningstar into retirement, so they said, leaving a vacuum for all of two minutes until someone with a lyrical Mediterranean name stepped in to fill it.

"Aren't you Merle Donophan?" I asked the bodyguard.

He lamped me with ceramic eyes. "What if I am?"

"You were a Detroit Red Wing three years ago. I caught your act a couple of times at Olympia."

"Yeah?" Out the side of his mouth now. He was stepping into character. "The last one, too?"

"I didn't see it. I heard about it. A fight. You let some guy on the Maple Leafs have it with your stick."

"He hit me first. Only difference was I used two hands and he only used one. So how come they gave me the boot and not him?"

"You aren't still sitting in a sanitarium watching the wallpaper."

"Christ's sake, Merle, let them in and close that fucking door. Draft's worse than a bullet."

If you've never heard a man speaking with the aid of a mechanical voice box, I can't describe it for you. A Dempsey dumpster or an automatic garbage disposal unit that's suddenly found itself capable of human speech doesn't cut it. Alvino Rey came close when he used to make his electronic guitar talk on the old "King Family Show." That was what came to my mind when the monotonic complaint broke in from across the room.

The place had all the warmth and security of a dentist's waiting room. The only light came from one of those copper Christmas tree floor lamps with funnel-shaped metal shades drooping from it like leaves on a rubber plant. Like those in most rental homes, mansions notwithstanding, the room had no personality at all. That had to be provided by the figure slouched in the green Lazy Boy next to the lamp.

Whether Benjamin Morningstar, no middle name, was pushing eighty or dragging it behind him was something nobody knew, not even Ben himself. The record of his first arrest in 1917 had 1900 marked in the box labeled "Date of Birth," but that was likely the educated guess of an overworked cop. A couple of years this way or that hardly mattered now in any case.

He was wearing a mustard-colored baggy sweater with a shawl collar over what was probably an expensive white shirt, limp for lack of starch and too big for his wasted frame. Equally as loose, his trousers were charcoal gray with a pearl stripe and cuffs two-thirds the length of his perforated brown shoes. A stout cane with a rubber tip was hooked around the chair's right arm. One hand lay twitching within its reach in his lap, a pale, spotted thing that reminded me of old blue cheese encountered unexpectedly in a wad of foil in the refrigerator. The other was raised to his face, where it clutched a flesh-colored cup of perforated plastic around his nose and mouth.

His eyes were huge wet plums that shimmered behind thick corrective lenses as they watched us come in. Farther up, hair as black and gleaming as a new galosh grew straight back from his forehead with a single, startlingly white gash of a part following the path of a bullet long forgotten by everyone outside this room. Not a gray hair in sight. It made the rest of him look that much more worn out, like a shabby old chair with a crisp new doily pinned to its crown.

When we were all inside and the doors were closed he lowered the filter, and then I saw his eagle's beak with the skin stretched taut and shiny across its bridge and the strings of loose flesh suspended beneath his chin over the scars from his throat operation and the downward turn of his wide, arid mouth. For a moment a bloom of life showed in a thin red line around his muzzle where the cup had been pressed, but it quickly fled.

The liquid eyes lingered on me for a beat, then flowed to the bodyguard. "Well, take his things, Merle," he ground out. "You can't expect a man to listen to a proposition when he's sweating like a broiled hog."

Now that he'd mentioned it I noticed that the room was overheated. The furnace was on blow and I could feel the hot air pouring through the square register in the floor behind me. I shrugged off my coat and handed it and my hat to the ex-hockey player, who had stepped forward to claim them.

"Jeez, a fedora," he exclaimed, still Allen Jenkins. He

could turn it on and off. "I ain't seen one of them on nobody under fifty in years."

I'd already used up my line for that one, so I kept silent while he crossed the room to a door on the other side, opened it, laid my things on a bed in the darkened chamber beyond, and returned to his post in the center of the room. He moved with a gliding swing, one shoulder thrust forward, as if he were still on the ice. His hands were clenched, hairless knots of corded muscle with two knuckles for every one of mine. Too many sticks had been laid across them in the heat of competition.

Cooke caught the black man's eye and nodded. The latter stepped forward and laid my .38 on the polished surface of the narrow end table at the old man's left elbow.

"We found that on him," said the Texan.

Morningstar hardly glanced at it. "Give it back."

No one moved. Cooke started to speak. The old man cut him off with a peevish gesture of his right hand.

"Damn it to hell, can't you see it's unloaded?"

The other hesitated, then strode up to the table and lifted the revolver to examine it. Light showed through the holes in the chamber. He looked at me.

"You didn't ask," I said.

He snarled and slapped it stinging into my outstretched hand. I returned it to its holster. I didn't mention the cartridge under the hammer. Sometimes it's useful to let them think you're afraid of guns.

Wiley, the black man, was beginning to sweat. It broke out in beads along his hairline and started the slow descent down his forehead. No one had asked him to remove his coat. He'd melt into a coffee-colored puddle before he took it off on his own. It was so dry in the room a match could ignite the air. I decided to risk it.

"Okay if I smoke?" Morningstar nodded. I won't say he smiled as he did so. What passed for one could have been just a nervous twitch of his dry slit of a mouth. I eased out a cigarette and touched it off, drawing the cool smoke into my lungs along with God knows what else. The man in the chair sat motionless except for quivering nostrils, as if trying to breathe the overflow.

"Proposition?" I prompted.

The mouth twitched again. "You're all right, Walker. You know enough to give an old man some slack. Not many of these young bastards would." As he said it his eyes circled the ring of help, lighting on Cooke. "Paul, get the hell out of here. Take Wiley with you. I've seen enough *shvartzes* for one day." He watched their retreat until the doors rolled shut behind them. "That was one of Paul's ideas, hiring the colored to keep an eye on things back here. I suppose he's all right, but that don't mean I got to like him. His kind's one of the reasons I left this town in the first place. You think I'm a bigoted son of a bitch, don't you?" He nailed me again.

"I don't think unless I'm paid."

"Strutting around in that fag getup." He didn't appear to have heard me. "He don't dress that way in Phoenix."

"Wiley?"

"Cooke. Sit down. I've got a larynx from Sears and Roebuck and a guinea pig's stomach and one lung and half of the rest of me is scattered in jars from here to the West Coast. I don't need no stiff neck too."

The only other chairs in the room were a vinyl number with a low back and no arms and a cushy leather overstuffed the size of the Uniroyal tire display south of I-94. I chose the vinyl. I didn't want to fall asleep during the conversation.

"Go to bed, Merle," he said then.

The bodyguard hesitated. "You sure?" His eyes told me I'd been weighed on his personal scale and come up short. I didn't figure I was alone in this.

"Damn it, Merle, one of these days you're going to ask me that question and I'm going to fry your ass."

Merle muttered something on his way out that I didn't catch.

Morningstar sat back and let out his breath in a long, rattling sigh. "Athletes," he said. "I never met one with brains you couldn't strain through a towel." He lowered his eyelids for a couple of seconds, and I was beginning to wonder if he'd drifted off or worse when they creaked open again. "Tell me something about yourself."

"Why? You've had me checked out or I wouldn't be here."

"Humor me."

"I'm thirty-two years old. I was raised in a little town you never heard of about forty miles west of here. I've a bachelor's degree in sociology; don't ask me why. I tried being a cop but that wasn't for me so I let myself get drafted. The army taught me how to kill things and sent me out to do it, but along the way someone found out what I'd done before and they made me an MP. I liked almost everything about it except the uniform, so when I got out I looked for a way to do the same thing without wearing one. I'm still looking."

"You dropped out of the twelve-week police training course after eleven weeks. Why?"

"Like I said, it wasn't for me."

"You can do better than that."

I shrugged. "Another trainee propositioned me in the shower room. He was very insistent. I broke his jaw."

"That doesn't sound like something they'd bounce you for."

"The trainee was the nephew of a U.S. congressman."

"I see."

"I thought you would."

There was a short silence. Then, "You're supposed to be a man who keeps his mouth shut even at the dentist's."

"Who says?"

"What difference does it make?"

"I like to keep track of whose mailing list I'm on from week to week."

He said he thought that was wise and gave me a name I recognized, never mind what it was. "I'll be straight with you," he said then. "Yours isn't the only name I had and it wasn't the first I tried. I called two others, but one's out of town and the other don't do this kind of work no more. They said. I think they backed off when they found out who was interested. Does working for Ben Morningstar make any difference to you?"

"It means I can charge more."

Twitch. I was beginning to think it really was a smile. Then it was gone. "I'm told you specialize in missing persons as well as insurance fraud."

He was having trouble getting into it. I crossed my legs and tapped half an inch of cigarette ash into the near cuff, sat back to finish the butt. I studied his face through the smoke.

"Who's missing?" I asked.

4

HE SLID A WALLET-SIZE photograph out of his shirt pocket and handed it to me. Our hands brushed as I leaned forward to accept it. His had a temperature and consistency to go with its blue-cheese appearance.

It was a high school graduation portrait of a dark-haired girl with even darker eyes that looked as if they flashed and a complexion like twelve-year-old Scotch going down. She seemed pretty, but you can't trust school photos. Those touchup artists can make the picture of Dorian Gray look like Robert Redford at the beach.

"Relative?" I held onto it. Giving it back would be a gesture of rejection and if I put it in my own pocket I was hooked.

"Ward. Her father shot himself in '63 when the government indicted him for smuggling Mexican Brown across the border and I raised her. Her name is Marla. Marla Bernstein."

"Leo Bernstein's girl?"

He nodded. "I see you're up on your Cosa Nostra history. Yeah, Leo Bernstein. Son of Big Leo Bernstein, king of Robbers' Roost. But of course you wouldn't remember that. Your father might. That's what the papers called him when he was down in Ecorse during Prohibition, running Old Log Cabin across from Windsor. But he wasn't really big, just five-five, weighed maybe a hundred and ten pounds. They just called him that because Big Al was what the Chicago papers was calling Al Capone, the fat-ass guinea bastard. He was my partner. Leo, not Al. I guess I can say that now that the statute of limitations has run out. Not that it matters much anymore.

"I brought Marla up the best I could after my wife died. I must have done all right because she never gave me a reason not to be proud of her. Not until—" He stopped and cleared his stainless steel throat. The sound was like fire-crackers exploding inside a drainage pipe. "Last year, when she graduated high school in Phoenix, I sent her back here to a finishing school in Lansing. I haven't seen her since."

"Why Lansing? Why not some place in Arizona?"

"They don't have finishing schools in Arizona. They have spas and dude ranches and co-ed colleges, complete with hot and cold running gigolos and vending machines with rubbers in them in the men's rooms. I had my fill of them health nuts and horsey cowboy types hanging around her when she was living at home. Besides, I sent my kid sister to the same school in 1928 and I liked what they did for her there. Miss Fordham's School for Young Ladies, they called it then. Now it's the Miriam H. Fordham Institute for Women. The same woman runs it now that was running it then. Esther Brock. She's a good ten years older than me, but you wouldn't know it to look at her. You'd say it's closer to a hundred. But she hasn't changed her methods of teaching, so off went Marla to Lansing.

"She stopped writing home almost a year ago. I didn't think much of it at the time. Christmas vacation was coming up and I figured she was saving up news for when she came to visit. When Christmas came and went and she didn't show up I got Miss Brock on the horn.

"She said that Marla dropped out two weeks before the Christmas break. She told Miss Brock that she was going to get married and was on her way back to Phoenix with her fiancé to introduce us. She wouldn't be coming back to school. Later, one of her roommates saw her getting into a car parked in front of the school with a man behind the wheel. They took off before the roommate could catch up. That was the last anyone saw of her."

"Any description of the man or the car?"

He shook his head. "The car was either green or blue, or maybe black. The man was in shadow and had on a dark suit with a dark tie. You know kids. They never look at anything."

"Did you go to the police?"

"I got out of that habit fifty years ago when I found out you could blind most of them with a twenty-dollar bill. First thing they'd do is tip the press and then it'd be all over the country. 'Police Seek Mob King's Ward.' That's the kind of attention I raised her to avoid."

"Publicity could help turn her up."

"Not in this case. Just the opposite."

"What does that mean?"

The look on his face alarmed me. If he had a bad heart, and there was no reason to think he hadn't with everything else that was wrong with him, that grimace was as good an indication as any that an ambulance was in order. But then he resumed speaking and I realized the pain went much deeper.

"I hired a private dick in Lansing right after she disappeared, but he didn't have enough to go on and gave up when his last lead came up empty two months ago. He's thrown over his practice since and moved to California along with all the others who can't take this climate. I found out he'd gone the other day when I tried to reach him to tell him about this."

Slowly, much more slowly than the first time he went for it, he reached into the same pocket from which he'd drawn the graduation picture and came up with another square of white cardboard slightly larger than the first. He held it out for me to take as if the weight of it were too much for him to push. I had to come part way up out of my chair and seize it from his fingers.

I was holding a black and white snapshot mounted on heavy stock designed to withstand a lot of handling. It wasn't good photography. The lighting was bad and it was hard to tell at first glance just what was going on in the shabby room with a print of *September Morn* just visible in one corner on the wall. What was going on was a hell of a lot less subtle than the artist's rendition of a coy female bather. A pretty, dark-haired girl, nude except for a black garter belt, net stockings, and high heels, was down on one knee performing what the Supreme Court calls an unnatural act upon an amply endowed male. The girl could have been Marla Bernstein. Nobody had touched it up and the mortarboard was missing.

"Could be any one of a hundred girls," I said. "What makes you so sure it's her?"

"It's her." The tuning fork or whatever it was that imitated the vibration of vocal cords was barely buzzing. "I watched her grow up. I know. If I had any doubts, that mole on her right shoulder blade would clear them up."

I looked again. I hadn't seen it before. It wasn't the sort of picture in which you noticed such details right off.

"Have they seen this?" I inclined my head toward the sliding doors.

"They know about it. You're the only one I've shown it to since I first saw it a week ago. I wasn't figuring on pasting it in no scrapbook."

"Are you a collector?"

"Certainly not." A spark glowed in the viscous eyes. "An old associate of mine, never mind who, has part interest in a business that wholesales this garbage to porno shops and grindhouses in the area. It's a sideline. He hardly ever sees the stuff that passes through, but ten days ago he happened to drop in on the man who runs the place and this was laying on his desk. This associate has spent a lot of time in my home and knows Marla almost as good as I do. He recognized her right away and came to me in Phoenix."

"He say who took it?"

"He questioned his man. He wasn't sure. It could have come from any one of a dozen studios he deals with here in town or he might have bought it in a package from some hophead punk off the street. Hundreds like it cross his desk every day. He can't be expected to know the source of each one."

"Swell. How about mail order?"

"No way. That's a federal rap."

"I'll need his name."

The lines in his face tightened. "My associate?"

"The guy who works for him. Also a list of the studios he does business with if you've got it. If not I can get it from him."

"I guess I can give you that much. His name's Lee Q. Story. That's important, the Q. I hear he's particular about it. Runs a dump called Story's After Midnight on Erskine. Another *shvartze*, but I don't suppose I got to tell you that in this burg. Frankly, I was surprised to hear you was white, name like Amos."

"There are a few of us left. I guess I have to get it from him."

"Get what? Oh, the list. Yeah. I didn't have the stomach

for it. Bad enough I got to see that garbage from the outside on my way down Woodward without going in. When I was young those were all theaters, you know what I mean? Theaters. Paramount, Roxy, Bijou. Clara Bow. Ramon Novarro. Dick Arlen and Buddy Rogers in *Wings*. I seen that one three times, each time with a different girl. You know what's playing at the Roxy right now? *Sluts of the Third Reich*. What the hell kind of a thing is that to slap up on a sign a yard high for kids to read?"

Color came to his face like blood on a galled fish. I tried to break in before he had a stroke, but he was just warming up.

"This morning I had Wiley take me down Twelfth Street where I grew up. Rosa Parks Boulevard they call it now. It made me sick. They burned down the house I was born in. Burned it to the ground during the riots. Same thing with all the places I used to work to help support the family after my pa got killed. Nothing but black holes in the ground with here and there a chimney or a cast-iron sink sticking up out of them. I remember thinking as a kid how ugly it all was, that neighborhood, how it would be a blessing if somebody put a match to the whole thing. I was wrong. It's worse."

I had been scribbling the essentials of the case into my soiled notebook with a pencil stub I'd dug out from among the lint and paper clips in my pocket. Now he noticed that I had stopped. Something that passed for a wry look slithered over his fallen features.

"Go ahead and say it," he said. "I'm one of those old farts who talk too much."

I turned that one aside. "A man in your line has enemies. Could it be she was forced into this to get you?" I flipped the photo.

"The last of my enemies died ten years back. I'm retired. Everything I own now is in the form of investments, and Paul Cooke looks after those for me. Even if I had something they wanted, it wouldn't do them much good keeping me in the dark. I found out about this by accident."

"Through your associate."

He smiled thinly, without twitching. "I thought of that. I don't trust him any more than I do anyone else, but he's above suspicion in this case. He has no family, and the cancer that's eating out his stomach is going to kill him before the one in my lung kills me. We had a saying in the business. I guess it's still used. You can't take it with you."

"Anything else I should know about Marla? Hobbies? Ambitions? Needs, medical and otherwise?"

"Her health's good, so there's nothing there. She's a real good singer. Nice voice. Plays the piano like a pro. She always wanted to sing for a living, but I hoped the Brock woman would put a stop to that. Show business is full of fags and whores. I know. I used to own a nightclub."

I sat quiet for almost a minute, lips pursed, tapping the edges of the two pictures against the palm of my hand. I could feel his eyes on me. Finally I took a deep breath and put them away in my inside breast pocket along with the notebook and pencil. The pictures, not his eyes. They were right behind them without my having to do anything. I got up.

"My fee's two hundred a day plus expenses. First day in advance. I report when I have something, not before. Does that suit you?"

"The money's all right. I don't know about the report. I'd like to hear something daily if that's possible."

I was going to say no, but something had happened to

his eyes. The plums had dried. The shine was gone, I sighed. Walker, you weak-kneed son of a bitch.

"I'll give you what I can."

He nodded. The mere effort of moving his head down and up seemed to have taken his last reserves. "See Paul on your way out. He'll give you your first day's fee and a copy of the other dick's report, if it's any help."

I stepped into the bedroom and got my hat and coat. "One thing," I said, stopping before his chair. "I'm working on an insurance case at the moment. I'll be spending some of my time on that. But you'll get a full day's work every day. I don't sleep. Got out of the habit."

"So did I."

I said a farewell of some sort and set out for the door.

"Walker." Barely audible. I turned back. His lids were closed behind the thick spectacles and his head was leaning back against the chair's cushy support. His weight wasn't enough to make it recline.

"If I see my name in tomorrow's paper, yours will be in the next edition. Bordered in black."

I let myself out.

It was after two when Wiley dropped me off back at my place. I was too keyed up to sleep and all the good movie stations were off the air, so I snapped on the lamp next to my chair and settled down with a glass of Hiram Walker's, no relation, and the sheaf of papers Paul Cooke had given me to read. The Lansing P.I., some guy named Stillman, couldn't spell FBI and his grammar was strictly Remedial English 302, but he had a definite flair for narrative. The record of his nine-month search for Marla Bernstein engrossed me for a full five minutes before I passed out.

The strident jangling pierced whatever I was dreaming without deflating it and I slept on, waiting for the alarm to wind down. It didn't, and after a moment I realized it was the telephone. I untangled myself from the chair and the litter of typewritten pages scattered over my lap, stumbled over to the irritating instrument, tried to pick it up with my left hand, the one that was still asleep, gave that up and used my right.

"Twelve rings. That's some kind of record even for you."

It was John Alderdyce. I let my eyes focus on the dial of the watch strapped to my slowly wakening appendage and asked him if he knew it was 4 A.M.

"I've been telling time for years now," snarled the voice. "I want you to get your ass down here yesterday."

"Down where?"

"The morgue. You ought to enjoy it. It'll be like an army reunion."

That took a second to sink in. When it did I told him to expect me in twenty minutes and had my coat half on before I realized I was still holding the receiver. I replaced it and finished the job on my way to the garage.

5

I DRIVE THE KIND of car you don't park next to if the itemized price list is still stuck to your side window. As Cutlasses go it's no heap, but it has that archaic look that falls to any automobile more than two years old in this day of neurotic change, and in the right light it shows more dings than I can properly blame on General Motors. You'd never think to look at it that there's a 455 Cadillac Coup de Ville engine under the hood, or that it can hit sixty-five while you're still closing the door on the passenger's side. Part of that is due to the fact that it has less pollution equipment to drag it down than a Model T Ford, but so far I've been able to duck those periodic traffic stops the cops engineer to make sure no one's putting anything past the EPA. Since there's almost nothing moving before dawn, however, I took it easy on my way down the Walter P. Chrysler to Brush and Lafayette, where the county morgue is located behind Traffic Court, to avoid calling attention to myself, at no time exceeding the limit by more than ten miles an hour.

Alderdyce's name got me into cold storage, where I found him standing next to a wall full of things that looked like oversize file drawers but weren't, with a white-coated attendant and Inspector Proust, whom I recognized from my last visit to headquarters. I went over there anyway.

John Alderdyce is the only truly black man I've ever known. His skin is the color of the business side of a fresh sheet of carbon, with the same high gloss, and nobody looks better in a yellow silk bowling shirt. Not that we'd bowled together in a long time. Today he was wearing a pastel blue number with matching tie, a well-cut herringbone over it and a hip-length belted leather coat over that. If you can be a fashion plate on a police lieutenant's salary, John's what you'd have in mind for a model. Like something from the pages of a magazine if *Vogue* and *Police Times* ever merged. He has pugnacious, simian features with a brain behind them and wears his hair cropped short in a style that in the right light does a fair job of concealing the thin spots. This wasn't the light.

Proust was white, very much so since he practically lived under a fedora that made mine look like a Shriner's fez, and was partial to suits as gray as his hair and as rumpled as his face. He was a holdover from the days of the old city STRESS crackdown unit, before they started shooting at each other and arresting too many citizens of the wrong color. Part of the reason for his attitude toward people in general, and private investigators in particular, was that he thought he should be an assistant commissioner by now. That dated back to 1970, when, stepping out of a New York Central boxcar that had just been broken into by a young Negro, he screwed his .357 magnum into the youth's ear and said, "Guess who, you black motherfucker!" This unorthodox method of identifying oneself as a police officer was recounted widely after the young man testified in his own defense at his trial, and had a habit of cropping up again every time the subject of Proust's promotion came up before the predominantly black police commission. An inspector he remained.

"You got square wheels on that buggy of yours?" he said as I approached. He was considered the cophouse wit, which should give you some idea of the caliber of the humor down there.

"There's an energy crisis," I reminded him. "You want me to break the law?" I nodded at John, who nodded back. That was the level to which our friendship had deteriorated since the day the state police issued me my license. He nodded hardly less effusively at the acne-faced kid in the white coat, who grasped the steel handle of a nearby drawer and tugged it out a third of its length.

The harsh overhead light did little for Francis Kramer's baby-fat features, which had crossed that line and were on the path to total obesity. The thumb-size black hole in his left temple did even less. The bullet had burrowed behind his eyes, bulging them, and exited with more fanfare than it had made going in, blowing out the right side of his skull like an overinflated tire on a hot day. The color of his skin made me wonder if I'd ever again be able to enjoy a jar of homemade preserves once I'd seen the paraffin with which it was sealed.

I gave them a positive ID and added, "That left a mess somewhere." My throat felt tight.

"All over the back seat," confirmed the lieutenant. He nodded again and the attendant replaced the drawer, then left silently on rubber soles. "He turned up at City Airport at two-thirty, folded into the trunk of a blue '78 Nova. The license number you know. Ever hear the word stupid? A whole parking lot to choose from, and they dump it in the president's private slot. He called airport security; they noticed the blood and called us. The M.E. figures he left us about ten hours ago. That puts it pretty close to when you saw what you saw on Woodward."

"Told you so."

He scowled, an expression that gave his face a decidedly

African cast. "That's what I like about you, Walker. You never rub it in."

"What are we pissing around for?" snarled Proust. "Take him in and let's grill him."

"Mr. Walker is an eyewitness, Inspector, not a suspect. He came down here of his own free will."

"All right, it's your case and I won't interfere. But this son of a bitch knows more than he's spilling."

"I haven't spilled anything yet," I said.

"That's what I'm talking about!"

"Let's go down to headquarters, Amos." That was strictly for Proust. John never called me by my first name, not even when his father and mine ran a garage on McNichols and we played together as kids.

It was a brief, freezing walk from the morgue to police headquarters on Beaubien. I spent the next hour in a bare interrogation room in the C.I.D., repeating my story under questioning for the benefit of a squeaking tape recorder and a stenographer with nice legs but not much else, and when it was over we all knew exactly as much as Alderdyce and I had eleven hours earlier. I looked through mugs until my eyes got bleary, with results even less satisfactory. Then someone broke out the Identikit and together we came up with fair likenesses of the Hager Twins, which is about as close as you can expect from a department that's too cheap to hire an artist. When Proust left to have copies made, followed by the stenographer—make what you want out of that, I personally don't think he had it in him—I sat back in the scoop chair they'd given me and tapped a Winston, my third in that flyblown cell, against the back of my hand. The lieutenant watched me hungrily.

"Still off the weed, John?"

He nodded. "Eighteen days now. It's a bitch." In his pastel blue shirt sleeves now, he fished out a pen he had clipped to a plastic holder inside his shirt pocket, and rolled it back and forth between his dusty pink palms. I'd lost track of how many times he'd done that since we'd come in. "Off the record, Walker, what kind of guy was this Kramer?"

I started to touch off the cigarette, then thought better of it and blew out the match, letting the coffin nail droop unlit. There was no sense in torturing the guy. "Off the record, on the record, I can't tell you because I don't know," I said. "A Pfc doesn't get too close to his company commander, even in combat. He struck me as kind of prissy. Fatigues always pressed and spotless whenever we were near water and an iron, clean-shaven, necktie tucked inside his shirt. He wanted us to look the same, ignored it when we didn't go along. Kind of a junior league Georgie Patton, only without the blood or the guts. I don't think he was a coward. Timid, maybe. Overcautious, they call it in Washington. Near Hue we lost more men than we should have because he made up his mind to take a hill too late. The company was threatening a general strike when someone got wise and he was yanked back to a desk job in the States. This is hearsay, but someone told me he got to be captain by snitching on the guy that was there ahead of him. You can take that for whatever it's worth. But it would fit in with my opinion of his character. Yeah, and he was a nut on taking home movies. Picked up some nice equipment in Saigon for next to nothing."

"Real officer material. No wonder we lost over there."

"We didn't lose, we strategically withdrew." I did up my necktie. "What'd you get on the car?"

"I had Auto Recovery process the license plate number right after you gave it to me. It was reported stolen yesterday afternoon in Ann Arbor. The lab is doing a Sherlock

Holmes on the interior right now. The slug entered the back seat at a forty-five-degree angle downward and flattened against the frame. It was a forty-four, and judging by what it did to his head on the way out it was fired from a magnum. The car radio was tuned to a station that plays straight country and western."

"That plays with what I saw and heard. Not that it'd stick in court. That stuff goes big across the river. Or maybe the guy who owns the car listens."

He shook his head. "A.A.P.D. got him out of bed. He digs opera."

"Kramer might have lived in that building he was hurrying from on Woodward. Did you send anybody up there?"

"They're checking it out now."

"Get Johnny Cash on the horn. Find out where he was yesterday at six P.M." He wasn't laughing. I changed the subject. "What are you doing on this one, anyway? They take you off Freeman Shanks?"

"No such luck. Maybe you haven't heard. There are more than enough murders to go around in this town. Sure, the overall crime rate dropped last year, but the percentage of crimes of violence goes up as steady as the cost of living. The renaissance crowd tends to gloss over that last part. That's like rooting for the Pistons when they're down one-oh-three to sixty-four with two minutes to go in the fourth and they finally sink one; it's nice, but what the hell good is it?" He was rolling the pen more rapidly now. "I wouldn't mind it so much if it didn't slop over into the department. Now they've got us doing PR work for the Chamber of Commerce. It's worth a cop's badge to use the words 'Murder City' in his own home. Meanwhile it spreads like venereal disease because everyone thinks it'll go away if we stop talking about it."

"The GOP convention next year will change all that," I fed him.

"Bullshit. That's one more headache we don't need. What if, in spite of all the security, one of the candidates gets blown away? Dallas is still trying to live down November 1963. What do you think it'll do to Detroit?

"A popular young black labor leader disappears in the middle of a union rally and shows up fourteen hours later on East Grand River with three bullets in his back fired from a thirty-eight. Who did it? The man he beat out for the presidency of the local? The Mafia bigwigs he promised to purge from the union? Or some bigot who hates to see a nigger get ahead in anything? I used to go with his sister, so they tell me to solve it. Then they peel off half my manpower and put them to work busting whores and closing down porno shops because they're supposed to be bad for the convention trade, even though they know damn well that's what brings them here in the first place. And my kids ask me why I don't tell jokes like the cops on 'Barney Miller.' "

"Feeling better?" I asked.

He glared at me. Then, slowly, a grin broke through the stony facade. "A little," he said. "Walker, we wouldn't be so far along on this Kramer thing now if you hadn't made that call last night. I owe you one."

"Every citizen's duty. If you don't want it hanging over your head, though, there's one thing you can do for me." I slipped the graduation photo Ben Morningstar had given me from my pocket and read off the description someone had penciled in a tight hand on the back. Alderdyce jotted it down on a yellow scratch pad with the pen he'd been trying to remold.

"Placing an order?"

"Too young for me. Her name's Marla Bernstein, but if she's still using it she's even more naïve than I figure her. Almost a year ago she split with an unidentified male, age and race unknown, from the waltz-and-pinky school her old man had her enrolled in up in Lansing. There's some evidence she's got herself mixed up in the porno trade here. Hooking too, most likely. They go hand in hand. You used to work Vice. Got any friends there?"

"My brother-in-law. He's a plainclothesman."

"If anybody who answers that description has been hauled in since last December, I'd appreciate hearing about it."

"Who's your client?"

It was my turn to smile. "Go to hell, Alderdyce."

The city was getting in its last winks when I fired up my crate and left the morgue behind me. There was some traffic, but it was still dark and the early rush hour was more than an hour off. A couple of times I looked up in my rearview mirror and spotted what I thought was the same light-colored mid-size trailing me two or three blocks back, but when I turned west on Milwaukee it rolled past without stopping and I relaxed. As I approached the General Motors Building, however, it or one like it swung in behind me off John R.

I decided to give it the benefit of the doubt a little longer. The city was full of yellow Pintos.

6

IF FOR ANY REASON you should ever find yourself
looking through the microfilmed copies of the *News,
Free Press,* or the old *Times* for the year 1931 at the
Detroit Public Library, you may come across a photograph
of a nondescript building with a Maltese cross superimposed
over one of its windows. If you read the accompanying
piece, you'll learn that the window marks an apartment
where three men were gunned down by the Purple Gang
one night in what was immediately tagged the Collingwood
Massacre. The building still stands at the corner of Collingwood and Twelfth—excuse me, Rosa Parks Boulevard—and
while it's no more remarkable in appearance than it was
during those days of Prohibition, it does hold the dubious
distinction of being one of the few structures left intact
there by the rioters a dozen years ago. There were lights on
in a few of the apartments when I parked on Rosa P. and
entered the sooty foyer, but I was interested in only one.
The Pinto was nowhere in sight as I left the street, which
meant exactly nothing.

I selected a grubby black button under an even grubbier
rectangle of paper bearing the name I was looking for and
pressed it. It wasn't the name my quarry was born with, nor
as far as I knew was it one he used anywhere else. As a
matter of fact, for someone as cautious as he was, his choice

of buildings, considering its forty-eight-year-old reputation, was nothing less than perverse. More of that later.

I had just about made up my mind that the buzzer wasn't working when a lean figure I knew well appeared atop the landing of the staircase on the other side of the locked glass-and-grill door. He spotted me and came bouncing down the stairs with a friendly grin on his face that did proud the plastic surgeons who had labored so many hours to put it back together. Straight up he crowded something over six feet of athletic build with sandy hair and the kind of jaw they used to go nuts over in Hollywood, square but not too square, and set off by a pair of level eyes whose color you couldn't appreciate if you've never seen Lake Superior on a clear day. He opened the door and offered me his left hand. He had a white cotton glove on the right to mask the missing fingers, and if it moved at all it wasn't without the other's help.

"Hello, shamus." His grip never crushed any bones or tendons he didn't want it to. For me it was the same strong, self-assured grasp he reserved for friends and his tennis racquet.

"Hello, newshawk."

"Business or pleasure?"

"Both, if you can get two drinks poured before sunrise."

"I can sure as hell try." He turned and took the stairs two at a time back up to the second floor. I took them as they presented themselves.

Barry Stackpole had trod the *Detroit News* police beat for five years before becoming a columnist whose exposés of organized crime were beginning to attract the attention of newspapers across the country. The way he carried himself, you'd never have guessed the bottom third of his right leg was fiber-glass or that the plastic on his face concealed

a titanium plate, two mementos of a TNT surprise left beneath the hood of his car shortly before he was to testify
before a Grand Jury on labor racketeering in the auto industry. The bomber needn't have bothered. After Stackpole
recovered from his injuries he spent a total of three months
behind bars on contempt of court for refusing to reveal his
sources. The word on the street was that his ears were worth
a handy twenty-five grand apiece to the soldier who
brought them in. The word was wrong, or he'd be sharing
quarters with Francis Kramer already.

Right or wrong, he lived as if he believed the rumors.
There were three people in town who knew where he was
staying at any given time, and he was one of them. That
left his mother and me, and there were times when I wasn't
sure he trusted her. Me? Like his, my livelihood depends
upon how close I can come to starvation before I open my
mouth.

He had a bottle and a suitcase and a portable typewriter
in his two-room apartment and that was it. Everything else
was furnished. The typewriter could be operated while still
in its case, which was the way he had it. The suitcase was
open on his bed with all his clothes in it except for the polo
shirt and flared cotton slacks he was wearing. The bottle
had two drinks left in it, and a minute and a half after we
entered the room it didn't have that. His entire life was spent
poised with one toe on the starting line. The difference was
that he had to be off and running before the opening shot.

"What phony story you want me to plant this time, op?"
He handed me one of two plain water tumblers he had half-
filled with McMaster's, his favorite, and motioned me into
my usual seat on the edge of his bed while he sank into the
chair at the typewriter, crossing his right ankle over his left
knee. Brown fiberglass peeped above his sock. He shifted

uncomfortably, then reached into his right hip pocket and pulled out the nine-millimeter Luger I had never seen him without since the day we had met in a mudhole during a MIG strafing south of Phnom Penh, when he was a correspondent and I was a dogface. It landed with a thud atop the papers on the desk. "Cold steel," he said, lifting his glass.

"Hot lead." We drank. It was a ritual we used every time we got together. "Cold Steel, Hot Lead" was the title I had suggested for the book he'd told me he was writing on his experiences in Vietnam and Cambodia while we were up to our chins in yak urine and motor oil. He never got around to finishing the book, but the title made a hell of a toast.

"No planting this time," I said, balancing my glass on my knee while igniting the cigarette I hadn't smoked in Alderdyce's presence. I didn't offer him one; he didn't indulge. Sometimes I think I'm the only one keeping Tennessee from going bankrupt. "This time I want you to do some digging." I reached him over Marla Bernstein, before and after.

He gave them equal time. His eyes didn't even flicker as he shifted his attention to this year's model. Sometimes I wondered about him. He handed them back.

"Hold onto them," I said. "I can stop by the *News* later and pick them up."

"Don't need them."

I'd forgotten his photographic memory. I deposited the evidence and gave him the *Reader's Digest* version of what I'd been told earlier.

"Bernstein," he echoed, the computer clicking. "Ben Morningstar's bogus daughter."

Damn him and his encyclopedic knowledge of the underworld. Aloud I said, "I don't have to tell you not to scribble it on any men's room walls. If it got out I'd even showed

46

these to a reporter, there's a certain ex-hockey player who'd turn my head into a puck."

He smiled, not the open grin with which he'd greeted me. "Merle Donophan. I'd heard he was under contract to a new team. What do you want, the usual arrest story?"

"If there is one. It shouldn't be too difficult, this not being an election year. Cathouse raids only get popular when the mayor smells re-election. Deeper than that, though. Hookers have been known to advertise. Roommate Available, Model Willing to Work Nude, Lay-a-Day Escorts, You Tap Her, We'll Wrap Her—you know the lyrics. Check out everything likely since the beginning of the year and when you find something get hold of my answering service. They'll page me."

"There won't be much. The *News* is so staid the editors sleep with their nightshirts knotted between their legs. The boys in advertising won't even accept business from X-rated movie houses."

"It's the girls in classified who take the calls. If you've got any bottle buddies on the *Free Press*, you might put them to work on it over there. It's worth a C for half a day's work. My client won't starve." I got out my wallet and spread one of the two Franklins Paul Cooke had given me on the bed.

"Keep it. I'm no menial." He drained his glass at a jerk. I always admired anyone who could do that.

"Since when? I never saw the day you wouldn't snatch at a quarter so fast you shook feathers off the eagle."

"You've seen it now. I got a call last week from New York. They've offered me a slot on *Today*, shoveling the same crap I shovel here, only out loud and for a dozen times what these cheap bastards are stoking me to sweat behind a typewriter six days a week. I'm leaving tonight to meet the head of network programming, whatever the hell that is."

"That's a relief."

"Why?" His blue eyes grew crystal sharp.

"Because I think some of Ben Morningstar's hired help followed me here this morning."

I was looking out the window at my right, above the sill of which, from where I was sitting, I could just make out the top of a yellow roof parked across Collingwood as dawn broke. Stackpole shot to his feet with a curse and limped over to the window. The only time he didn't walk like you or me was when something happened to remind him of his loss.

I finished my drink, a swallow at a time, the way I took the stairs. "I'm sorry, Barry. I thought I lost him on Trumbull. Anyway, it's not you he's after. I doubt if he even knows who I came to see."

"Well, it doesn't really matter." He left the window without presenting his back to it. Whether or not he bought that story about the price on his head, the chance that someone did was enough to make him act like Bill Hickok most of the time. "I'm leaving for Metro straight from the office. I won't be coming back here. If, that is, checking into your girlfriend's past doesn't make me miss my plane."

"You're still doing it?"

"My column's done through next Tuesday. If you hadn't come along I'd just be wasting time resting."

I offered up the hundred. "To grease the skids over at the *Free Press.*"

"Keep it," he said. "I've been wondering how to collect on the favor Freddie Sloane over there owes me before I leave."

I put away the C-note and stood up. "That's one I owe you."

"Two." He smiled. "Don't forget that redhead from composing I fixed you up with last summer."

Wiley had last night's edition of the *News* open to sports behind the wheel of the Pinto when I approached him across the street from the side entrance.

"The Wings dropped it in the last two and a half," I informed him.

He'd been watching me out of the corner of his eye. He turned to comics. "Basketball's my sport."

"So I noticed. You've been playing guard to my center all morning. How come?"

"I do what I'm told. You're pretty chummy with the cops, I see. Drop in on them any hour of the day and they're so happy to see you they entertain you for seventy-two minutes. Or maybe it's the other way around."

"You've been wasting gas. Your boss isn't the only client I've ever had. His name never came up."

"I hope not, for your sake. Who lives in the dump?" He inclined his modest afro toward the building I'd just left.

"What if I told you it's a reporter I know?"

He looked at me for the first time. "I'd say it's a sad day for a certain peeper," he replied after a moment.

"Like I said, I don't work exclusive. The deal was your boss won't see his name in the paper. Until that happens I visit who I want. Take that back to Grosse Pointe."

I spun rubber on Rosa Parks to get him out of there before Barry left the building. On West Forest I lost him, but picked him up again on Woodward and from that point on he was a bumper sticker. He was good. I grabbed a light breakfast at a lunch counter—don't laugh, it's your language too—and at eight sharp was parked on Watson kitty-corner from George Gibson's apartment when the subject in question stiff-legged it out the door and hobbled down the street with the aid of his canes toward the nearest bus stop. He was a skinny, white-haired little guy with a determined face that looked ten years older than it was. I laid aside the morning *Free Press* I'd been reading (there was nothing in it about Francis Kramer, but then I hadn't expected there to be, considering the lead time involved) and swung out into the main gut, where I rolled along discreetly amid the congealing traffic until he reached his destination, then double-parked next to a van in a loading zone and waited for the DSR to pick him up. It was only fifteen minutes late, just enough time for me to check my mirrors and determine that Wiley's bilious economy job was gone. Which meant that he'd either swallowed the line I'd offered or gone back to confirm the old man's suspicions.

When the bus pulled out with Gibson on it I drove past it and was waiting across from the unemployment office when he got off and went in to pick up his check. My Nikon was on the seat beside me with a telephoto lens, but it might as well have been one of those toys you crank to deliver a picture that develops in minutes, too dark and primarily green, for all the chance I got to use it. He stayed between the sticks on his way out of the office and through a brief shopping trip downtown without the slightest indication that he could get along without them. When he returned to his apartment a little before ten I kept going. Maybe this time my cynicism was misplaced. Maybe he was a straight guy with a streak of hard luck. And maybe the mayor voted Republican in the last election.

7

MY OFFICE IS A third-floor wheeze-up in one of the
older buildings on Grand River, a pistol-shot from
Woodward. The last time I scrubbed it, the
pebbled-glass door, which always reminds me of the window
in a public lavatory, read A. WALKER INVESTIGATIONS in
flecked black letters tombstoned tastefully across the top
and in need of touching up. The man from whom I inherited
the practice, who had himself inherited a bullet meant for
me, used to call it APOLLO CONFIDENTIAL INVESTIGATIONS, after
the Hellenic god who brought light to the darkness, but I
changed it after I got fed up with taking calls from people
who wished to speak with "Mr. Apollo." It's a pleasant
enough little burrow, and while the place has never seen a
featherduster or broom with bristles stiff enough to reach
into the corners, let alone the Silver's touch, it has everything a P.I. requires, including a file cabinet with the worst
dents shoved up against the wall, a backless sofa suitable
for snoozing one off, and a desk with a bottom drawer deep
enough to store a bottle of Hiram Walker's upright, suitable
for tying one on. I admit it's a hike south from my dump
near Hamtramck, but then the internal combustion engine
has spoiled us all for those copper towns in the upper pen-
insula whose residents slept and ate in company-owned
homes built in the very shadow of the mines that employed
them.

I'd started the day on Scotch and don't mix my drinks, and in any case the sun was well up and watching me, so it wasn't the bottle I was going for when I unlocked the door and crossed through the outer office. Today my own office telephone was the only one available that hadn't already received the attention of some industrious fellow with a crowbar and a yearning for a pocket full of quarters.

I made two calls, one to information, the second to the number the impatient-sounding operator gave me for the Miriam H. Fordham Institute for Women in Lansing. Esther Brock turned out to be a mannish-voiced matron who claimed direct descent from General Sir Isaac Brock, the canny old Britisher who shelled Detroit from across the river in 1812 and marched a motley assortment of guerrillas, British regulars, and Indians up Jefferson Avenue to make this the only major American city ever to surrender itself to occupation by a foreign power. She told me all that in the first five minutes, which should give you some idea of how garrulous the beldam was once you broke through her crust. I was touching base. Yes, Miss Bernstein told her two weeks before the Christmas break that she was leaving school to get married. No, she didn't say who the young man was. Yes, her roommate was certain that it was Miss Bernstein she saw getting into a car with a man later that afternoon. No, the young lady was no longer enrolled at Fordham. Married, don't you know, and living in Maine or Maryland or some other place that begins with M. So few finish these days. Miss Bernstein herself had entertained hopes of leaving school for a theatrical career, of all things. Have you a sister or a daughter of college age, Mr. Walker? Oh, that's unfortunate. Yes, you'll be the first to know if Miss Bernstein is heard from. Good-bye, Mr. Walker, and do remember Fordham when you marry and are blessed with female progeny.

I could still smell lemon verbena and starched white gloves when I hung up. I glanced at the calendar on the wall with the picture of a pretty girl on it whose clothes went up with the clear plastic flap to make sure I hadn't slipped back fifty years during the conversation. Then I consigned the mail I'd picked up on my way in to the wastebasket and left for Erskine Street, where they took down the red lights a long time ago for the same reason a church needs no sign to tell you it's a house of God.

Story's After Midnight shared a block of age-blurred building with half a dozen similar establishments on the north side of Erskine, a street where business was conducted behind graffiti-smeared clapboard fences and from the back seats of spanking new Caddies and Lincolns, where cops paired up on sticky August nights to patrol on raw nerve-ends, thumbs stroking the oily black hammers of the holstered magnums they preferred to the .38 specials issued by the department, ears tuned for the quick scuffing of rubber soles on the sidewalk behind them and the wood-on-metal clacking of a sawed-off pump shotgun being brought to bear just beyond the next corner, a street where a grunt of uncontrollable passion and a stifled scream in the gray, stinking depths of a claustrophobic alley could mean a ten-dollar quickie or a rape in progress. With its stripped, wheelless hulks that had once been cars and aimlessly blowing litter, it was the kind of street you never saw on the posters put out by the Chamber of Commerce. If you got a glimpse of it at all it was on the eleven o'clock news, whose cameras had recorded hundreds of feet of rubber-wrapped corpses being trundled out of narrow doorways into the rears of ambulances backed up to the sidewalk on streets like this, while in the foreground earnest young reporters with microphones in their hands and blow-dried hair stirring in the wind rattled off names and facts in modulated baritones, acting as Greek chorus to a scene that was dyed-in-the-wool American. It was an area that spawned a mindless, disorganized brand of violence, and once every few years, as it had less than a mile south of here not long ago, it spawned a Cass Corridor Strangler, who killed for a time and then faded into terrifying obscurity. But you could still hear good jazz in the right bars.

I parked next to a hydrant heaped high with rusty snow in front of the store, where I could keep an eye on the car through the window, and went in, easing my way past a knot of sullen-looking black youths in scuffed Piston warm-up jackets who were sharing the same twisted cigarette in front of the entrance. My nerves tingled as I did so. I'm no more prejudiced than the next guy, but I tighten up whenever they band together like that.

It was one of those places where you had to tip the guy at the counter fifty cents before he'd let you in. In this case he was a bony young black seated on a high stool behind a display of latex breasts and plastic phalluses. He had an afro you could lose a shoe in and invisible eyes behind mirrored glasses and needle tracks all over his mahogany wrist where it stuck out of his cuff as he reached for my two quarters.

"Cold out there," I ventured.

"So's the world, man."

A philosopher. His accent was Mississippi straight up with a Twelfth Street twist. I left him to ring up the alloy in a big, old-fashioned register and began browsing.

The place had everything the well-dressed degenerate could want. It was stocked primarily with books and magazines, from near-legitimate classics like *A Man With a Maid and The Story of O* to the more contemporary *Hot*

Snatch and *Anal Delight*, with covers featuring various sexes and species engaged in provocative pursuits which, according to the title splashes, only hinted at the literary and pictorial treats to be found inside, shrink-sealed in plastic. But miscellaneous grunts and squeals that seemed to emanate from everywhere and yet nowhere, and a sign made to resemble an interesting anatomical pointer, indicated that a peep-grind "with sound!" was available in the back for the admission price of one dollar, There were the usual revolving wire racks containing the kind of greeting cards you didn't send Grandma at Christmas time, the standard bin filled with fifteen-minute reels of Super 8 film with titles like *A Lesson From Miss Dove* and *Blowing Wild*—not the one starring Gary Cooper and Barbara Stanwyck—and, beneath the glass counter near the entrance, a fascinating collection of gadgets, among which was a device which, its tag pledged, would Increase the Size of Your Organ in Minutes, an ingenious contraption with a glass tube and a vacuum pump that seemed ideal for rescuing golf balls from mud puddles.

The only other customer in this part of the store was a heavy-set businessman-type, black, with a brown cashmere overcoat buttoned over his spreading middle and a sprinkling of gray in his kinky, receding hair. He seemed oblivious to everything but the fag corner in the back, where a study of the photographs on the covers of the magazines, in the proper order, provided a crash course on how to get along with your fellow man. A sales executive, I figured, killing his coffee break in a way his fellow employees never suspected.

It wasn't the dank hole the folks in the suburbs had in mind when they formed their Sunday morning decency leagues to keep pornography out of their neighborhoods.

Fluorescent tubes in the ceiling shed plenty of light over the merchandise, and the tile floor shone beneath a seal of fresh wax. The plate glass window was spotless. You'll find stores like it in any shopping center. The only difference is the stock.

The snowbird behind the counter was dividing his attention between a convex shoplifters' mirror in the corner and a paperback in his hands. I caught a glimpse of the title when he shifted it to turn the page. *Catch-22*. That was like finding an "Out to Lunch" sign on the door to a McDonald's. I approached him.

"Lee Story?"

"Lee Q. Story." He didn't look up.

"Sorry. I'm told you wholesale."

My reflection came up to meet me in the mirrored cheaters. "Who's asking?" He turned down a corner of the page he'd been reading and laid the book aside.

"Andy Jackson." I waved a shopworn twenty under his nose.

I couldn't tell if he was looking at the bill. Lamont Cranston would have trouble reading a man's thoughts behind those Foster Grants. "You a pig or something?"

The guy over in fairyland overheard him and strode swiftly past me out the door, fat legs working despite the hobbles of his calf-length coat.

"Or something." I put the double sawbuck on the counter and hauled out my wallet, flipping it open to the license and sheriff's buzzer. When he'd had an eyeful I returned it to my pocket and planted the more interesting of the two pictures Morningstar had given me atop the twenty.

"Maybe you could see it better minus the shades," I suggested.

He had wide-set eyes with pupils that reacted slowly

when they were exposed to the light. He was a user, all right. He barely glanced at the photo.

"I seen it before, man. That what you wanted?" He reached for the bill. I speared his wrist.

"What I want is the name of the person who saw it before you did," I said.

"I done told somebody else I don't know." That gave him an idea. "Say, we working for the same boss?"

"Not hardly. I want a list of your picture sources."

"Is that all?" Acidly. "Look, man, I got people to answer to. Leggo my hand."

I held on. "How long can it take to jot down some names? Five minutes? That's two hundred and forty an hour. Henry Ford, Jr. doesn't pay that. Senators don't make that much in graft." He still looked doubtful. "The people you answer to have people to answer to," I added. "I answer to them."

Whatever the hell that meant, it hooked him. I raised my hand and he withdrew his, leaving behind the green.

"Second." He swiveled to face a small desk beneath the display window strewn with grainy snaps like the one I'd shown him, snatched a pen from a glass of them, and spent some minutes scribbling on the back of a page from a large receipt book. Then he tore it off and spun around on his stool. He passed it over with his right, grabbing the bill with his left at the same time.

There were thirteen names on the sheet, a few of which I recognized. I pocketed it, along with a blister card from a display of stick batteries on the counter "For the Junior Miss Vibrator," and gave him a dollar, telling him to keep the change. He rang it up without asking questions.

"Anything else?" I asked.

"You been a pig somewhere down the string, man." He

looked exasperated. "You wring a buck till Washington sweats."

"MP," I said. "Three years, after Nam and Cambodia."

"You was in Nam?"

"Were you?"

"Damn near. I done a year in Leavenworth for lighting a joint with my draft card."

I tapped the picture. "There's a piece of paper tacked to the door in this shot. Could be a list of rules and checkout times. Which of your sources works in a hotel or a motel?"

"Which of them don't? This ain't L.A."

"How about the girl? Know her?"

"Man, they all look alike with their threads off."

"Give me back my twenty. I don't buy crap."

His bony face twisted into a mask. "Get out of my place, honky."

When I didn't move he reached beneath the counter and clanked a battered .22 with a seven-inch barrel down on top of it. I moved.

The youths were still gathered around the door when I stepped out. I moved to pass them. They moved with me. I shifted in the other direction. They went the same way. There were four of them. One, who acted a half-beat ahead of his companions, was a tall, rangy cager-type with a small head and too much untended afro atop a long, skinny neck and wrists that protruded several inches out of the sleeves of his warm-up jacket. He said something about my mother in an Erskine Street drawl and started to push me.

That's how it always starts, with a push. Most of us learn that in grammar school and some of us never get over it. When he thrust his big palms against my chest, I took advantage of the opening and gave him as much knee in the groin as I could afford without sacrificing my balance. It was enough. He exhaled a double lungful of stale marijuana into my face and jackknifed.

Among the others there was a moment of shocked indecision. Then a short, chunky black with a firmly rounded belly, Jeff to the other's Mutt, rushed me, arms outstretched to take me in the bear-hug that appeared to be his specialty. I sidestepped him and gave him a judo kick in the well-upholstered seat of his pants that sent his woolly head crashing into the building's block corner. The plate glass window shivered but didn't fall apart. Neither did Fatty, but not for lack of effort on the part of heels suddenly gone round as he staggered aimlessly across the littered sidewalk.

That left two I hadn't tried, but they had to wait their turn. The beanpole I'd kneed had recovered himself, and now he went for the pocket of his jacket.

The switchblade darted from the steel and plastic handle like a serpent's tongue and jiggled up and down lightly in his hand with the confidence of a sixth finger. A grin that didn't remind me much of Cab Calloway spread across his face as he watched my reaction. Then he lunged.

The blade scraped some fiber off my coat as I threw myself hard against the other side of the entrance niche. I moved to kick him as I had Fatty, but he anticipated that and twisted as he went past. My foot scuffed his pocket, nothing more. He came up against the door with a shuddering bang.

The years between me and my last workout on the mats were offset to a degree by the mild narcotic in his system, but he had youth and reach on me. It was time to stop playing. As he came away from the door, I fisted my Smith & Wesson and sent three pounds of steel, bone, and flesh smashing into his grin. It gave way with an audible crunch; he slammed into the door once again, and dribbled down it like Pepto-Bismol.

My fist was beginning to ache when I turned the revolver around and Wyatt-Earped my way through the ominously growling knot of toughs to my car. As I pulled away from the hydrant I got a hinge of Lee Q. Story watching me through the display window. His expression put me in mind of a fight manager who had laid everything he had on the wrong guy.

On St. Antoine I took advantage of a stoplight to study the list Story had given me. Then I crumpled it and tossed it to the floorboards. The one name I wanted would be the one he hadn't written down. For that I'd have to wait.

8

I WAS HITTING ALL the red lights today, which was okay since I didn't know where to go and was in no hurry to get there. At the next stop I broke out the batteries I'd bought at Story's and replaced the old ones in the pencil-like paging device I wear clipped to my inside breast pocket. It was a struggle; the knuckles of my right hand were burst and bleeding and the fingers were beginning to stiffen. I barely got everything screwed back together when the damn thing started beeping.

I made it to a public telephone between the repairman and the neighborhood vandal and got the girl at my service, who bawled me out for not answering the page half an hour sooner and gave me Barry Stackpole's private number at the *News*. He stabbed it halfway through the first ring.

"We lucked out, shamus," he said, after I had identified myself. "Thursday, January twenty-fifth, a couple of days after the GOP picked Detroit for next year's convention. The city council put the cops to work scouring the red light districts. We had a photographer on it. If that isn't your girl standing behind the one being handed into the police van on John R I'll tear up my press card."

I breathed some air. "That's fast sliding for someone who was the apple of her guardian's eye in December."

"They don't call it the skids for nothing. That's not all. It was a slow news day. The *Free Press* covered the same raid, without pictures. But they did publish the girls' names. How does 'Martha Burns' sound?"

"Just like something an eighteen-year-old girl named Marla Bernstein might pick if she wanted to remain incognito without giving up her identity. Give me the rest of it." He did, along with the names of all the others, just in case. I took them down in my notebook. "Thanks, Barry. By the way, how are you guys planning to handle the Kramer killing?"

"What's the Kramer killing?"

"Maybe the cops haven't released his name. They found him imitating a spare tire in the parking lot at City Airport this morning. He had a hole in his head the size of the Windsor Tunnel."

"I was just talking to the city editor. He said that unless the mayor sticks his Size Nine in his mouth again, tonight's front page is going to be all state and national."

I gave that a couple of seconds. Then, "Keep scratching, newshawk." I pegged the receiver before he could ask any questions. But as I stepped aside for the delinquent who was waiting to smash the telephone I thought up some questions of my own.

The address he'd given me on John R—a street named, along with Williams, after the city's first mayor, who left no other legacy—belonged to a large, neat-looking brick house with a fenced yard that even under a pile of snow looked as if it complied with the antiblight ordinance, no matter how many others it might ignore. A big, square man, black, in a green polar coat with a fur-lined hood, was busy shoveling out the front walk when I let myself in through the picket gate. When he saw me he stopped shoveling and straightened to his full height, which turned out to be a lot fuller than I'd expected. If he was less than six foot six I had shrunk.

He wasn't ready yet for the River Rouge scrap heap, but his best days were forty years behind him. His skin was the faded gray of old age, and where scar tissue had not formed there was not an inch of it that wasn't cracked and squeezed into dozens of sharp creases like a crumpled sheet of foil that's lost its shine. What I suppose he called a nose had been bent and straightened out so many times that now it was just something on his face. His shoulders were broad and square and he had no waist to speak of. He wouldn't be any harder to stop than a runaway oil tanker.

"You got business, mister?" Nobody had ever punched him in the throat. He had plenty of volume but there didn't seem to be any anger behind it, just suspicion.

"I do if you're in charge." The way he peeled back his hood on one side and cocked a cauliflower ear in my direction told me he hadn't heard. He wouldn't, at any normal level. Now I understood why he shouted. I repeated it, louder this time. His eyes narrowed as far as they were able.

"You a cop?"

I shook my head. "Just a guy."

"Miss Beryl, she don't do no business this time of day."

"I'm here on another kind of business."

He jerked a gloved thumb back over his shoulder. "See the lady. I just shovels snow and turns back cops." As if to prove it he resumed his labors, taking forty pounds at a swing. I sidestepped the flashing blade and mounted the stoop.

A doe-eyed black maid answered the bell. I flashed my license for the third time that day, minus the badge this time, and asked for the lady of the house. She wasn't impressed. Confronted with a faceful of door, I was about to try again when it opened back up and I was ushered inside. I gave the maid my coat and hat and she blew. If she could speak at all I didn't hear it.

I was marooned for a time in the middle of a bourgeois little salon or family room or whatever the architects and real estate agents are calling the living room this season, complete with a baby grand piano in one corner and rows of leather-bound books arranged in unread elegance behind glass. Three arched doorways led into adjacent rooms and a thickly carpeted staircase wound toward the second story a short hike from the entrance. A Presto log burned blue in the fireplace. In another minute I expected Perry Como to stroll in singing "Home for the Holidays." I wasn't so far off.

"Mr. Walker?"

The beige carpet beneath my feet was so deep I hadn't realized I was no longer alone until I heard the voice behind me. I turned to face the same arch of the same doorway I'd seen when I'd looked in that direction before. Her head didn't start until two feet below that point. She was pink and fluffy and squeezed into a pink and fluffy dress that fit her like the casing of one of those tiny, expensive sausages they sell in the chain stores in packages of six that nobody ever buys. She had bluish hair carefully brushed and sprayed into soft-looking waves that framed a round, pink little face with a round, pert little nose and round, bright little eyes that sparkled from the depths of her plump flesh like glass buttons machine-punched into a throw pillow. Her Cupid's-bow mouth was fixed in a rouge-tinted smile of greeting as she approached with dainty steps, making a journey out of the few yards that separated us.

I admitted to the Walker part but said I wasn't so sure

about the mister. Up close I caught a scent, or rather the impression of a scent, of delicate toilet water, or maybe it was just her.

"I'm Beryl Garnet." A plump, moist little hand slid into mine, fluttered there for an instant, and was gone.

I leered charmingly. "Parents play some awful tricks on defenseless babies, don't they?"

Her laughter tinkled as if the tin and crystal pendants of a Chinese mobile dangled in her throat.

"You're perfectly awful, Mr. Walker. And perfectly correct. But then I haven't met anyone named Amos in over forty years."

"My father named me after half a radio show."

The pendants stirred again. "Shall we sit down?"

We should and did. Beryl Garnet assumed a ladylike little pose on the edge of a Louis XIV or some such number chair with her tiny hands folded in her lap while I foundered in a maroon overstuffed sofa. By the time my keel had righted itself the maid was standing over me. The vow of silence was broken. Did the gentleman wish a cup of coffee? I looked at the two white cups painted with tiny flowers steaming on the silver tray in her hands, decided I couldn't get enough grip on one of them to lift it without shattering it, and said no thanks. It should have been tea in the first place. My hostess fluttered a hand and the maid glided off.

"May I smoke?" I kept away from my pockets. I'd been caught once too many times with a Winston in one hand, a flaming match in the other, and a big fat No staring me in the face.

"Try one of these." She opened a hand-worked wooden box on the glass coffee table between us and held it out. "They're Turkish."

I selected one of the oval cylinders arranged inside and

lit up. The tobacco had been mixed with shredded fiber from some sultan's flying carpet. By the time my match was ready for it, a glass ashtray had appeared on the arm of the sofa. The maid seemed to operate by remote control.

It looked as if it was up to me to open. I was gearing up for it when the floor shook and a Great Dane the size of last month's utility bill came bouncing into the room through the arch to my right and planted its huge paws on my shoulders with the light touch of a pair of battering rams. My teeth ground halfway through the cigarette. Through the smoke a great square head with hornlike ears and ivory teeth bared in a blue-black muzzle breathed hot air into my face with a taint of stale meat. Its growl was a dynamo rumbling deep in its powerful chest.

"Ulysses! Down!"

The weight lifted suddenly from my shoulders, leaving only its ghost behind as the blood rushed in to fill the dents. The great beast turned a bobbed tail on me and went over to its mistress, its head lowered for petting. It planted its feet carefully this time, like an elephant testing the ground before trusting its weight to it.

"You bad dog," she said, but it didn't sound as if she meant it. She scratched behind its ears. It closed its eyes and gave vent to a long, groaning sigh, like a record winding down. I hadn't seen anything like it since the last time I fell off the wagon. From snout to truncated tail it stretched four feet and stood a yard high at the shoulder, with almost two feet of that gobbled up by its chest. From there its underside swept back up in a graceful scoop to taut flanks and narrow hips and muscular haunches, between which its nub of tail moved from side to side with a measured beat as its mistress' pudgy fingers stroked the sensitive hollows behind its skull. Even when it wasn't moving, its muscles seemed to throb and ripple with restless power beneath a thin coat of flesh and short hair the color of gun bluing.

"You mustn't let Uli frighten you, Mr. Walker," she said, staring into the dog's nut-brown eyes as with both hands she smoothed back the seams that ran down both sides of its neck. "He's really very gentle. He wouldn't hurt anything larger than a rabbit. Would you, dear?" Ulysses craned forward to lick her ear with a tongue like a wet facecloth.

"Does that go for the guy that looks like Kong and talks like Willie Best out front?"

That took a moment to seep through. Then she laughed that tinkly little laugh again. "You mean Felix. Yes, he's harmless. If you believe what he says, he'd have been the world heavyweight champion in 1936 if they hadn't forced him to throw his biggest fight. If they did, it was the only time he was ever paid for something he did all the time unintentionally and for free."

While she was talking, a slender black girl with very closely cropped hair drifted down the stairs, smiled at me dazzlingly, helped herself to a cigarette from the box on the table, and retreated back to the second story. I watched her openly. Anything else would have been ludicrous, as she was wearing a pair of rubber shower clogs and nothing else. Her skin was deep brown with a purplish tint. She had conical breasts and round, firm buttocks and a pubic patch that grew wild over her small mound, untouched by any razor. As she walked, the loose clogs came up and slapped the soles of her feet, but aside from that she made no sound at all. The dog watched her movements with a bored expression. Naked females were nothing new to him.

I won't say I wasn't stirred. I've slept with women who didn't move like that when they were fully clothed. But drinking's the only vice I indulge in before noon. I reached over and stubbed out what was left of my cigarette and hoped to hell my hand wasn't shaking as noticeably as it seemed.

Beryl Garnet looked amused. She was still scratching Ulysses, who was sitting beside her chair now and, it appeared, studying my throat closely. "Don't let Iris embarrass you," she said. "She's new. They're like children at that stage, always trying to shock the grownups. I've found that if you ignore them when they do something outrageous, they soon become embarrassed themselves and stop." She let her hand drop back into her lap. The Dane swung its mammoth head in her direction, looking for more attention; when none came it got up, stretched, its bones cracking, and trotted out the doorway through which it had entered.

"You're dying to know what a sweet little old lady like me is doing running a whorehouse." She brushed fussily at the dog hairs adhering to her pink skirt. "When you're my age you'll realize that you don't get to be a sweet little old anything without seeing a lot of life whether you want to or not. My husband was a pimp. In some circles that's considered an insult, but it never was in our house. The money he made doing what he did best gave us both a very handsome living and I saw no reason to give it up just because he died. It pays better than Social Security, and if I have to spend a night in jail now and then, those are the chances I take, like falling out of bed and breaking my hip. Only it's less painful and in the long run much more rewarding. But listening to an old woman's prattle won't help you find the girl you're looking for, will it?"

My hand stopped halfway to the pictures in my pocket. "Who talked?"

The Cupid's-bow took an adorable dip. That was the word, adorable. "You did, Mr. Walker. You told my maid you were a private investigator. They're nothing new here. We average two or three a year, hired by some father or mother or uncle or grandparent who hasn't seen Suzy since the senior prom. They usually come during business hours, though, so that if nothing comes of it the trip won't be a total waste and they can charge it to expenses. Sometimes I can help them, sometimes not. If it weren't for runaways, I'd have to advertise under Help Wanted. I don't get many calls from placement services."

"How about her?" I gave her the graduation shot. She fished out a pair of gold-rimmed reading glasses and peered at it as if it were a doubtful twenty. Almost immediately she broke into a smile. A real smile this time, showing a row of perfect teeth molded and matched by a dental technician's patient hand.

"That's Martha." She handed it back. "A lovely girl. I knew she belonged to somebody."

"Martha Burns?"

She nodded. "You've done your homework."

"Someone's been doing it for me. Is she here?"

"Heavens, no. Not since early February. She left on Groundhog Day. Don't ask me why I remember that."

"Did she say where she was headed?"

"No again. Girls in this business seldom leave forwarding addresses. Or their right names, for that matter."

"Tell me a story." I got out my notebook and pencil.

She removed her glasses and put them away. The sparkle in her eyes had changed. "No, you start. My girls call me Aunt Beryl, Mr. Walker, because I look after them. I wouldn't want to turn any dogs loose on them. Especially not on Martha. I have to know why you want her."

I gave her my spiel, minus names and specific places. She watched me the way an auditor studies the books.

LOREN D. ESTLEMAN

"Have you ever considered grifting, Mr. Walker?" she asked when I had finished. "We get a lot of confidence men here. Most are like you, polite and youthful-looking and brimming with sincerity, but you've got something most of them haven't. I think it's the brown eyes. They make me think I can read your mind. Anyway, I'll take the chance."

She talked. I wrote.

9

"SHE SHOWED UP ON my doorstep December twenty-eighth."

The old lady folded her pink, useless-looking hands and stared at me with her brilliants, waiting for me to ask the question. When I didn't, she continued as if I had. "I know it was the twenty-eighth because that's the only slow day we get during the holiday season, midway between Christmas and New Year's. 'I'll Be Home for Christmas' is a nice song, Mr. Walker, but that's all it is. If everybody who sang it meant the words, I'd be working for the Post Office come December. Right away I could see she was a young lady. That seems to be a dirty word among women these days, but there's an art to looking like you belong everywhere you're seen without becoming part of the scenery. She had that. She had a great deal more, not that it did me any good."

"I'll bite. Why not?" I looked up from my scribbles.

"I'm coming to that. She was with a young man. At least I think he was young. It was so hard to tell with his collar turned up and that hat he had jammed down to his eyes. And it was dark, about three o'clock in the morning."

"Hat?"

"Gray felt, with a wide brim. A fedora, we used to call it. Like the one my maid said you were wearing when you arrived."

I was beginning to think I could walk around town naked except for that hat and it would be the only thing anyone noticed.

"Black? White? Oriental? Aztec?"

"He was black. Well-built, leaning toward heavy. He seemed young as I said. On the green side of forty anyway, and to me that's almost adolescent. I didn't recognize him. He seemed to be afraid someone would though, judging by that costume." She giggled girlishly. On her it fit. "Men are amusing creatures. Of course he didn't realize that all he was doing was calling attention to himself, rather like those movie stars who go around wearing dark glasses on cloudy days. His features were very average. I'm sure I could pick him out of a lineup, but I'd never be able to describe him so that you'd know him if you met."

"What did he do?"

"Well, to put it bluntly, he shoved a fistful of fifty-dollar bills into my hands and told me I had a boarder. Actually he was much more tactful, but that's what it amounted to. I got the impression I had no choice in the matter."

"Aren't you the boss in your own place of business?"

"Are you?" She smiled again. "The point is, young man, that we all take orders from someone. In my case the someone can be particularly unpleasant when you ask too many questions. Ask Felix. If you'll pardon my being coarse, his kidneys haven't functioned properly since he started complaining too loudly about having to lose that fight I told you about. Besides, I was holding eight hundred dollars in cash, which makes a compelling argument even when you're not assured, as I was, that the incident would be repeated twice a month for as long as the gentleman chose to keep her beneath my roof."

I whistled. It seemed called for. "How did she act?"

"Shy. She let her escort do the introducing. I think you suspect she was a prisoner. That may have been the case, but if so it was the strangest relationship between a captive and her keeper I've ever heard of. She was hanging on his arm as if he were the only thing that kept her from plunging forty stories to her doom, as the announcer used to say at the end of each chapter during those marvelous old Hollywood serials. But of course that was before your time. Television is a poor substitute. I never watch it myself, nor read the newspapers. I'm prattling again." She shrugged daintily. "She seemed reluctant; nothing more."

"She wasn't turning tricks?"

"No. He was specific about that. Brutally specific. If he got wind that she was anything more than a guest in this house, he explained, I'd be wise to hold onto the money for plastic surgery." She heaved a ladylike little sigh. "It was such a waste, too. There are men among my clientele who in a moment of inebriation would have signed over controlling interest in their companies for one night with a girl like Martha."

"She was that much of a looker?"

"Not just that. She was lovely, yes, but at this level of the business nothing less would be acceptable. Detroit isn't some dusty cowtown in Reconstruction Texas, where anything in skirts was enough of a novelty to be worth a month's hard wages. It was everything about her: her carriage, clothes, the way she behaved toward others, aloof yet unspoiled. Women like that are walking aphrodisiacs. Men dream of obtaining them in the same way the captain of a scow fancies himself at the wheel of the Queen Mary. That simile's as mixed up as it is anachronistic, but I think you know what I'm driving at. The lady was just that, a lady. God help her, there aren't many left."

LOREN D. ESTLEMAN

"How did it work out?"

"Better than you'd think. A situation like that is bound to cause jealousy among the other girls, but despite her obvious breeding Martha was such an unassuming, likable individual that the others took to her right off. She was a talented singer with a remarkably good voice, and knew her way around a keyboard. On a slow night the girls would spend hours around that piano just listening to her. If there was any conflict I'd have known about it."

I scratched a handful of meaningless signs on the page to make her think I considered that worth preserving. "What about the raid last January?"

For an instant she stopped being Aunt Beryl, and I found myself looking at a whorehouse madam. Then she pulled her gentility back up. "That, Mr. Walker, was double-dealing of the vilest sort. I pay good money to people in high places to prevent that kind of thing from happening. I'm not naïve. I understand politics and I realize that arrests must be made from time to time for certain officials to remain in office. All I've ever requested is advance warning so that people like Martha and my maid and my more important customers may be spared unnecessary embarrassment. Ten months ago they forgot that part, and I assure you that there have been some nervous people in the City-County Building ever since."

"Is that why she left? Because of the raid?"

"Yes. It was a foolish business. They had no evidence, and so everyone was released the next day, after the media had lost interest. Most of the girls took it in stride, but not Martha. She locked herself in her room and none of us saw her for days. Even took her meals there. When she didn't answer my knock the morning of February second, I got my passkey and went in. She was gone, along with her clothes and luggage. She'd sneaked out early that morning after everyone had gone to bed to stay."

"Alone?"

She nodded. "Her gentleman friend fairly raised the roof a couple of nights later when he came to visit her and found she'd left. He made all sorts of threats. I had to call Felix to persuade him to leave."

"Any idea where she might have gone?"

She started to shake her head and stopped. She called the maid. "Corinne, dear, do you recall that funny Greek fellow who was here New Year's Eve? You know, the one who said he owned a recording studio? Didn't he give us his card?" When Corinne withdrew to fetch it: "You see what I mean by 'funny,' Mr. Walker. Any man who would leave his right name, let alone his card, in a place like this—" Corinne reentered and handed her a small white pasteboard rectangle with printing on it. "Barney Zacharias. That was his name. He heard Martha singing and playing and told her she'd make a fine recording star. Of course that's just a variation on a line as old as the Greek theater, but she seemed mildly interested."

She gave me the card. It read:

APHRODITE RECORDS
Bernard Zacharias, Prop.

The address was clear out in River Rouge. I pocketed it. Then I passed over the other picture of Marla Bernstein. She hauled out her glasses again.

I hadn't expected it to shock her and I wasn't disappointed. "Martha?" she asked calmly, peering at me over the rims.

"If Martha's the girl I'm after. Would you know where that was taken?"

"I have no idea." She returned it. "You see, Mr. Walker, the market that buys pictures like that is entirely different from mine. People who look don't do, and vice versa."

I put away my paraphernalia and got up. "Thanks, Mrs. Garnet. I wonder if I might talk to one or two of your girls before I go? Just to make sure I haven't missed anything."

"That won't be necessary." She arose gracefully except for a little hop at the beginning to bring her tiny feet into contact with the floor. "They couldn't supply anything more than I have. As I said, I know everything that goes on here."

"Just to make sure."

"I'm sorry, but I must insist. I don't want my girls talking to men before business hours. It makes them independent." Her eyes now were hard little steel pellets sunk in folds of fat. I studied them a while and nodded. The maid glided in with my coat and hat, helped me into one and handed me the other. Beryl Garnet restrung the Cupid's-bow. "Good-bye, Mr. Walker, and don't forget us after sundown. Corinne, show him out."

"No need. I'm a detective."

She laughed as I made my way to the door, then turned and waddled airily back out through the arch. The maid vanished again. I had my hand on the knob when someone whispered my name. I turned around, but there was no one there. I made another assault on the door.

"Mr. Walker. Up here."

I looked up. Iris, the black, horseless Godiva of a few minutes before, stood on the staircase landing leaning over the bannister. She had drawn on a diaphanous lavender something that concealed her dark body about as well as vermouth conceals an olive. She signaled for me to join her.

"You changed costumes," I commented cleverly, as I mounted the landing. She shushed me and swished down the carpeted hallway in a manner that bore following. I didn't resist. The view from up here was better.

She led me through a door near the end into a no-nonsense bedroom with a number of feminine things scattered about the pile-covered floor and, so help me, a waterbed big enough to freeze and use for a skating rink, with a mirror mounted on the ceiling over it. I wondered if Aunt Beryl deducted the furnishings from her taxes. On signal I pushed the door shut behind me.

We stood a couple of yards apart facing each other in silence. I finally tore my eyes away from the silhouette beneath the dressing gown long enough to note that the Turkish butt she had bummed downstairs was crushed into the bottom of an onyx ashtray on the dressing table, got out my pack, and offered her a Winston. She didn't snatch at it; she lunged for it as if it were a piece of flotsam from the *Titanic* and she were a survivor. I took one for myself and lit them both, starting with hers. A quarter of it went in the first drag.

"God, that's good," she said. "I've been smoking those fuses of Aunt Beryl's so long I'd forgotten what a real cigarette tastes like."

I said nothing. She had a West Indian accent that went with her exotic figure. Her legs were long and slender, not the sticks they use in the pantyhose commercials, and ended in small feet with unpolished nails. She had a heart-shaped face and big eyes and regular islander features. The rest you know. She was devouring the cigarette, but it wasn't what she really wanted.

"What do you do, shoot it between your toes?" I asked.

Her eyes expanded. "What are you talking about?" She fired it too fast.

I seized her wrist and turned it over. "No tracks. Behind the knees is just as popular, but I've seen those too. That leaves between the toes, which is a painful place to stick a needle unless you care about your looks."

She snatched back her arm. White marks showed where my fingers had dug in. "How'd you know?"

"You could be just naturally nervous, but you're a hooker too. The rest was guesswork."

"Big deal detective stuff."

"It works one time out of six. What've you got for me?"

She turned it on. Her hand went up and down my arm. "Maybe I just wanted to be alone with you."

"Truckers don't go for Sunday drives." I knocked her hand out of the way. "Spill it."

I braced myself for her palm. They don't take it kindly when you turn down a freebie. At the last moment, however, she jammed the butt between her lips and sucked it down to the letters. Then she stabbed it out beside the Turkish.

"All right, damn you. Aunt Beryl wasn't telling you the truth when she said Martha wasn't tricking."

"You were here then? I thought you were new."

"Everyone's new the first year. It's like tenure."

"Why would Aunt Beryl lie?"

"She wasn't lying. She didn't know. Martha was taking them up here after working hours when the old lady was asleep."

"What about Felix?"

She laughed. "Who do you think brought them here? She had him in for a third. That wasn't hard for him after dealing smack and coke to me and some of the others as long as I've been here."

"How'd you know about Martha?"

"She had the room next door. There are twice as many now as when the place was built. The partitions are made of Kleenex and spit. She cut me in for another third for the big hush."

"Why was she tricking?"

"Why else? Money. She told me that boyfriend of hers didn't give her any because he was afraid she'd leave. He was hiding her here for some reason; I never knew why and she never said. But she was climbing the walls to get out from the first night. Besides, I kind of think she needed it. To get laid, I mean. There aren't as many like that in this line as most people think, but when one does come along she's hell to compete with." She shook her head, smiling. "One night she had two brothers up here at once. Jerry and Hubert Darling. I don't know what they were doing exactly, but it sure made entertaining listening."

"She was doing this all the time she was here?"

"Not for the first couple of nights. I guess she wanted to be on her good behavior until she got the lay of the land. Excuse the expression."

"What do you know about her boyfriend?"

"Nothing. I never even saw him. Neither did any of the others. He only came to visit her two or three times, always after business hours when the rest of us were asleep. She clammed whenever anyone asked about him."

"Why this concert?"

Her eyes went down, then up. "Look, you're after Martha, right? Don't answer that, it's a bonehead question. What do you charge?"

"Like the man said, if you gotta ask, you can't afford it."

"It's not a question of affording it. It's not being able to afford not doing it. When Martha left she took something of mine with her. I want it back."

"Cash?"

"She took some of that too, but I can get that much back on a good night. I'm talking about a little gold heart."

I grinned. "A prostitute with a heart of gold?"

"Shut up, damn it! A little gold heart, about like this"—she made a circle with her index finger about the size of a collar button—"with a tiny loop for a gold chain but no gold chain. It and the cash were missing from my jewelry box the morning she split. It was a present from my mother the day I left home. I can't go back without it."

"When are you planning on going back?"

"Someday."

"Uh-huh."

The big eyes flared. "That means what?"

"Just uh-huh. What makes you so sure she took it?"

"She was the only one who knew where I kept the box. She saw me once through the connecting door when I was putting it away."

"Why don't you just get another one? They aren't rare and they can't cost any more than fifteen or twenty bucks."

"Twenty-five. It's got to be that one. I can't explain it, but I just can't see myself—without it I can't go back. It's the only thing I have that—" She trailed off.

"This is why the slow streak through the living room? To get my attention?"

She nodded.

"I'll do what I can." Before she could collapse on me I stuck the black and white snap under her nose. She took it in one hand, stared at it blinking, wiped a forearm across her eyes, sniffed, stared again.

"Is this Martha?"

"You tell me."

She shrugged and gave it back. "If it is, she's got a lot to learn."

"Recognize the room?"

She shook her head. I disengaged myself and struck out for the stairs. On the landing I paused, then went on more slowly. Beryl Garnet was waiting for me at the base of the staircase with Felix and the great dog Ulysses.

10

STANDING BESIDE HIS COMPACT employer, the black man looked impossibly huge, his shoulders nearly as broad as she was high and each of his paws large enough to palm her fluffy head as if it were a regulation-size basketball. He had shed his parka, and the late-morning sunlight slanting in through the east windows shone off his shaven skull, an enormous, melon-shaped mass with thick veins drawn like cargo netting across the top. His oriental eyes, made so by the mantle of scar tissue that scabbed his forehead, did a slow burn as they watched me come down the stairs. They were as baleful as those of the big Dane standing on the other side of Aunt Beryl and just about as intelligent.

The lady herself eyed me with none of the sparkle I'd seen earlier. The more I saw of her the less she looked like a comfy throw pillow.

I stopped two steps from the bottom. This gave me an inch on Felix and, if I was alert, half a second to get to my Smith before he connected with one of those trained sides of beef he called fists. Having thirty years on an ex-prizefighter wasn't enough, not even when he was a bad ex-prizefighter. I fished out my last cigarette and placed it in the corner of my mouth without lighting it, keeping my eyes on his left shoulder all the time. When it dropped I was going for the gun.

"What were you doing up there?" demanded the old lady. It was hard to imagine a voice like that laughing with a tinkle.

"You can't blame a guy for trying," I said. "I used to be pretty good at sneaking in for a free matinee when I was a kid. Guess I've lost the knack."

"Am I supposed to believe that?"

"I had hopes."

"Felix."

She might have been calling to the dog. The big man's shoulder dipped a fraction of an inch and I scooped the gun out of its holster and planted the muzzle between his eyes with a hollow clop. The fist stopped, hardly airborne.

"Brains don't scrub out of carpets." I spoke around the cigarette.

It would have gotten very quiet then if Ulysses weren't growling.

"Pretty brave, ain't you?" Felix rumbled. "With a piece."

I said, "Thanks. That was all this scene lacked. A good cliché."

"What were you doing up there?" Aunt Beryl repeated. "I have a right to know that, Mr. Walker. This is my house."

I kept the gun and my mouth where they were.

"I have friends in the state police," she said. "I can have your license revoked. Trespassing is an illegal act."

"Do that. I'll tell the board of inquiry I was trying to get information out of one of your whores."

"You've made your point, Mr. Walker. Put the gun away."

"Call off your animals."

Felix, his fist still cocked, made a noise in his throat that drowned out the dog. I crunched back the hammer of the Smith, which was as effective as it was unnecessary.

"See to the rear walk," directed his boss. "Take Ulysses."

The fighter held his ground long enough to save the face of half a million Chinese, then lowered the massive left and shambled out, whistling through a space in his teeth for the dog to follow. I put away the revolver and was on my way past Beryl Garnet when she placed a hand on my arm.

Her tiny eyes glittered up at me. "I let you have that one, Mr. Walker. Next time I won't be so sporting."

I removed my arm from her hand and left her to her hookers and her big pets.

My usual space across from my building was taken by a dark green Mercury without a speck of chrome on it, one of the new small jobs, so I parked around the corner. I noticed as I walked back around to the front door that there were two men in it, the one behind the wheel reading a newspaper. Automobiles had become surprisingly popular study spots of late for November. I noted the license plate number as I went in.

Lunchtime found me at my desk polishing off one of those modern rarities, an unadorned hamburger, and washing it down with Pabst. Those finished, I dialed police headquarters and got a receptionist who explained that Lieutenant Alderdyce was on another line and put me on hold. Five lonely minutes later I got John.

"Got another number for you," I said. "I may be getting paranoid, but I think my office is being watched."

"So what's new?" He sounded harried.

I gave him the number. Paper rustled, which could have meant that he was either writing it down or mopping up a coffee spill with an old report. That's why I don't trust telephones.

"Anything else?"

"Yeah. What's the Kramer burn doing under glass?"

"Forget it." It came too fast.

"Come on, John. You know I'm good for it."

"Goddamn it, I said forget it!" He caught himself shouting. He turned down the volume but left the intensity where it was. "Walker, I'm sick to Christ of you sticking your snooper into police business. I'm warning you, stay out of the Kramer case or I'll see they yank your ticket for good!" He banged off.

I replaced the receiver as if it were a live bomb, zipped the top off a fresh pack of Winstons, and sat and smoked and wondered. I tried the number for Aphrodite Records, just for fun, and got a recording that told me Mr. Zacharias was out for a while, would I please wait for the beep and leave my name and number? I didn't wait. I snatched up the morning *Free Press* and attempted to interest myself in Part One of a windy series on the life of the late Freeman Shanks. A stirring account of his struggle to survive a diabetic childhood. It didn't stir me. Halfway through the second paragraph the door to my outer office opened and closed. When my visitor's shadow appeared on the pebbled glass of the inner door I cranked down the drawbridge.

It was Rosecranz, the building super. He was a little man with a fraying face and scruffy hair from which all the color had run years ago and a posture so stooped he seemed to be lugging two thousand years of misplaced guilt in the bib of his overalls.

"Hope I ain't caught you busy, Mr. Walker," he squeaked. His vocal cords seemed always to be in need of a lube.

"Nobody's timing is that good, Mr. Rosecranz."

"I just wanted to remind you of the clause in your lease that says you can't change what's on the windows."

I turned around to look at the single square window behind me, partially hidden behind the dusty, half-drawn venetian blinds. Then I turned back to give him the same blank expression.

"That fellow I let in an hour ago," he said helpfully. "The one come in to measure for curtains. Your lease says you got to stick with them blinds. How'd it look to the folks outside if every office had something different on its windows?"

"What did this fellow look like?"

He frowned. "Not tall, not short. Dark hair. Kind of average. Looked like a lot of other fellows."

"That's probably what makes him average. Black or white?"

"Oh, he was white. I'd of said so if he was otherwise. He had on a blue suit, though, which struck me as kind of queer."

"That it was blue?"

"That it was a suit. Where would he carry his folding rule?"

I thanked him and told him not to worry about the blinds. After he left I sat and smoked and crushed out the stub in the glass ashtray on my desk. I looked in all the drawers and underneath them. I checked out the file cabinet. I crawled on my hands and knees along the floor and ran my fingers over the baseboards. I stood on the desk and peered inside the glass mantle of the overhead fixture. I found a gum wrapper and six dead flies. Finally I sat back down, lifted the telephone receiver, and unscrewed the mouthpiece. A disc about the size of a dime and twice as thick was taped inside the rim.

I didn't touch it. I screwed the whole thing back together and cradled it and lit up and sat and smoked and stared at the wall on the other side of which, three stories down, two men in a green Mercury were staring at the door of this building. Then I grabbed my hat and coat and headed for the hallway.

The sedan didn't pick up on me right away. They were too good for that. It came into my rearview mirror when I was two blocks down Trumbull, and maintained that distance until I turned onto Michigan, where it fell back. That was what I'd been waiting for.

I had time to kill before Barney Zacharias came back from lunch. Without signaling I hung a sharp right onto Harrison, cutting across two lanes of traffic in front of a tanker with good air brakes and a healthy horn, squealed into a private driveway and sat there pretending to consult a map of Indiana while I waited for the fireworks. I barely got the thing unfolded when more rubber screamed, accompanied by fresh horns, and a dark green bullet shot down Harrison past the end of the strip of concrete where I was parked, rear end fishtailing on the slushy street surface. I banged the indicator into the R position and swung out behind them, gunned the engine, spun slush and snow until the tread caught, and tore off in their wake.

They must have seen me looming up in their rearview mirror, because I was almost on their bumper when they began pulling away. There was more mill under that nondescript hood than the engineers had in mind when they'd designed it. Even with my disguised Caddy I couldn't take time out to burn tobacco without losing half a block. Bravery and cowardice had nothing to do with it; it's disconcerting to go along thinking you're the hunter and then suddenly find yourself the quarry. You need time to get away by yourself and think it out. I wasn't letting them have it.

In a chase, all the advantage belongs to the guy doing

the chasing. If the driver of the Merc knew where he was going, I knew where he'd been, and if he could take a forty-five-degree curve at eighty without turning his car into a football, or plow through a snowbank without getting stuck, I knew I could too. There were a couple of times when I could have swept alongside and forced him over, but I resisted the temptation. That kind of stuff works on the tube, but the only time you can expect the odds to be in your favor east of Hollywood is when you're at the wheel of a semi or a tanker or a Sherman tank and your quarry isn't. What I was doing was waiting for him to make his second mistake. His first was tailing me to begin with.

We shot past a couple of stop signs and splattered dirty spray over a pedestrian or two, and I was beginning to wonder if the eighth of a tank of gas I had left was going to hold out, when the idiot up ahead stood on his brakes. I was two car lengths behind him when I reacted. I floored the brake pedal, twisted the wheel left, and let the ice and snow under my tires do the rest. When Detroit stopped whirling I was parked facing in the direction from which I had come, one wheel was crammed up over the curb, and my right rear fender was snuggled against a stout maple planted in a box on the sidewalk. The tree would never be the same and neither would my bridgework.

My mirror had been knocked askew by something, probably my head. In the rectangular job mounted outside the driver's window I could see the familiar rear of a dark green sedan and, hurrying toward me, the most average-looking guy I'd ever met. He had on a blue suit and a black topcoat and his hair was dark and the automatic in his left hand shone like a movie starlet's hopes.

My revolver was in the glove compartment where I kept it while driving, a whole arm's length away. My engine was still running. I punched the accelerator. The rear wheels whined merrily and that was it. I was stuck in a snowbank. My mirror was full of Mr. Everyday. I lunged for the glove compartment, but before I got there a hot light exploded at the base of my brain and suddenly it didn't seem so important anymore. Stretching out on the seat did.

"He's down, General," said a voice on the other side of a blaze orange nightmare.

11

FICTION'S NICE. WHEN A writer hits his golden-armored alter ego with the Penobscot Building, the lucky slob gets a few minutes of much-needed sleep and comes out of it with no headache that three fingers of Hiram Walker's won't cure. He takes the count quiet and gets up disheveled but clean, his necktie romantically askew and a lock of hair hanging Gable-like over one eye. The rest of us go down shouting and swallowing our tongues, and when after a lifetime we finally slog our way back to the surface, we're crumpled in the dusty corner of a rumbling automobile in a pool of our own vomit, our pockets hanging out and the linings of our thirty-dollar overcoats flapping where the stitches have been popped loose by a sharp knife.

I hadn't been completely out, naturally. If in the course of your daily routine you've ever been sapped on the underside of your occipital lobe by something like a pistol swung sideways, you know that it's your motor functions that go first, making so much spaghetti out of the intricate nervous system that carries electrical impulses from your brain to your various muscles and turning your limbs into dead weight. Then your brain cells begin to blink out in clusters, then just one by one, until you're left with just enough to wonder what was so bad about staying in bed that morning, and precious little else. Had the blow been just a little lighter I'd have tingled all over and caught myself before I'd gone down, and that would have been it except for a sore spot on the back of my head. Had it been just a little harder I'd have qualified for bed space in the produce section of the local supermarket, next to the other cabbages.

I knew it, but was powerless to stop it, when two pairs of hands working from opposite sides of the car turned me over and emptied my pockets and went through the linings of my coat and jacket. When I was lowered to the floor and folded into the corner under the dashboard to make room in the driver's seat I knew that too, but only by the change of scenery since I was as numb as a victory party in the losing candidate's campaign headquarters. My head began to throb dully as it rocked from side to side over the squishy spot with the lurching of the Cutlass being freed from its snowy prison.

For a while I fluttered in and out, and then reality slammed into me as suddenly as it had been taken away. I turned my head and retched again. That brought me up a rung or two from the bottom of the barrel, but it was a deep barrel and there was a lid on top. I attempted to spit out the farmer's brogan in my mouth, but the taste was there to stay. Then I said something that wasn't a sentence in any language I'd ever heard of and started the long crawl up to the seat.

"He's coming around, General."

The voice, which belonged to the driver, was the same one I had heard reporting my condition just after my lights were shot out. It was ordinary like the rest of him, innocent of regional accent, and about as distinctive as a paper clip. I sneaked a look at him as I was scaling the seat. He had a good profile, with a straight nose and clean line of jaw and dark, wavy hair, not short, not long, the way even politicians are wearing it these days. He could have been thirty or forty-five.

The guy in the back seat, whom I glimpsed while shifting around to sit the way I was designed, was older, about fifty, with crisp gray hair cut severely without sideburns. His face, naturally lean but beginning to go slack in the standard places, was all planes and sharp angles, like something blocked out by a sculptor before placing the finishing touches on a statue. He was bareheaded and wore a tawny car coat with a black fur collar. He didn't pay any attention to me at all, but kept his flinty eyes on the scenery rolling past the window. His wide, lipless mouth was tugged downward into a wooden-Indian scowl that looked as if it might be terminal.

We were doing twenty-five down a street I recognized, one of the better residential sections along the river. All the houses looked alike and their snow-clad lawns sloped at the same angle down to the sidewalk. Only the colors of the Cordobas and Sevilles parked in the asphalt driveways changed.

"Stop here," I said, through a throat thick with phlegm. "Going somewhere?" The driver's tone was casual enough. The threat was there without his having to be obvious.

"Not as long as you've got my car."

"General?" He shot a glance back over his shoulder. The General didn't say anything, but he must have nodded because the car swung in toward the curb and glided to a stop.

I got out, breathed some cold fresh air, stooped, and rolled up the square plastic mat containing the remains of my lunch. I hiked back to where someone had left his garbage out for pickup and thrust the roll inside a plastic trash can.

I had an egg on the back of my head you could have

served to a Boy Scout troop. But you wouldn't have wanted to, because it was sticky with blood. A white-hot bolt of pure pain shot clear down to my toes when I touched it. The ache that came back afterward was blinding. As the car slid into motion I closed my eyes and slouched down to rest my neck on the back of the seat.

"Cigarette?" The man behind the wheel nudged me. I opened my eyes and stared for a moment at the package of Lucky Strikes beneath my nose as if it were a picture of his kids. I patted my shirt pocket, found that my Winstons were still there, got one out, and shook my head. Something rattled inside. He withdrew the pack.

"The trouble with Luckies is they never came back from the war." I couldn't find my matches. He finished lighting one of his own and tossed his lighter toward me. I caught it and looked at it. It was a silver and pigskin job with the initials J. V. engraved on one side. I lit up and tossed it back.

"Jim Vespers," he introduced himself. "Colonel Vespers, if you want to be formal about it. The gentleman sitting behind you is General Spain." He scooped something out of a pocket and flipped it open in front of my eyes. It was a leather folder with gold corners and something behind a celluloid window.

"Which one am I supposed to read?"

He laughed, a short, ordinary laugh, and put it away. "I forgot. You're probably seeing double about now. The General and I represent Army Intelligence."

"That's depressing."

He laughed again. He enjoyed a good joke as much as the next guy. They were regular fellows, these quiet men with guns who went around tapping people's telephones and following them from place to place. He caught me eyeing the glove compartment.

"Is this what you're looking for?" Without taking his eyes from the road he held out my Smith & Wesson in its snap holster. "Go ahead, take it. It's not loaded anymore."

I accepted it, took a minute to establish that fact, and snapped it onto my belt.

"You've a permit to carry that, I hope," he said.

"You ought to know. You went through my wallet."

He let that one slide. "That was a stupid trick you pulled back there. How come?"

"Force of habit. I can't seem to stop myself from going for iron whenever somebody comes running up on me waving a pistol."

We drove for a while in silence. We weren't going anywhere in particular, just swinging in a wide circle back to where we'd started. Vespers pulled into the filling station at Fort and First and told the kid attendant to top off the tank.

"This one's on the taxpayers, Walker," he explained as the pump clanged.

"Thanks," I said. "That's worth a fractured skull anytime."

"Where's the film?"

I looked at him through the smoke of the cigarette I wasn't supposed to have going now that the pump was working. Nobody enforces the rules anymore. I reached over and crushed it out in the ashtray. Vespers made no effort to ditch his.

"What film?" I said. Someone had to.

He changed the subject. They teach them to do that in Washington. "We ran down your record after Alderdyce told us you were the one clued him in on Francis Kramer. Pretty impressive. Six years' military service, a tour in Vietnam and Cambodia, a DSC for saving your platoon at Hue, three years in the MPs stateside. How'd you end up in this greasy line of work?"

"Where'd you learn to tap a telephone?"

He smiled. That amused him. He took a last drag on his butt and killed it beside mine. "So you found it. I told the General you would. We also tossed your office and your house, but you wouldn't know that."

"I knew about the office. I haven't been home."

"You did? How?" He seemed genuinely interested. I'd stumbled on a chink in his defenses and he was waiting with mortar and a trowel.

"You left it neater than you found it. What's on the film?"

"We waited quite a while for you to show up. What've you been doing?"

"Working."

"Working on what?"

I stared out the window. "Did you know this is a historic site? This was the first drive-in gas station in the world. It's been operating since 1901. The roots of the automobile era go down deep in this town."

"What the hell has that got to do with anything?" He was miffed. That was the word for it. His type never gets howling mad. It would draw too much attention.

"Exactly," I said.

That bought me a few seconds of confused silence. Then the fellow in the back seat spoke up. "Tell him, Colonel." His voice was General Patton filtered through George C. Scott.

The kid in greasy coveralls and a two-tone high school jacket appeared at the driver's window and quoted an astronomical figure, which Vespers paid without glancing at the pump. People like him put kids like that through college. Back on the road: "Have you ever heard of something called the Black Legion?"

"A Warner Brothers flick. Bogart made it in '37."

He nodded, as if that was what he'd been getting at. "I've seen it. That's basically what I'm talking about."

"Where does Ann Sheridan come in?"

"Cut the comedy, Walker. The Legion was a northern branch of the Ku Klux Klan that kept its headquarters in Detroit during the thirties. It boasted a membership of two hundred thousand, but it was a few hundred bully boys at the center that caused most of the trouble. Mainly they were a bunch of frustrated WASPs who blamed blacks and for-eigners for their inability to get anywhere in the world. What they should have done was blame their mothers for giving birth to a herd of narrow-minded malcontents who had neither the brains nor the stamina to rise above their station without resorting to violence. Midnight rides in white robes and peaked hoods, lynchings, cold-blooded ex-ecutions in lonely fields in the wee hours—that was their style. It's estimated that between 1931 and 1936 they were responsible for at least fifty killings in the area. There's no telling how many more might have died if the police and the public hadn't banded together in '36 to put most of the leaders behind bars. After that, publicity and unmasking laws sent them scrambling for the tall timber."

"Does this history lesson take long?"

"Jesus, but you're impatient for a cop, even a private one. The Black Legion's been staging a come-back over the past two years. Someone down south is financing a Klan franchise up here. We know who it is, but we can't prove it, and even if we did what could we do about it? It's per-fectly legal."

"So why worry?"

"Don't be naïve. It's our job to see it stays that way. Detroit was chosen for tradition's sake, but since the GOP's announcement that it would hold its next convention here the whole movement's gained real impetus. Word has it that one of the candidates for the Republican nomination is marked for assassination and that the Legion's behind the plan. The system can stand it, but all hell's bound to bust loose for a while, and chaos is what these quasi-revolutionary groups thrive on. There's no telling what they'll do for an encore. We've all learned something from the troubles in Ireland and the Middle East."

"Sounds nutty."

"Read the papers, Walker. Watch television. The world's gone nutty."

"How does Army Intelligence figure in? Why not the FBI or the Secret Service?"

"The army's got as much stake in seeing this thing put to rest as anybody. The Legion's infiltrated our ranks. I'm not just talking about the guys you see on furlough at the local whorehouse, privates or sergeants or even second lieutenants. I'm talking pentagon. Care to see your country defended by rank after rank of ridgerunners in sheets and pillowcases, carrying flaming crosses? Stick around."

I started to hum "Marching through Georgia." It hurt my head. I stopped.

"Okay," he said, "so maybe I'm being melodramatic. That doesn't throw any sand over a sticky situation. We had a man among the local nightriders. He's dead."

"Francis Kramer made Army Intelligence? You really ought to change your name. Too many jokes come to mind."

"He wasn't one of our regulars. He knew some people in the group and he was familiar with most kinds of photographic apparatus. We got him out of the reserves, where he was a major, taught him how to avoid tripping over his own feet, armed him with a movie camera, wound him up, and turned him loose. For six months he furnished us with reports and some interesting footage, then missed an appointment with a field agent and cropped up nine hours later with a hole in his head an army physician couldn't miss. No film. No camera. We threw wraps over the case and tossed his apartment. We found the camera, but the only film kicking around was unexposed. He had something or he wouldn't have made the appointment. Question is, what was it and who has it?"

"Which is why I'm sitting here holding my brains in while you run up miles on my automobile."

"We'd attract too much attention sitting where we were. As for the state of your health, I'm sorry about that but you begged for it. You were the only lead left. As far as we know you were the last one to see Major Kramer alive—except for his murderers—and by your own testimony at police headquarters he was your company commander in Southeast Asia. Furthermore, you're a private dick, a profession that has not been known for an astonishing lack of blackmailers and ripoff artists. Look at it from this side and see how it plays. You run into an old war buddy who may already be in fear of his life because of some incriminating evidence in his possession. He gives you some song and dance and places the evidence in your care. He gets dealt out; you realize what you've got is dynamite and sock it away for future use. What could be more natural?"

"Except that you didn't find anything."

"Yet."

I laughed dryly. That hurt too. Not much didn't. "You didn't even turn a key to a safety deposit box. If you looked up my background you know I don't own a summer house in Grosse Pointe. Where else could I have ditched it?"

"You tell us, Walker. Look, I didn't say you were the only possible suspect, just the only one we had. That play you pulled back there makes me wonder if we've even got you. That isn't the kind of thing someone with something to hide would do. Someone who isn't wrapped too tight, yes, but not someone with something to hide. So we're back to square one. Less than that. We're out a deep cover agent we couldn't afford to lose. What's the case you're working?"

"Missing person. Nothing to do with Kramer."

"Who's the person?"

"It's either Judge Crater or Jimmy Hoffa. I keep forgetting."

"All right, smart guy."

We were back on Harrison. The green Merc was parked in front of a ranch-style home on a low hill as if it belonged there. Vespers coasted up beside it took the Cutlass out of gear and got out, tipping the driver's bucket forward for General Spain to climb out of the back. I'd almost forgotten he was there. Colonel Average Guy stooped to peer in at me through the open door.

"You roll out first," he said. "I don't want this hot rod in heap's clothing behind me again. Oh, and a word of warning. Just in case I'm wrong, and you *have* got something to hide, stand clear of a pair of blond hicks who call themselves the Darling brothers. They dusted Kramer because they found out he'd been spying on them. You they'd do just for practice."

He circled around the front toward the sedan, leaving me there to think. Somewhere in the wreckage of my memory a coin that had been rattling around for a while dropped through a slot and things started clicking. I was too groggy from the blow and from too much all at once to figure out why. I wasn't any closer to it when I slid beneath the wheel and got moving. It bothered me all the way into River Rouge.

12

FOR THREE HUNDRED YEARS, the broad, flat, sluggish artery men call the Detroit River has brought life to the community that flourishes, more or less, at its base. Before that, like every other waterway in North America, it brought the Indians, Sac and Fox and Miami and Huron and Potawatomi and the mysterious Copper People, who paused not long enough to leave a disfiguring mark on the land they loved, then continued on their predestined way to oblivion. Then came the *coureurs de bois*, the "runners in the woods," who paddled their birchbark canoes with strong sure hands, leagues ahead of the powerful fur-trading companies in whose territory they were poaching. They left behind their stamp in the depletion of the beaver that once swarmed the grassy banks, but they too moved on. One of them, Etienne Brulé, came to explore one time too many and left his brains in an Iroquois camp. Missionaries followed, bringing with them their robes and sacraments and wafers and Bibles and the destruction of the old ways, and the land began to conform to their will. Among these were the Jesuits Dollier and Galinée, who, chancing to pass a stone idol erected by Indians near the mouth of the River Rouge to ensure safe passage across the treacherous waters of Lake Erie, hove to, smashed the pagan abomination to bits, and hurled what was left into the river. In 1701 Antoine Laumet, a well-traveled adventurer with no more scruples than he could carry comfortably in his parfleche, and whose title, Antoine de la Mothe, Sieur de Cadillac, was so new it squeaked, stepped ashore where the Civic Center now stands, sank the foundation for the first of many log structures to be erected beneath his supervision, and eventually got a car named after him. If he'd known what he was starting he might have taken advantage of the first favorable wind and set sail for home. Probably not, though, or he might not have died rich.

The river has brought death too. During the siege of Detroit, Pontiac, a great chief and not a bad automobile, turned a successful ambush of British reinforcements into a powerful psychological weapon when he sent logs floating past the fort at irregular intervals with the mutilated corpses of soldiers strapped to them in 1763. Prohibition turned it into a river of beer and blood as rumrunners on their way to and from Windsor shot it out in the names of the Purple Gang and the Licavolis and certain high officials later indicted and sent up for complicity. Every few years someone dredges up another rusted hulk that's sat on the bottom for half a century, sometimes with a skeleton in it, sometimes not. And there's no telling how many wops and sheenies are sleeping the long sleep down there wrapped in concrete. In the early summer of 1943, Belle Isle, a spit of land bulging out of the water just this side of the international border and the scene of the massacre of a family of hog-tenders by Pontiac's warriors during the Battle of Bloody Run, was the origin of one of the worst race riots in modern history, with thirty-four deaths the consequence. Now it's a park with a grimy fountain named for a notorious reformed gambler, boozer, and womanizer, and Bloody Run hauls sewage and death beneath the pavement to Lake Erie.

An ore carrier wallowing beneath fifteen or twenty tons

of iron pellets was crawling through the rust-colored waters at the mouth of the River Rouge on its way to the Ford plant. I watched it through the big picture window on the north side of the truss barn that housed Aphrodite Records on Marion while Barney Zacharias, standing with his back to the window, bored me with his oral history of the rise and decline of the music industry in Detroit.

"Stevie Wonder," he was saying, oblivious to the manic chords barreling out the open door of the glassed-in recording cubicle to his right, where a stout, bearded white man in a funeral suit sat banging New Orleans boogie-woogie out of a battered upright piano. "He called himself Little Stevie Wonder in those days. He cut a couple of discs in my place on Michigan. Diana Ross, Aretha Franklin, the Rationals, SRC, the Ones, the Woolies, Bob Seger, Streisand. That was a riot, Streisand. She didn't look like nothing coming into the studio, and one of the engineers comes in and says, 'Hey, babe, she don't look too cool, but, boy, she's got a hell of a voice.' And there she is, and she don't even give Big D a tumble no more. She did then, though. They all did. What's Nashville? We turned out more real stars in one month than they have in five years."

"About Martha Burns," I put in.

It was no use. Once he got started you had to wait for him to wind down. He was an excitable little guy with a bald head nesting in a fringe of black hair and a body you could pass through a pipe if it weren't for his forearms. Sticking out of his turned-back cuffs, these were thick, powerful things overgrown with coarse black hair and terminating in large, hard hands that he might have had trouble keeping still if he bothered to try. It's bigoted to generalize, but I've never met an Italian or a Greek who could hold up his end of the conversation if you tied his wrists behind him. His face was round and he had lively eyes the size and color of olives and a five-o'clock shadow that gleamed dully like blue steel beneath his skin.

"It was big money did us in." He spread his hands to show how big. "A group cuts a disc here, it sells, they get an offer from New York or L.A., and they hop a plane and we never see them again. Which is the stupidest thing in the world, because this is where they got their sound. That don't come in packages. The riots finished us off. When them windows started busting, the writers lit out, and when they lit out the talent followed them. Then Motown went out to L.A. and died. Those of us that decided to hang on and ride it out got law down our necks and we're still trying to shake it loose.

"My old man used to tell me about the Old Country, where you would bring the judge a jug of goat's milk and win any case. To me, if I put a record out, and the jock is instrumental in putting it over, it's no different from tipping the waitress a buck for doing a good job. But some jocks got hungry. The government looks into it and fines the pants off me so bad I got to sell out and take this dump outside the limits. You'll see, though. It'll turn around. Motown's back now, and pretty soon it'll be 1965 all over again. Just wait and see."

He cocked his naked pate toward the recording room, where the pianist had switched to a low, lingering blues. "Hear that? That guy's a Methodist minister, but by the time he gets done fooling around and puts that stuff on wax and we push it in all the right places he'll have a brand new calling. He's just the kind of talent we need to get the whole thing rolling again. Just goes to show you don't have to be black to play good nigger jazz. What'd you say your name was?"

I gave him my card. He studied it, fingered a corner absently, and consigned it to his shirt pocket. He wore neither jacket nor tie, and his white shirt was dark around the armpits. It wasn't that hot. The room we occupied was a cavernous hall lit by fluorescent tubes in three long troughs suspended from the ceiling twenty feet above our heads, its dusty cement floor littered with cables and alive with icy drafts that skirled gleefully about our pants legs. The steel door on the north side banged in its casing with each gust off the river.

"Martha Burns," he reflected, as if I'd just mentioned the name. "I'm not sure I—"

"Beryl Garnet said you offered to record her," I said.

A sly look came over his features. His expressive face must have been something to see when they had him in court on the payola charge. "She's marrying money, I bet," he said. "He's paying you to look up her past. I bet there's big dough in it."

"Wrong twice. Her father's looking for her and I'm getting my usual fee. Which is probably less than what you'd slip a deejay to turn a bomb into a hit."

"Hell. The way she carried on I thought she had William Clay Ford on the hook at least."

"She was here, then. When?"

"What's it worth?"

"Depends on what you've got to sell."

"I got expenses to meet. Rent. Utilities. It's gonna be a long winter. I'm gonna burn a lot of gas."

"Not as much as you're burning right now, brother."

"I need some guarantee I'll get paid for what I give."

"Sorry."

He thought about it a minute. The minister had stopped playing in the next room and was scratching something on his sheet music. Zacharias stepped over and pulled shut the soundproof door.

"It was February," he said. "Early part. She comes in one morning, tells me she's taking me up on my offer. I said what offer. I didn't even know her. She says I told her I could make her a star. Hell, that was New Year's Eve and I was three sheets to the wind. There's damn few I don't say that to when I'm off the express. I say, 'Okay, let's hear what you got.' She sits down at the box. She's got sheet music in her purse. Something from Broadway, I forget what exactly. I expected to get my eardrums warped, but she surprised me. She was good."

"Star material?"

He shook his head. "Not by ten miles. A good voice I can get by raiding any church choir in town. There are lots of tricks for making a terrific singer sound better, but no amount of backups and echo chambers is gonna put in something that wasn't there to begin with. Good isn't good enough."

"You tell her that?"

He started to go sly on me again. I squashed it early. "It might be worth something."

"A century?"

"Trot it out. I don't buy horseflesh I can't see."

"You wouldn't trust Jesus with a used rubber."

"Jack, you don't look a bit like him."

"All right." He swiped a hand over his scratchy chin, smoothed it up and over the top of his head as if there were something up there to smooth, let it slide down the back of his neck, and left it there. "I told her I could do something with her, but first she'd have to invest a couple of hundred dollars. I needed the money. My landlord's halitosis was in my collar and the phone company was gonna shut off my service."

"What made you think she had it to invest?"

"Hell, I saw it. When she hauled out that music the inside of her purse looked like the Valley of the Jolly Green Giant. She had a portrait of Madison in there. You know what he's on?"

"A thousand-dollar bill."

"That's right! Say, what kind of fee do you charge?"

"I read a lot. How much she pour down your little rathole?"

"Watch it, smart mouth! I held up my end. We cut the records, I took out ads, got a jock friend of mine to spin it on the air. I'm not a crook."

"We had a president who said that. Okay, you bought a tombstone in the neighborhood shopper and sank a fin to play the disc at five A.M. in between farm reports. How bad you burn her?"

"Fifteen hundred."

I laughed. "How come you're not mayor?"

"She had plenty to spare." I'd wounded him. "I got one of her singles here if you don't believe me. Care to hear it?"

I said sure and followed him into the recording room and across to the door of the engineers' booth on the other side. The minister didn't look up from his keyboard as we passed behind him on a wave of ragtime. The booth was deserted. Inside, Zacharias stooped to slide a master disc with a plain label out of a cabinet beneath the gaudy control panel and skimmed it at me. I had to clap it to my chest with both hands to keep it from falling. By the time I had it I was staring into the hole of a .25 automatic in the Greek's right hand. At that range it might as well have been a Howitzer.

"Cute, huh?" he said around a grin. "I saw it done once in a movie. Only they used an inner tube."

"I guess you didn't have one handy."

"Shut up. I got this baby two years ago after a kid I was training to be an engineer got held up and shot right about where you're standing. Junkies. He died. They got six dollars off him and some change. Call it River Rouge or Ecorse or Hamtramck or Farmington or Dearborn, it's all Detroit and it stinks. Now suppose you tell me how much you're willing to spend to find out what I know. Sight unseen."

I was holding the record overhead where I'd raised my hands when the gun came out. I let it drop. It didn't break. They don't nowadays, though they scratch when you look at them. It hit on its edge and rolled across the floor toward Zacharias. People are like dogs, attracted by movement. His eyes followed the rolling disc and I reached out and snatched hold of the gun.

His forearms were as strong as they looked. He held on and we closed and grappled, four hands fighting for a gun that could be concealed in any one of them. There was a loud, sharp rapping sound and a bullet chipped the concrete between my feet and whizzed off to bury itself in the sound-proof wall. The recoil, tiny as it was, was unexpected and it made him loosen his grip momentarily. I twisted it out of his grasp and kneed him in the groin in the same movement. He doubled over gasping.

On the other side of the window the minister was pounding away on the piano. Not a note came through with the microphones turned off. The soundproofing worked as well in reverse. I left Zacharias to wait for the pain to tingle up through his stomach and out while I pocketed the little pistol and stepped over to retrieve the record. Martha Burns' name was scratched on the label in block Magic Marker capitals. Below it was the title: "Body and Soul." She had a sense of humor. I found a turntable and spiked it and fiddled around until I found the knob that started it turning. Half-way through the vamp I came across the volume, which damn near brought the booth crashing down around me before I got it dialed down. Then I stood back to watch Barney Zacharias and listen.

She had the kind of voice you find in the better bars, the kind you don't really hear until you're three-quarters shellacked and the number you courted the wife by comes up and you poke a dollar into the tip glass and you go home feeling a little sad and wake up the next morning without remembering anything but the drinks and the sadness. It was good enough to hum along with when you weren't too preoccupied to notice it, but not so good it interrupted the serious drinkers. It was low but not low enough, sultry but shallow. You wouldn't pay to hear it.

The small combo Zacharias had hired to back her up was cut from the same bolt. There were a lot of them out there. One out of every hundred thousand made good money for a while, then dropped out of sight and ended up with a tag on his toe and an inch on page twenty-three of a newspaper small enough to take notice: "Johnny Hercules, one-time guitarist with the Winged Wonders vocal group, was found dead on the bathroom floor of his Dearborn Heights home yesterday afternoon. Death is believed to have resulted from drug overdose." I wondered if Aphrodite Records offered the musicians the same deal as Martha Burns, née Marla Bernstein.

By the time the record ended, Zacharias was sitting on a stool at the control panel with his head in his hands. I asked him if he was feeling better. He didn't call me anything I hadn't been called before.

"Let's start with the money," I said. "Where'd she get it?"

"Go piss up a rope." The words were squeezed from his diaphragm. Either I'd kicked him harder than planned or he was faking. I decided to test the second hypothesis.

I took the little widowmaker out of my pocket, made sure the safety was on, gathered it up in my fist, and, moving so that my back was between him and the window, tapped the bald Greek on the tip of his chin between his supporting hands.

As an improvement on nature the compact firearm was fully as effective as my own Smith had been on Erskine. His hands sprang apart, his teeth snapped, and his head went back and rapped the fiberboard on the wall behind him. He gasped and shook his head as if to see if I'd knocked anything loose inside. I was sure as hell trying.

I massaged my knuckles where they'd split open again and stepped in for a second blow. He saw me coming, yelled, and threw his hands up in front of his face. It was like hurling a shotput through morning mist. His nose flattened like so much papier-mâché and blood spurted from his nostrils over his white shirt front.

"I don't like people who pull guns," I explained, through my teeth. "Sooner or later someone's got to show your brand of punk that a peashooter in your hand doesn't necessarily mean the world in your pocket. I guess I'm elected."

I was proud of myself. I'd been insulted by cops, swiped at with a shiv, frisked, brained, shot at, and threatened, and I was taking it out on a guy half my size with an artificial aid I didn't need just because he swindled kids who had nothing but hope and a little money and pulled guns he had no intention of using. I was in a league with the brainless slugs at Olympia who sat swilling beer out of paper cups and screaming for one overpaid athlete to splatter another's gray matter over the manmade ice. The only difference was that I was the one doing the splattering. I spread my feet for another crack.

"No!" It was a shriek of uncut terror. He had his arms crossed over his swollen and bleeding face and his head was pressed back against the wall so hard it dented the brittle material that covered it. "I don't know where she got the money! I didn't ask. She just had it. I swear!"

"That'll buy you a ticket to yesterday's ballgame," I said. But I backed off. Slowly he lowered his arms. His nose was puffed and still trickling and a dirty bluish patch had begun to spread over his chin and jaw. He'd be living on oatmeal and eggnog for the next week.

I got out my handkerchief and wound it around my sore right hand. The blood seeped through the white cotton, something else to be added to the expense account I would submit to Ben Morningstar. "Try guessing," I told him. "She didn't make that much hooking."

"How should I know? Maybe she got it from her boy-friend."

"You mentioned that before. Who was he?"

"Search me. I never even saw the guy. She used to get calls from him in the studio. I overheard enough to know he was loaded. That's it."

"You sure?"

"No, I'm holding out. I like to do that when somebody's working me over real good. I'm into S/M."

"When did you see her last?"

"Sometime around the end of July. We had problems getting a good cut and knocked off around seven. She said she'd be in to try again in the morning. She wasn't. I haven't seen her since, and don't think I didn't try to find her, a sweet deal like that. No soap. I never even knew where she was staying."

I broke the clip from the automatic, jacked the shell out of the chamber, wiped everything off with the end of my handkerchief, and laid the works on the control panel out of his reach.

"Why'd you air the iron?"

He had his own handkerchief out and was using it to staunch the flow of blood from his nostrils. If we used the same laundry there were going to be rumors circulating come wash day. "Sooner or later everybody gets to pushing me around," he complained. "I figured it was time I did some pushing of my own."

I left the booth. He scrambled up off the stool. "Hey, what about paying me for the info?"

"Your turn at the rope," I said, and left. The minister played on.

13

SINCE ANYONE DESPERATE ENOUGH to steal second-hand furniture and magazines old enough for Medicare deserves a break, I leave the door to my outer office unlocked during the day for the convenience of those customers who don't mind waiting. There was one on the pew behind a copy of *Life* when I got back.

"Where'd you park the yellow bomb?" I asked as I drew the door shut. "I didn't spot it out front."

"Around the corner." Wiley returned the magazine to the coffee table and got up. The more I saw of him the more he looked like an ad for campus fashions. I kept wondering how he got into the business. He didn't look the type to go the standard dope route, but you never know.

I got out a cigarette and rolled it around in my fingers. "What can I do you for?"

"You can start with a full report. You promised Mr. Morningstar you'd check in daily."

"That was only fourteen hours ago. The day's not up yet."

"Let's hear it anyway. I don't smoke."

I'd offered him a Winston. I shrugged and lit mine. "Thanks. I'll make it to Mr. Morningstar in person." I waved out the match slowly. He was watching me, not the movement. Well, it didn't always work. That was good to know for future reference.

"Come along, then."

"Sorry. I'm busy."

"He's an old man," he said calmly. "That's why he hires people like Paul Cooke and me to look after his interests. Which includes making sure he isn't taken by down-at-heels private eyes with friends on newspapers and in the police department. He can holler nigger all he wants and I'll still do it because that's what he pays me for. Do we understand each other?"

"Not quite. I'm down at heels because I'm honest. Some of us are in this business. We're the guys the slick ops in the sharp tailormades hire at the professional courtesy rate of fifty or a hundred a day to do the work their clients engage them for at three hundred. Your boss may can me and throw his green into office bars and computers and flashy receptionists with nothing to do all day but answer the telephone and ball the department head, but he'll still be hiring me or someone like me. He'll just be shelling out more to the middleman. I may charge whiskey to expenses, but when I do I write it out clear and firm on the accounting sheet. He won't get that from anyone in a higher tax bracket."

He watched me in silence a moment longer. It was hard to believe I'd ever compared his looks with Stevie Wonder's. "Is that what you want me to tell him?"

"That and one more thing. Ask him if he was sending Marla any money while she was in finishing school."

"I can answer that. He did all his banking here, through me. It was the one link he had with his hometown he wanted to keep. He paid for her board and tuition directly to Esther Brock. Marla never saw a penny. I think it was his way of keeping her mind on her studies and out of trouble."

"That seems to have been the popular notion."

"Meaning?"

"Meaning I've got a big mouth. Forget I said it. Tell your boss I'll call him tonight. Unless, of course, you've got orders to take me for a ride or something like that."

He grinned. That's what was missing. It transformed his whole face. "Man," he said, "you've really got to stay away from that late-late show." Then the bottom dropped out of the grin. "Just keep in mind that fiction is always based on something known."

I met his gaze. "Message received."

The latch had just snapped home behind him when the telephone in my office started ringing. I unlocked the door and went in and sat down and answered it.

"Walker's Funland. Hit the private dick and win a cigar."

"Can the jokes, Walker. This is John Alderdyce."

"Second, John." I unscrewed the mouthpiece and tore out the tap. "Go ahead," I said when I had it back together. I dropped the junior-size mike into the file drawer next to the office bottle and pushed it shut. If it was powerful enough to pick anything up through all that oak it was worth hocking.

"Listen," Alderdyce was saying. "I traced that license plate number. Know who was on the other end?"

"Yeah, Uncle. Why didn't you tell me you had orders to sit on Kramer?"

"How in hell—" He sounded awestruck. I affect people that way sometimes.

"Skip it. Someday I'll write a book. Everyone else does. So why the tantrum this afternoon instead of telling me?"

"It's not something a cop cares to talk about. Not long after you left headquarters this morning, Proust calls me into his office where these two birds flash their ID's at me and say they're taking over the investigation. Proust says he called the Pentagon and confirmed their authority, tells me to turn over everything I've gathered. A case I've just about got solved, thanks to you. Later on you call and ask me why I'm keeping it under glass. What would you have done?"

"Bent some noses, but then I'm not a public servant. Listen, John. What've you got on a couple of billies who call themselves the Darling brothers? Jerry and Hubert."

"This wouldn't have anything to do with Kramer, would it?" His tone was baggy with warning.

"What if it does?"

"How does twenty years in the Milan pen sound? Anyway, if we had anything on these two in the mugs you'd have found it this morning. That is, if they're the pair you saw snatch Kramer."

"I'll take my chances with Uncle. Can you get anything on Telex from Atlanta P.D.? If these dudes weren't a hundred percent Georgia I'll give up my membership in the Professor Higgins Association of Accents and Linguistics."

"Forget it, Walker. I'll be damned if I'll use police facilities to obtain information on a case I've been warned off."

"Excuse it please, is this the Lieutenant Alderdyce who told me this morning he owed me one?"

"Hold on! You called us square when I agreed to find out if this Marla broad you were looking for had a record with Vice."

"So you remember," I purred. "I was beginning to wonder."

"Christ's sake, Walker, I can't do fourteen things at once!" He paused. I could almost hear his digestive juices working. They'd have finished with his lunch by now and would be starting in on his stomach. "Okay," he sighed, "you win. A guy I went through training with wound up a captain down in Atlanta. I'll call him and charge it to my home phone. If they suspend me I'll come looking for you."

He was about to hang up. Hastily I said, "Anything new on Shanks?" If he rang off mad at me I might lose him. Better to turn his anger in some other direction.

"Please," he growled. "This case has more angles than the Hope diamond. He made enemies like you and I make toast. He was going to shake the Mafia out of the union brass. He was organizing the military, starting with the transport services. He had his opponent in the last election investigated and dug up a thirty-year-old assault rap that never got to court. He had ties to Core and the Panthers but severed them when he went into union politics. Want to hear my theory? The guy was twins."

"Feed that to the press. It'll keep them off your back while they fulminate over it."

"Great. Now tell me what I can feed Proust. He's convinced I'm dragging my feet on this one."

"Try arsenic. Oh, what'd you turn up in Kramer's apartment?"

"Apartment?" The swift change of subject left him hanging. "Oh yeah, the place on Woodward. That wasn't his. Turned out to belong to an assembly foreman at GM. A bachelor. He's up north this week deer hunting; we couldn't reach him. Looks like your old C.O. was a thief. The place was torn inside out."

I gripped the receiver until it creaked. "What was he after?" The voice wasn't mine anymore. It belonged to a loose board beneath the linoleum.

"You tell me. All I know is this foreman has a porno collection you'd have to see to believe. Stills, books, rags, posters—"

"Films?"

"Those too. Real filth." He yawned. His day had been as long as mine. "We thought for a while that might have had something to do with the shoot. Maybe somebody was blackmailing somebody else. Anyway, that's the line we were following when Uncle came and took it away. Walker?"

I scraped my voice from the ceiling. "Thanks, John. I'll be here when you get word from Atlanta." I depressed the plunger before I could betray myself and just missed my thumb with the receiver.

I sat and drummed fingers on the big flat scribble calendar that took the place of a blotter. Then I opened the file drawer and hoisted out the office bottle and a glass and poured myself a slug and trickled it down my throat. The warmth was just beginning to spread through me as I stepped into the four-by-four bathroom and bathed the back of my head with cold water from the tap. At first it was like ramming in an ice pick, but as I toweled off gently the throbbing dissipated a hundredth of a percent and my stomach stopped doing gymnastics. I returned to the desk then and got down to some serious solitaire.

The telephone went off toward the end of the third game and halfway through the fourth glass. It interrupted a debate between my conscience and Hiram Walker over the morality of diving for the four of spades, which was snickering at me from its hiding place beneath the king of hearts. I scooped up the instrument's business end.

"John, knowing you is keeping me honest."

"What the hell are you talking about? Have you been drinking?"

It was John all right. I struck a match where he could hear it and touched off a weed. "Not too much," I said, spitting smoke. "I'm not burning."

"Grow up and listen. My buddy in Atlanta couldn't raise anything on anyone named Darling. Screwy thing. When he fed the names into the computer it referred him to Grand Theft Auto, but when he tried that he drew a blank."

"I half expected something like that."

"In English, please."

"We're dealing with Washington here. Most of our tax dollars go for electric wastebaskets and paper shredders. They learned how to erase tapes a couple of administrations ago. Computer tapes can't be all that different. Thanks twice, John."

I hung up long enough to haul out the city directory and run my finger down the G's until I found the name I wanted. Damned if she wasn't listed. I dialed. It purred twice and then Beryl Garnet's sweet little old voice came on.

"Hello?"

"Hello yourself." I did my Bogart impression. That one always worked. Nobody ever guessed who it was. "Let me talk to Iris."

"She doesn't usually come to the telephone. May I take a message?" She didn't sound as if she suspected anything. But then she never did.

"Quit stalling, sister. I got dough to spend and a plane to catch at seven. It's Iris or nothing."

"One moment, sir." No pause, no sharp intake of breath, not even a change in tone. Just, "One moment, sir," as if I were placing an order for party drinks and she had to grab a pencil. I listened for a while to the miscellaneous bumps and footsteps and unintelligible voices that came to me as if from the other end of a hollow tube and smoked my cigarette. Somewhere a TV set was playing: loud, blaring music, shots, a shriek of tires followed by the smashing of glass. A cop show. I checked my watch. 3:52. That made it either the teatime movie or a rerun of an old program. Aunt Beryl's girls didn't get to do much viewing in the evening. Someone lifted the receiver.

"Hello?" A unique voice, timid at the same time as it made promises. A hint of island in the cadence. Iris.

"I'm a customer you had a while back." I used my natural voice. "Don't let Auntie know I'm anything else. Say yes if you understand."

"Oh, yes!" She sounded tickled pink. That put the old lady right there in the room.

"Okay, here's where it gets sticky. I have to ask you some questions without you tipping off the boss with your answers. Is there another extension in the house? Don't just say yes or no. Be inventive."

"I'm afraid not." She sounded as if she were playing hard to get.

"Good. Two pairs of ears is all we want on this. Get rid of the old lady. Tell her I'm shy and you've got selling to do. If she balks tell her I'm loaded and so are my friends. Make it sound long and boring. If that doesn't work we'll try something else."

"Oh," she laughed, "I'm sure we can work something out." There was a pause. Then, in a low voice: "It's okay, she's gone. Good thing, too, because that story would never have worked in a million years. What is it?"

"The loonier the line the better it works, usually. These Darling brothers you mentioned, that romped once with Martha. Were they regular customers?"

"Not really. I saw them once or twice before, several months apart. That's how I knew it was them when I heard their voices on the other side of the wall that night. They sounded like the Dodge Sheriff in stereo."

"Either of them ever go with you?"

She laughed shortly and without mirth. "Lord, no! I don't think those good ole boys went for dark meat."

"Don't be coarse. Seen or heard anything of them lately?"

"Not since that night."

"What happened that night?"

Her voice rose. A coy note crept into it. "No, I don't think I'd like that." Someone had come into the room. There was another pause, then she resumed in hushed tones. "Felix walked through. There was a lot of talking that night, but I couldn't make out what they were saying. Some of it sounded kind of angry. There were a lot of bumps and smacks and squeals, as if someone was getting worked over good."

The butt was burning my fingers. I'd forgotten about it. I smashed it into the glass bottom of my souvenir ashtray from Traverse City. "Didn't that seem strange?"

"Not here. It takes all kinds to pay the bills in a whorehouse. I'm being coarse again, aren't I? But she had a black eye when I saw her later that night."

"Who? Martha?"

"Mm-hm. I didn't have much chance to talk to her about it, though. That was the night we were raided."

"What'd the old lady say when she saw the shiner?"

"She didn't. She was out of town when the cops hit the place, and we were all released together the next morning. Some crummy newshawk snapped us during the bust, but the eye didn't show up in the shot. It was right afterward that Martha locked herself in her room. Aunt Beryl thinks it's because she was embarrassed at being hauled in like a common hooker. I know better. She had no excuse for that eye. A few days later she lit out, taking my gold heart with her."

"What about Jerry and Hubert? They get picked up too?"

"They left an hour before the cops showed. Does this have something to do with finding Martha?"

"It may have everything to do with it. Sit tight, angel. You'll be hearing from me soon."

"Wait! Am I going to see you, too?"

She had turned it on again. Not that it was ever really off. "Did someone just come in?" I asked.

"No."

I grinned. "See you later, angel."

I stared at the office bottle for a few seconds. Then I seized the half-full shot glass and poured its contents down the neck, screwed the cap back on, put them both away in the drawer, and reached for my hat. Who needed liquor? I was getting my highs off life.

14

THE TEMPERATURE HAD CLIMBED twelve degrees since noon, according to the radio, and now big fat drops of freezing rain were starring the windshield after the wipers had made peanut brittle out of the wafer-thin ice that had already formed. My tires swished on the slick wet pavement. All around me cars were hydroplaning on the sheen of water atop the glassy surface, and here and there curbs, gutters, and hydrants had begun to blossom with fender-benders and six-hundred-dollar suspension replacement jobs. Some people have to learn how to drive all over again each winter.

The overcast had reduced the complexion of the city from its usual smog blue to a smeary gray, through which swollen headlamps gleamed resignedly like candles beneath a filthy wet undershirt and were reflected even more dimly in the puddles ahead. I reached over and tugged mine on just for appearances. The car smelled of warm, wet wool. Tires swished and wipers thrummed and rain pattered on the vinyl roof and the heater fan pushed warm air at my feet, drying my socks, soaked from slogging through puddles. I felt cozy and relaxed and protected from the cold, wet, noisy world by a palpitating wall of warmth. Then I swung left onto Woodward and an icy stream of water that had been trapped beneath the dash drooled over my right ankle and the feeling was gone.

Just for the hell of it I cruised past George Gibson's building at Woodward and Watson, but this time my attention was fixed on the place across the street, where Francis Kramer had knocked a match out of my hand while he was hurrying out the door. No soap. A guy with a back like a marine drill instructor's—straight as a rifle shot—in a necktie and brown, knee-length trenchcoat was standing in that very doorway looking miserable and sticking out, in that neighborhood, like a pair of black formal shoes at a love-in. Only he wasn't marines, he was army. Which when I thought about it wasn't such a tough break after all, since if there had been anything worth looking for in the GM foreman's apartment they'd have found it by now, and there wouldn't be any need to post a guard. I rolled on past and lit a shuck east to Erskine.

I parked in a lot a couple of blocks down from Story's After Midnight and walked back in that direction with my hat brim down to my eyes and my collar turned up around my ears, leaning into the driving rain. The drops crackled when they pelted my face, burning the skin on contact like showering sparks. The wind picked up my coattails and flapped them noisily about my legs. Along this block the street rose at a thirty-degree angle, and the run-off made rivers out of the gutters and gurgled greedily past naked branches and gobs of wet newspaper in the sewer grates. The world was very much with me here.

There were no toughs waiting for me this time, but I nearly brained myself anyway when I swung into the deep doorway and grasped the brass handle and pushed and the door didn't budge. I stepped back and read CLOSED on a dun shade on the other side of the glass. I cupped my hands around my eyes and leaned against it, but the shade was opaque and so was the one over the window. My watch said

4:33. It seemed a strange time to close, but he might have worried about getting home later because of the road conditions. I didn't think so. Something that wasn't a drop of cold rain crawled down between my shoulder blades.

There was an alley two doors down. I took it, walking as nonchalantly as the rain and my own gnawing hunch would allow, around to the back and counted the brown steel doors I found there until I came to the one I figured led into Story's. Two black plastic garbage bags lounged beside it. One of them had a hole chewed in it near the bottom and something was squirming around inside. Rats. When we've all been blown to atoms, they'll still be around. I made sure they had room to scurry out without running up my pants leg and stooped to inspect the lock.

It was a dead bolt, which came as no surprise in a country where mace manufacturers advertise in women's magazines. The brass strikeplate didn't wobble when I shook the door by its dull metal handle, and what I could see of the screws wasn't encouraging. If they were longer than half an inch they might pose a problem. I looked around, took two steps back, raised my foot, and threw everything I had behind the heel, smashing the lock square on the keyhole. It shuddered a little.

I tried the door a second time. It seemed to have given some, about as much as Gibraltar settles into the ocean each day. The old wood had begun to release its hold on the screws that kept the strikeplate in place. I took a deep breath and stood back with my foot poised. It wasn't just the loss of my license I was flirting with now; it was a year in the slam. Judges don't take to private sleuths any more than cops do, and they'd been coming down hard lately on cases of breaking and entering. The hell with that. Amos Walker had a hunch.

It didn't happen on that one either, or on the next, but the fourth blow tore the screws from the casing and sprang the door inward, twisting my ankle at the same time. The molding and a fist-size chunk of worm-eaten oak went with it. I limped inside and pushed the works as shut as it could get behind me.

I was in a storage room of some kind, windowless and as black as Hitler's heart. I knew it was used for storage because I tripped over a long box of something parked across the entrance and had to twist so that I sat down on it instead of pitching forward into God knows what. The force of my weight moved it about the width of a butterfly's eyelash. I fished out my pencil flash and snapped it on to examine the box. The flaps were open and it was full of hardcover books shrink-wrapped in plastic and packed for shipping via whatever parcel service Story subscribed to. I got up and, using the flash to prevent a similar accident, made my way over a jumble of other cartons to a door that presumably led into the shop proper. Satisfying myself that it was reasonably airtight and would leak no light where it could be spotted from the street, I grasped a chain I'd noticed earlier dangling from a naked bulb on the ceiling and gave it a jerk.

It was a claustrophobic little cell, hardly eight by ten, and the walls were fuzzy yellow lath with plaster the color of old ivory squeezing out between the slats. Cardboard cartons of various sizes filled the room. If someone had stacked them, someone else had pulled the stacks apart. Every one had been opened, and although from where I stood the boxes of books and rolled posters and packets of stills had been left as they were, those containing films had been dumped out, the canisters pried open and the celluloid strips uncoiled from the metal spools and left in tangled, glisten-

ing piles like wet black tapeworms. There was no use ex-
amining them. Someone already had.

I tugged off the light and tried the door. It was unlocked.
I stepped into the shop, where the soggy gray afternoon
light slanting in through the transom over the front door
was all I needed to see that it was in even worse shape.
Here, even the books had been torn from their racks, their
plastic seals slashed open and the books flung to the floor
in a riot of pages. The drawers of the desk beneath the plate
glass window had been pulled completely out, dumped
upside-down, and their contents scattered over the floor in
that pawed-through pattern you see only when every item
has been closely examined. Even the glass picture frames
containing obscene photos suitable for desk-top display had
been taken down from their shelves and pulled apart. The
sale films were in the same condition as their cousins in
back. Someone with a lot of time had been through the place
with a thorough hand, and the odds were he didn't get what
he had come for. People usually stop searching when they
find what they want.

There was one door left to try, a narrow job with a poster
tacked to it of a nude girl with breasts the size of water-
melons and the face of a prominent feminist superimposed
on top of her neck. This one was locked, but not nearly as
securely as the one that led into the building from the rear.
I produced my pocket knife, inserted the blade between the
edge of the door and the jamb, slid it upward for six or
seven inches until it clicked against metal, then gave it a
firm upward jerk that flipped a little steel hook out of a
little steel eye. There was no latch. The door creaked inward
of its own weight like Boris Karloff Night at the movies.

Lee Q. Story sat fully dressed on the toilet seat facing
sideways so that he could lean his forehead on the edge of

the matching white porcelain sink, just as you and I might do if we got up to get ready for work before the flu was out of our systems and a fresh dizzy spell hit while we were tying our shoelaces. Only the flu wasn't anything he had to worry about, ever again. He was long past worries of any sort. My fingertips on his throat where the pulse was supposed to be told me that much. The rain outside wasn't as cold as his skin.

He wasn't wearing his mirrored glasses, but I was still unable to determine what color eyes he had because they were rolled back beyond the half-closed lids. His mouth hung open and his head rested on the edge of the sink a quarter-turn sideways. He might have drooled out the bottom corner. The saliva would have dried long since. Below the sink his long, bony arms dangled as if limp, but they'd be stiff as icicles. I didn't feel them to make sure. His right sleeve was rolled up past the biceps, where tiny, gray-white circles of scar tissue peppered the mahogany flesh. He had a clotted patch on the back of his head that spoiled his afro, but that wasn't what had killed him.

A spoon with a bent handle and a blackened bowl lay on the top ledge of the sink beside a hypodermic syringe and a pair of burned-out matches. Something had dried into a brownish pink crust in the bottom of the bowl, sealing a wad of starchy white cotton the size of a thumbnail to the stainless steel. Nearby lay a razor blade with a corner broken off. A tiny crumple that had been a cellophane packet floated in a quart of gray water that refused to go down the sink drain, next to yet another charred match. Something was missing. I took a step forward and kicked a plastic vial that had fallen to the floor, spilling more fine white powder out onto the worn linoleum. Milk sugar, probably, or something else that melted easily.

The spoon was a holder, the bend in its handle designed to keep heat from reaching the fingers that grasped it while one of the matches was held burning beneath the bowl. Another would have been used to sterilize the needle. The presence of a third was a puzzle, but it might have taken more than one to melt the stuff or maybe he was more careful about the needle than most. The milk sugar, or whatever it was, was the pony on which the brownish pink stuff had ridden to its destination. The cotton was a filter to prevent impurities from being sucked up into the syringe along with the brownish pink stuff and the sugar. The razor blade was for scraping callus off an old needle hole so that the brownish pink stuff could be pumped directly into the vein. The brownish pink stuff was heroin. Mexican Brown they call it in Detroit, after its color and the country of its origin. It isn't as refined as the white stuff you see circulating on the cop shows on television, but too much of it at one time is every bit as lethal. After a thousand dollars or so of taxpayers' money had been spent on an autopsy, I'd bet the unregistered Luger I kept in a special pocket in the trunk of my Cutlass that that's what they'd find Lee Q. Story had died of.

The door to the medicine cabinet was a sheet of tin with a mirrored front badly in need of resilvering. I tugged it open with the back of a knuckle. Inside was a can of Afrosheen, half full—I took it out and shook it with a hand wrapped in my handkerchief—an abandoned cobweb and winter air. I snicked it shut. I didn't bother to search Story's body. Someone would already have done that. Even the top of the toilet tank was sitting at a slight angle, as if it had been lifted off and replaced by someone whose time was running short.

As a homicide it had something for everyone, including

a locked-room mystery. There was nothing to that. There are a dozen ways to close a door so that the hook slips into place with no one on the other side to guide it. It can even be done by accident. I know, because it did it again the third time I tried it on my way out. I smeared the knob carefully behind me.

The air in the shop breathed easier, and not just because I'd been in a cramped bathroom with no ventilation. Story's .22 wasn't under the counter, but that wasn't what I was after. The hunch I was following had all the foundation of a houseboat. I navigated my way around the disturbed inventory to the front door to prove to myself how shaky it was.

The mailman had been by since the killer. Either that or whoever it was had gone through the mail and then put it back into the comparatively neat, fanned-out pile it had assumed on the floor after passing through the brass hatch in the door's bottom panel, which was ludicrous considering the condition of the rest of the place. And he wouldn't have ignored it, not someone who would peep inside a toilet tank or pull apart a picture frame. Or hit a man over the head and feed him an overdose of his own dope. I nudged the pile gently with my toe. That gave me exactly nothing. I stooped and shuffled through the envelopes.

Most of it was bills and circulars, the stuff you and I glance at every morning except Sunday and then file either in a drawer or the nearest wastebasket. There were a couple of businesslike items in typewritten legal envelopes and one three-by-seven with the address scribbled in a cramped, nearly illegible hand.

I'd seen the hand before. Seated in my car at a stoplight, looking at the back of a sheet from a receipt book with a list of names written on it in ink. Story's hand. He was writing letters to himself these days. I broke a federal law opening it. I didn't hear any sirens, so I looked inside.

It contained nothing but a short thick key wired to a worn paper tag with a number on it and the name of a public food storage locker on Gratiot, which made as much sense as anything else had in this case so far.

15

I LEFT THROUGH THE back door as stealthily as I had entered, obliterating as many traces of my presence there as I could think of on the way. There was nothing I could do about the damaged door, which might send the cops off on all sorts of wild theories, but in that neighborhood maybe they'd disregard it as an unconnected break-in. Which it was, kind of.

The street shone like a hippo's back. The rain had slowed to a freezing drizzle, as relentless as a collection agency and nearly as dangerous. The homeward-bound traffic was inching along at fifteen miles per hour. On the way I was witness to two low-velocity collisions and a couple of dozen near misses, one of which involved my car and an empty haul-away en route to one of the auto plants. It was six o'clock and past dark when I got to the address I wanted on Gratiot, spun into the little customer parking lot in front of the building, swallowed my heart back down where it belonged, and climbed out. The Indians had the right idea: Who needs wheels?

The place was a butcher shop and cold storage plant combined, with a partition in between and a narrow doorway barred by a counter flap through which, the sign warned, only employees could pass. Beyond this stood a hard-faced woman in her late forties and a white smock whose dyed black hair and scarlet lipstick made her look sixty. At her elbow was an old-fashioned cash register and, on the wall above that, a pegboard with rows of hooks from which hung dozens of keys with paper tags similar to the one in my pocket. I figured I could get past the counter flap but not her.

As it turned out, I didn't have to. I held up the key and she pointed a skinny finger with a crimson nail at a heavy wooden door at the end of an aisle that led past her station and between a pair of long, refrigerated glass cases full of steaks and chops and pale chickens and packages of sliced bologna the color of scrubbed dead flesh. Feeling foolish, I swung the great door open by its huge steel handle and stepped into Siberia.

I was inside a cavernous chamber, cold as death from the refrigeration unit that hissed hollowly in the space between the top of the left wall and the ceiling, and furnished with rows of heavy racks like library shelves containing square metal drawers that reminded me uncomfortably of the bigger ones in the morgue. The walls were hoary with frost. I made sure that the push handle that was supposed to operate the latch from inside was in working order and let the door close itself against the pressure of the pneumatic whozis mounted on top. I felt very, very alone.

The number I wanted was located at the far end of the fourth rack. I inserted the key in the slot near the top of the drawer and twisted. The tumblers shifted reluctantly, as if the extreme cold had driven them into hibernation. I took hold of the handle and tugged. The drawer opened on noiseless casters.

It was nearly full of foil-wrapped packages. I ignored the ones that seemed unlikely, the smaller, bulgy ones that could have been hamburger or bulk sausage and the flat, solid ones that were probably steaks bought on sale and put away for later consumption, and settled on a disc near the bottom, about an inch thick and a bit wider than my hand. It felt like a canister of eight-millimeter film. I unwrapped it nervously and stared for a moment at a wheel of Pinconning cheese.

I sealed it back up as carefully as if I planned to eat it myself later, put it back, and scowled at the rest of the drawer's contents. I couldn't have been wrong. Food prices were climbing, but mailing a key to a locker full of nothing but meat and cheese to yourself for fear of its being lost or stolen seemed a bit drastic. I placed a hand on either side of a rounded something twice the size of my head and lifted it out. It wasn't any heavier than an anvil. I took a deep breath and shook it. Something inside may have wobbled. Balancing it on the edge of the drawer, I peeled aside the foil. Inside was a plastic bag. Inside that was a fourteen-pound turkey. Inside that, jammed sideways into the cavity, was another foil-wrapped disc that I didn't think was cheese.

I got it out and let the turkey fall back into the drawer with a thud that shook the rack. Then I tore the foil from the smaller package. Brown butcher paper was next, secured with matching tape. I unsecured it and did the same with the plastic wrap beneath that and found myself holding a flat, gunmetal-gray canister without a label. I had a hunch it didn't need one. I admired it for a few seconds, then slid it into the saddle pocket of my overcoat and pushed the drawer shut. I took out the key and pocketed that too. Then I returned to a world that was a little less cold and a hell of a lot less remote.

Outside, the temperature was dropping again and there were flakes of soggy snow the size of quarters mixed in with the drizzle. They slithered down my face and melted beneath my collar, but compared to the atmosphere in the place I'd just left they were warm as spit. Cars crept down Gratiot, their headlamps hardened by the soft black backdrop of night into bright diamonds whose facets sent out shoots that wheeled around their hot white centers and trapped flakes glittering in midair, stopping time like pent-up breath. Behind the wheel of my own crate I waited forever for an opening, then swung out to join the plodding march. It was another hour before I reached home.

The house looked lonely and dark until I flipped on the overhead light and then it was just lonely. It didn't look as if anyone had been in it since I'd left that morning. It wouldn't, except in the tiniest details. I threw my keys onto the stand that held up the telephone and went straight to the closet just inside the door without bothering to take off my hat and coat.

A client for whom I'd done a service, never mind who or what, had paid me off a couple of years ago with a movie projector in lieu of the cash she said she didn't have after taking care of the pool man and the beautician. It had cost me fifty bucks to get it into hockable condition, and then I'd lost interest and shoved it away, I thought, in this closet. I wasn't mistaken. I found it, battered black case and all, on the bottom of a pile containing such items as a hairless horsehair blanket inherited from my grandfather and a leaky feather mattress acquired from my ex-wife. I hauled out the projector, set it up, and plugged it in. When it didn't explode, I got rid of my outerwear and opened the canister and leaned the contents, a metal spool of glossy celluloid some four inches in diameter, against the baseboard near the hot-air register. It would be too brittle to run in its frozen state. Then I went into the kitchen to heat up the supper I'd had defrosting since the night before.

After two hours I woke up in my easy chair and went to

check the film. It was still there—I'd locked the door, not that that had stopped anybody before—and it looked and felt like film. I threaded it into the machine, picked out a fairly clean section of wall, pointed it in that direction, took a deep breath, and turned it on. The image flickering on the wall looked pale. I called myself a name Barney Zacharias hadn't thought of and went over and snapped off the over-head light.

I was looking at a long shot, in black and white, of a grassy vale, framed, as any photographer who had had three lessons would know enough to do, between a pair of maple trees in the foreground. Their branches were fully leafed, which made it summer or late spring, and they cast impos-sibly long shadows that stretched along the ground to the left and ended somewhere outside the shot, which made it late afternoon or early morning. A slope fell away from where the photographer was standing, at the base of which five men were gathered. I assumed they were men. Four of them were wearing pale robes that swept the ground and matching hoods with high, pointed peaks. Their eyes were black holes in the part that came down to cover their faces. The fifth man, a black with a medium-heavy build, wore an ordinary suit with the necktie undone. There seemed to be something familiar about him, although at this distance his features were impossible to pick out. He appeared to be struggling against something. I had been watching for ten or fifteen seconds before I realized that his arms were pinned behind him, and that he was being held—barely—by two of the robed and hooded men. He stamped the ground with his short, powerful legs and twisted his barrel torso until a third stepped forward to help the others subdue him. He was still coming when the prisoner broke free.

The third man made an ineffectual lunge to take him in

a bear-hug, but the black swept him out of the way with a mighty backhand sweep of his arm and took off running up the shallow grade to the right. He ran swiftly but awkwardly, pumping his arms and legs more than he had to and bent forward a little too much at the waist, not so much because he wasn't used to running or that he had been held in confinement too long, but as if an old ailment of some kind, possibly a back injury, hindered his movement. Nevertheless he had a head start on his pursuers and was halfway up the slope when the fourth man brought a dark object up from under his robes and it bucked three times in his hand and the running man jerked three times and spilled forward onto his knees and then his face. His back hunched once as though he was trying to get up, but then he stopped trying and rolled over onto his side and didn't try again.

The other three snatched off their hoods and ran up to the fallen man. One of them knelt beside him for a moment while his companions stood around with their hands on their knees. Then he got up. The man with the gun put it away and pulled off his own hood. Then one of the men standing around the body happened to turn in this direction and his hand came up as if to point, and at that moment the camera panned away crazily. The last shot on the roll was of bouncing sky. The rest of the film was blank.

The match with which I had been about to light a cigarette when the action started burned down to my fingers. I cursed and shook it out. Then I spat bitter tobacco off my tongue. That was the second time Francis Kramer had made me bite through a Winston.

I reacted finally to the flapping that told me the feed spool had run out of film and switched off the projector. That left me in the dark. But the little projector behind my eyes was casting its own images on the wall where the bright yellow square had just faded out and I was watching those.

Francis Kramer was dead because he'd been seen filming a Black Legion execution straight out of the Depression. Lee Q. Story was dead because he'd had the film and somebody had lost his head before Story could tell them what he'd done with it. Any amateur shutterbug with a good darkroom could blow up those final frames big enough to stand up as identification in court. As for the victim, I didn't need a blowup to identify him. Footage on him had been taking up quite a bit of air time on the local news programs over the past three months. I knew him chiefly from that running gait, made awkward by a well-publicized football injury suffered during his freshman year at the University of Detroit.

I needed no blowups to know that I had just witnessed, secondhand, the murder last August of Freeman Shanks, the ghetto-bred darling of the union rank and file.

16

F OR A LONG TIME after the film ran out I sat there in the dark and smoked and thought, but mostly I just smoked. My throat was beginning to feel like the inside of a stack at the Ford plant when I mashed my umpteenth butt into an ashtray rounded over with them and got up and put on the light and bought myself a drink. As I stood there pouring it into a tumbler I thought some more. My head began to hurt.

The Kramer burn was related to the Shanks killing, which was related somehow to Marla Bernstein's/Martha Burns' disappearance. If Beryl Garnet was telling the truth, her description of the man who bankrolled Marla's room and board in the cathouse on John R fit Freeman Shanks as well as it fit a thousand other guys. That explained the attempt to disguise himself during his visits, which was unnecessary if the old lady never watched television or read a newspaper as she claimed, but he wouldn't have known that. Interracial affairs weren't good politics, any more than one between a racketeer's ward and a labor leader who had pledged to purge the union of Mafia influence. He would have been running for office last December when he stashed her.

What stank was my stumbling into the same case, if it was the same case, from both ends on the same day. It reeked of coincidence, like the unbelievably complicated plot of a Victorian novel. But then, if coincidences didn't happen from time to time there wouldn't be a word for them. That was why two sisters born in Russia who hadn't seen or heard from each other since the Nazi invasion could meet by accident at the local shopping center in Oil Trough, Arkansas, and discover they'd been living within a couple of miles of each other for the past twenty years. So the jury was still out on that one.

I thought too hard on it and filled the tumbler to the rim and ended up having to pour most of it back into the bottle. I went into the kitchen and passed what was left in the glass under a damp faucet—only hopeless alcoholics drink their whiskey straight—and came back in and sat down and drank it off and thought. Then I got up again, got out my notebook, went over to the telephone, removed Spain and Vespers' tap, and dialed the number of the Miriam H. Fordham Institute for Women.

It rang eight times before I got a woman with a Mary Astor accent who informed me that Miss Brock had gone home for the day, would I care to call in the morning? It took me two minutes—a lot of time when you're on the horn—to wheedle La Brock's home number out of her. Esther Brock remembered me very well indeed. I asked her one question, she gave me one answer back. I thanked her and put the receiver back where it belonged.

Which left me holding both ends of the rescue line but still half a mile from shore and treading water like a rat. Even though the answer I'd gotten was the one I needed to tie the thing up with a dainty satin bow, I had no idea who had killed Lee Q. Story, which wasn't important, and knew as much about Marla Bernstein's whereabouts as I had twenty-four hours earlier when Merle Donophan's telephone call came to upset my peaceful poverty, which was.

Then I remembered something I'd forgotten to do, and immediately wished that it had stayed forgotten, because it meant going back to interview a dead man.

17

THERE WERE NO TACTICAL mobile units parked in front of the shop on Erskine, no bubble-gum machines splashing pulsating blue light over everything, no crowds on the sidewalk, no barricades, no frightened-looking young men in midnight blue uniforms as snug and new as the wrapper on a stick of spearmint, no weary-looking middle-aged men running to fat in rumpled over-coats speaking in played-out monotones over hand mikes attached to unmarked units, no police radios turned up to maximum volume to be heard over the controlled mayhem of a routine murder investigation. In short, no one who was still in the habit of reporting to authorities had discovered the corpse in the bathroom. Too bad. It would have given me an excuse to keep rolling.

There was just enough snow on the street to provide traction. I tooled into the lot I'd used earlier, left my car in shadow—of which there was plenty, the nearby streetlight having been broken out—and struck off on foot, taking a route I thought would bring me out behind Story's. I had my revolver in my pocket this trip. I would have in any case, in that neighborhood after sundown. Wet snow soaked my feet through my shoes.

I got lost for a time in the medieval maze of streets and alleys that wound Caligari-like through the area, but dead reckoning finally placed me under a working light that

stood kitty-corner from the blank expanse of building I was
after.

The two garbage bags were still there, but the rats were
gone, probably inside where it was warm. The door was as
I had left it. Inside I clicked on my pocket flash just in time
to avoid tripping over the same carton of books all over
again. No one had straightened up the storeroom in my
absence.

I found the shop in the same condition. No mysterious
footprints or garments left behind or lingering smell of exotic perfume. Nobody waiting to knock me over the head.
Death was never this quiet. Just for the hell of it I gave the
door to the bathroom a push. It opened to my touch.

That trickle of cold water that wasn't started down my
spine again. Hooks can fall into place without help, but they
don't come undone by themselves. As the door crept inward
without any further encouragement from me I put away the
flash, got my gun out, placed my free hand on the inside of
the door with my thumb on this side of the jamb, and forced
it the rest of the way with my fingers until it bumped the
wall. It met no obstruction, which left only the other side
open to speculation. I charged in, smashed shoulder-first
into the opposite wall, spun and drew down on the suspicious corner with the revolver clasped in both hands at
arms' length, police style. Nothing moved in the shadows. I
fumbled for the chain that swung from the bulb overhead
and bathed the tiny room in light. A crack in the plaster
yawned at me.

Story was still sitting on the john with his head on the
sink and one eye peeping up at nothing. My rude entrance
didn't appear to have disturbed him. Neither had any of the
others that had taken place since my last visit. He was just
another fixture in the room. I popped open the medicine

cabinet. Its contents didn't look to have been tampered with. Whoever had slipped the hook seemed to have come to the same conclusion I had.

It wasn't the police. They would still be nosing around, drawing chalk lines and popping flashbulbs and quartering the floor in search of buttons and butts and using the freshly dusted telephone to roust out their favorite reporters and see about snatching some space in the morning edition or half a minute on what was left of the eleven o'clock news. They'd have come in with sirens and defiled the air with their cheap stogies and everything would be lit up like a disco on Saturday night. I didn't think it was the killer, unless he'd had the same idea I had about the morning mail. In which case there was no reason for him to look in the bathroom, unless like me he was just plain curious.

Stepping out, I shut the door without bothering to reset the hook this time, traded the gun for my flash, and made my way over to Story's desk. There I squatted among the debris on the floor and used one of his pencils to poke through the items that had been dumped out of the drawers. I came across one of those little brown plastic-bound note-books you see on the impulse-buying racks near the check-out line in any supermarket, lying open face-down on the floor. I picked it up and shone my light on the pages.

It was an address book. The names and numbers were in Story's awkward hand and I recognized them as the ones he had written down for me that morning in exchange for twenty dollars. One page was missing. I fingered the bits of paper adhering to the metal rings and got crafty.

By now anyone who watches television knows that something written on top of a stack of pages makes legible impressions two or three pages down, and that even when the sheet on which the information was scribbled is missing, the edge of a sharpened pencil rubbed across the next sheet down will bring it out in negative. Story's pencil and a lot of squinting and turning the light this way and that—the page beneath had writing of its own on it—gave me more addresses I recognized and one I didn't. I wrote it out fresh on the other side of the page, tore it loose, and thrust it into my pocket. Then I gave the notebook's slippery covers a thorough wiping with my handkerchief, no doubt destroying valuable evidence in the process, and put it back more or less the way I'd found it. Then I had a premonition.

The telephone is a wonderful invention, whether you trust it or not; it conserves time, energy, and sole leather and has even been known to save a life once in a while, if you dial the city's emergency 911 and can get someone to answer before you choke your last. Considering that A. G. Bell lived in Nova Scotia, the instrument is one of a couple of things Canada has given us to justify its existence. So I tried to reach Barry Stackpole with the telephone on Story's desk and no one answered.

I'd forgotten about his trip. I hung up and thought. Then I called Beryl Garnet's house of ill fame.

"Yes?" A slow, honeyed voice, not Aunt Beryl's and not Iris'. The maid.

I fell back on Bogart. "Let me talk to Iris."

"Miss Iris is occupied. May I take a message?"

A friendly place. Everyone I spoke to there seemed to want to preserve my golden words for posterity. "I'll bet she is," I growled. "Drag her out from under whoever it is and tell her Lieutenant Fowler wants to talk to her."

"Lieutenant Fowler." She'd been around too long to show it in her speech, but if she hadn't gone stiff as Chester's leg on that one I'd turn in my license tomorrow.

"Yeah," I said. "One of her customers stuck up a gas

station tonight. Killed an attendant. I want to tell her to hang out her eyeballs in case he shows up."

"Please hold the line." She put down the receiver. Off to change her drawers, I suspected. There was conversation going on in another room, but I couldn't make it out. It sounded like a mouthful of bees. Once I heard a man's loud, drunken laughter. Business hours were in full swing.

"Me, angel," I said, when a familiar voice greeted me. "I'm calling you because right now you're the only one there is to call. Are you alone in the room?"

There was a pause, then: "Yes. Corinne said something about a gas station stickup. What—"

"That's my cover. Hang onto it if anyone asks what this was about. Listen, things have gone smoothly so far and I don't like it. I don't mean to say I like collecting lumps, but when there's too much time between them I get itchy, like when I used to box with my uncle as a teenager and he let me win three straight matches. Fourth time out I dropped my guard and he knocked me clean past my next birthday. After that I learned to look out for that sneaky left hook."

"What are you talking about? Are you drunk?"

That was the second time I'd been asked that. I was beginning to wonder. "The point is," I said patiently, "if I'm walking into a buzz saw I want someone somewhere who knows where the pieces go. What kind of terms are you on with the law?"

"I'm on a short fast slide to Dehoco with a banana peel under my butt. What's happening?"

Dehoco is the Detroit House of Corrections, and outside of playing host to bandit queen Belle Starr something over a hundred years ago, it doesn't have much going for it. I made a disapproving noise with my tongue against my teeth.

"You're being coarse again. Never mind. You don't have to give them your name, although they'll ask for it. It's now"—I inspected the luminous dial of my watch—"eleven-twenty. If you don't hear my dulcet tones by one-twenty, call the cops and send them to this number." I gave her the address I'd copied from Story's book. "Ask for Lieutenant Alderdyce." I spelled it.

"Just a second, honey. I'm busy."

She wasn't talking to me. I'd heard the footsteps approaching while waiting for her to finish writing. A man's tread, heavy and shambling, audible even on the fluffy carpeting that seemed to cover every floor in Aunt Beryl's house. Drunken footsteps. I'd also heard the rustle of paper as Iris hurriedly ditched the pad on which she'd been writing Alderdyce's name.

She wasn't fast enough. "Whassamatter, babe? I innerupt you or somethin'? You writing a love note to your fav'rite john? Mebbe thassim on the phone." The voice was as heavy as his walk and twice as drunk. He needed a winch to haul his tongue around each word. I tried the inebriated laughter I'd heard earlier on him to see how it fit. It fit fine.

"Leggo, honey," said Iris, trying to sound as if she couldn't wait to get back to him. "I'm on long distance. It's my father. Gimme a minute."

"First it was a second, now issa minute. Go on, no whore's got no daddy, leastwise not the blood kind. 'Specially not no nigger whore. Come on, whore." Feet shuffled rapidly on the other end. He was grabbing for her and doing plenty of missing.

"Put him on," I snapped.

There were a couple of seconds of dead air, then a muffled "Huh?" and then two big clumsy hands fumbled with the receiver and hot wet heavy breath wheezed into the mouthpiece. I drew back instinctively. I could almost smell the liquor.

"Yeah?" No word conveys a sneer so well.

"Captain Johnson, Chicago Vice." I put tough urban black into my voice. He'd be too drunk to wonder why there wasn't any island in it. "I want to know what a man's doing in my daughter's sorority house. What's your name?"

He said, "Urgalagurg," or maybe it was "Schlapadafrap." In any case it didn't sound like something I'd find in the city directory. There was more fumbling, followed by heavy footsteps moving away from the telephone, but this time they sounded hurried, driven in fact. There was a loud crash, as of a man's hip slamming into a door jamb or the edge of a table, and then a louder curse. I might have heard it even without the telephone.

"What did you say to him?" It was Iris. She had the hiccups, or maybe she was holding back laughter. "He turned three shades of green and took off running for the bathroom."

"Pretext and subterfuge." I felt for a cigarette, remembered where I was and vetoed it. "Some Michigan P.I.'s went to court last year over our right to employ it under certain circumstances. That was one of them. Got that name I gave you?"

"Alderdyce. I got it. Amos, what's going on?"

"Funny. I never did like the name Amos, but coming from you it sounds like 'Stardust.' Is it me you care about, or the gold heart?"

"Sh—" she started, and stopped. "Hang the gold heart. I don't want it if it means you coming out in a zipper bag. You're a nice guy. Maybe the only one I've met this side of the water."

"Don't spread it around. 'Nice' isn't one of the words I use in my Yellow Pages ad."

"Damn it, will you stop screwing around and be serious for a minute? Can't you see I'm worried as hell about you?"

It could have been a tender moment, but Beryl Garnet spoiled it by calling Iris' name. The second syllable was louder than the first. She was entering from another room.

"Don't be," I said hurriedly. "At least not until one-twenty. And don't leave that pad lying around. Nothing stays secret in Washington or a John R bordello." I hung up. Then I wiped everything off all over again and got the hell out of there.

It was on what had to be the last unpaved road within ten miles of the city limits, a narrow gravel job that ran north off West Grand River long after you'd forgotten what skyscrapers were like and begun to wonder if gas stations and roller-skating rinks and Big Boys were all the civiliza-tion there was left, and then this diagonal ribbon of dark slush sprang into your headlights out of nowhere with no sign to warn you it was coming up and you had to stand on the brakes and twist the wheel and skid and scratch mud and gravel to avoid having to turn around up ahead and go back. It wasn't on the map I kept in my glove compartment. I wouldn't have known where to begin looking for it if they hadn't found the nude body of a female rape-murder victim jammed into a culvert near the corner a year or so ago and splattered it all over the airwaves. Even then it probably wouldn't have stuck with me, but the girl was a secretary who had worked in an office on the floor below mine and we used to run into each other in the lobby and talk about the weather on our way up the stairs. I couldn't remember her name but I never forgot the road.

Phooey on the country. The Wayne County Road Commission spends all its time and appropriations keeping up the main highways leading into Detroit and lets these little half-forgotten paths wither into rutted things, along which trees with branches like the groping fingers of men long dead crowd the shoulder and thrust out solitary limbs you don't see until you're right on top of them, when it's too late to swerve and they crack up against your windshield and drag wrenchingly along the side of your vehicle, taking paint and metal with them. Then the salt they scoop up from the mines beneath the city and slather over the road to make up for the grading they don't do in summer splashes up and eats greedily of the exposed metal, and six months later you're sucking dust where your rocker panels used to be.

I drove past the place once, turned around in the driveway of an old farmhouse, went back and pulled into an even narrower private lane that led into the Vistaview Mobile Home Park. I pulled up in front of a six-by-six trailer mounted on a block foundation with a phony sign made to look as if it had been burned crudely into a hunk of bark riveted over the door, reading OFFICE. There was a light on behind the louvered front window.

I didn't like it. It was too remote and there were too many places to sink a body without someone getting suspicious about what you were doing outside after dark with a shovel. I killed the engine and got out and walked up the scraped flagstone path to the door and went in without bothering to knock.

18

"YOU FORGOT YOUR TRAILER." The comic was a chunky black in a faded blue and gold University of Michigan sweatshirt, seated behind a folding card table mounded with paperwork beneath the front window. He was looking through it at my Cutlass and chuckling. His profile in the light of the standing lamp behind his right shoulder was flat, as if someone who didn't care for his witicisms had squashed it with the heel of a callused palm. What I could see of his eyes beneath the puffy lids was rheumy and toadlike, the look of a confirmed alcoholic. It was something to keep in mind.

"I'm not after a spot," I said. "Just information."

"Try the phone company." He swiveled halfway around with a squeal of dry bearings to face me and leaned back, clasping his lumpy hands behind his neck and looking at me from under the heavy lids.

"Hilarious," I told him. "Like a whoopie cushion on a wheelchair." I fished out the later picture of Marla Bernstein and scaled it onto his makeshift desk. It skidded to a stop across a ledger sheet full of penciled figures slopping over the ruled lines. He watched me a moment longer, then allowed his eyes to slide down his nose to the photo. He came forward slowly, unclasping his hands and bringing them forward to handle it. A greedy light sprang into his eyes.

Guys like him were the reason guys who took pictures like that were in business.

The interior of the trailer was no better than it deserved to be. The walls were paneled with that cheap blond veneer they used to slap on furniture during World War II, the kind that fell apart months ahead of the Axis, and the ceiling just above my hat was a water-stained pegboard from which sprouted a light fixture with four blackened bulbs, none of them burning or ever likely to. There were a studio couch, badly worn, a safe behind the card table you could crack with a nail file and ten seconds to spare, a toilet behind a folding screen, an old-fashioned gray steel radiator beside it, and closets and cabinets built into everything. A couple of kitchen chairs made of tubing and cracked vinyl were arranged in front of the table, ostensibly for the conven-ience of customers. There were no other rooms.

After a minute or so he returned his attention reluctantly to me and held the item out for me to take back. "So what about it?" His tones were spare and northern. He was a na-tive.

I made no move to accept it. "Know where it was taken?"

"Copper?"

"Private."

He studied it again. This time he was looking at the room and not the two people in it. Finally he shrugged and re-turned the picture. "I might. For a price."

I played my hole card. "Let's discuss it over a drink."

"You got?" Suddenly he looked thirsty. His eyes frisked me, looking for telltale bulges.

"Wait here."

I went out to the Cutlass, got the fresh bottle I'd been meaning to take out of the glove compartment before the weather got too cold, and came back in holding the flat pint so that he couldn't miss the unbroken tax stamp on the cap.

"Haig and Haig," he said, approvingly. "You drink good." He was almost panting.

There were two one-ounce glasses waiting on the table. Sitting in one of the customer chairs, I broke the seal and twisted off the cap and poured amber liquid into both of them. He had his hands around one while the bottle was still airborne toward the second. They didn't shake any more than a go-go girl in an icebox.

"Sex and violence," he said, and tossed his down the pipe. I didn't try to compete. I emptied mine in two swallows and was still waiting for my breath to catch up when I poured him another. His hands now were as steady as the murder rate. That one died as painlessly as the first.

"God awmighty, that's good booze. Keep 'em coming, Mr.—I didn't catch the name."

"I didn't throw it." I poured. "What about the picture?"

"Picture?" He was slowing down some. His first sip had only cut the contents in half. "Oh, that. I ain't sure." He swallowed the rest and held out his glass.

I replaced the cap. He stared. I sat back holding the pint and drumming my fingers on the table. The plastic top was sticky from drinks long ago spilled and forgotten.

"You're playing blindman's buff. Gropin' in the dark." His snarl was bottled in bond. He raised a hand to clear away the cobwebs and missed. "What makes you think I know anything about this blue picture racket? What do I look like, a pervert?"

"This court was listed in Lee Q. Story's little brown book."

Surprise flickered briefly behind his eyes, which had begun to look even rheumier. Then he looked angry. Then he made his face blank. The changes came sluggishly, like a fluorescent lamp blossoming on in a cold room. "So who the hell is this Story? He tell you he knows me?"

"He didn't tell me anything. He couldn't, the second time I saw him. He was dead. Somebody treated him to a double dose of his own joy juice. Maybe you know something about that, too."

"I don't know nothin' from nothin'!" He tried to stand up, but his feet skidded out from under him and he crashed back down. He wasn't that drunk. He was scared clean down to his toes. I wondered why. I opened the bottle and reached out to pour him a slug. He cupped a hand over his glass. It was shaking again.

"I still ain't seen nothing that says you're not sloppin' at the public trough," he said.

I got out my wallet and tossed it atop the table. He opened it, spent some time focusing on the ID and the photostat license enclosed in celluloid, and flipped it back at me with a grunt.

"The cops don't know about the murder yet," I explained. "I stumbled on it. There was one piece of written evidence that linked Story to this address, and I've got a copy. Trouble is someone else got there ahead of me and swiped the original. I figure whoever it was came straight here. You've seen him?"

He uncovered his glass. I poured. He drank. His wide nostrils flared. I blamed his flattened nose on a youth spent in the ring, feather-or bubbleweight division, before high living caught up with him. The town turned out almost as many fighters as it did cars and hit men.

"Not him. Them." He was staring past me now at nothing. His hands were curled around the glass so tightly I winced, waiting for it to burst. "Hillbillies, both of them. Big guys, like you. One was bigger than the other and a year or two older, maybe forty. Blond. Big noses. Maybe they got that way by being talked through all the time, you know, twangy. Said 'hort' instead of 'heart,' 'thang' instead of 'thing.' Stuff like that. Figured they was brothers. They was here about an hour ago. That the straight dope you give me about them icing Lee Q.?"

"He was iced. I don't know if it was them did it. Probably not. A forty-four in the head is more their style. What'd they want?" I think I presented a calm exterior. I wanted to get my hands around his throat and force the words out.

" 'Cause, man, I don't want no conspiracy rap on my head. I done time once already. Them prisons is full of fags." He shuddered at some private memory. Then he looked sharply at me. "Them TV private guys always got an in with the cops. That so?"

I told him it was. I hated to lie like that. I waited. He drained his glass and held it out. I bought one for each of us just to be sociable.

"Maybe you can put a word in for me if things get hot? I co-operated with the authorities, stuff like that?" I nodded.

He sighed bitterly and ran a hot damp hand back over his balding head. "Oh man, I can get in trouble just sitting here. The big redneck done most of the talking. Asked me if I knew Story. I said what if I did? He hauls a roll of bills out of his hip pocket big enough to stuff a bowling ball with some left over, peels off a C-note and swats it down on the table on top of my cash sheet and says, 'This is what.' I make a grab for it, but my hand's just touching it when he slams his big ham-hook down on it so hard I can still feel it. Well, I keep a gun handy when I'm figuring receipts. I don't know if you noticed it."

"I noticed it." I had, the butt of what looked to be an Army Colt automatic being hard to miss sticking out from under a stack of scribbled-over sheets at his left elbow.

"Yeah, I figured you might." His eyes narrowed for an instant. Then they returned to limbo. "Turned out, so did the smaller one. He saw me looking at it and reached across his belly under his coat—he was wearing a suit, both of them was—and stuck a hogleg under my nose like I ain't seen since 'Gunsmoke' went off the air. 'Don't,' he says. Just that, 'Don't.' Calmlike, you know?"

"Was it a forty-four?" I managed to keep my voice off the light fixture, but just barely. His grip on his glass was nothing compared to mine.

He nodded. "Could of been, yeah. One of them magnums. You know, the kind that can turn a guy's brains into spaghetti. Everybody's carrying 'em these days. You'd think they didn't make nothing else. Anyway, I forgot all about my little Colt when I seen that. So the big guy says the century's mine if I tell him what my connection is—was—with Lee Q." He drank.

"You told him?"

"The bill's in the safe. Should I hang onto it for evidence or something?"

"What'd you tell him?"

"The truth. That these two honkies, a man and a broad, are using a trailer here to shoot dirty pictures and then turning around and selling 'em to Story. Hippies, but that don't make no difference to me. Hell, I was getting a cut. It's no skin off my ear if some guy out in Grosse Pointe or somewhere gets off on that crap. Anyway, it's legal now, ain't it?"

"More or less. What do they call themselves?"

"The brothers? They didn't—"

"The couple!" I grasped my glass as if it were his neck and inhaled the contents in a slow, steady draft. It wasn't enough anymore. I still wanted to throttle him.

"Oh, them. Rinker. Ed and Shirley, but if they're hitched I bet it's common law. Filthy, both of them, with hair out to here. I thought that crap went out with Watergate. But their money's clean." He grinned to show what good friends we were. His left incisor was steel and shone dully in the bad light.

"Are they there now?"

He stopped grinning and shook his head. The glow of the lamp played off the dents in his gleaming brown pate. He was a one-man light show. "The bastards split this morning without paying me my last cut. They left their trailer behind, though. Figure I might make some scratch renting it out."

"The girl in the picture. Ever see her?"

"I never got to see any of the models, worse luck. They didn't come through here. Too bad. I could of used some of that stuff. I like my white meat as well as my dark."

"Did anybody else ever ask about the trailer or Story? Maybe a black man, husky build, around forty?" Leading question, Walker. The drinks were screwing up my judgment.

"Nobody like that ever came here. Them two billies was the first ever asked about Story. Hold on." A vertical cleft marred the polished expanse of flesh between his skimpy brows. "One night I seen this guy. Some broad with a trailer on the other side of the park came in to complain about her plumbing. I went out with her to take a look. We was passing Rinkers' when the door opens and this guy steps down and almost walks into me. He was a brother all right, and husky."

"Did he act like he was in hiding?"

"Come to think of it, yeah. Furtive-like. You know?"

I said I knew. "Straight hair? Light eyes?"

"Yeah, that was him all right."

"What color was his flying saucer?"

He scowled thoughtfully, as if trying to picture it. Then he glared at me suddenly. "Flying saucer? Say, what the hell you trying to pull?"

"That's my line." I got up and ran straight into my drinks. I had to reach up and grab the brass arms of the dead ceiling fixture to keep from reeling backward. "Nobody sees everything," I snarled. "Why didn't you quit while you were ahead? You didn't see any husky black. You thought if you gave me everything I wanted whether you had it or not your chances would be better with the cops. Maybe the whole damn story was just that, a story. Thanks for the use of the glass, and be sure and show your best side to the artist from the *Free Press*. He draws the best courtroom pictures." I capped the bottle and swept it into my hip pocket. It was a lot lighter than it had been coming in. That was more than could be said for me. I set a tack for the door.

"Hold on!" His chair scraped backward. I kept moving. "It wasn't a story, not all of it. Just the part about the guy. Not all of that, neither. I seen a guy, but he was white, kind of blond and pudgy. Wore one of them Russian fur hats. Like the Commies, you know. About a week back. And the rednecks was real enough. Hell, you know that; you recognized the description. Hey!"

I had a foot on the stack of cinder blocks that did for a stoop outside the trailer. I turned back, as much to get away from all that cold oxygen as to look at him. My stomach did a slow, ponderous turn, like a whale rolling over in deep water.

"One more chance," I snapped. He was standing now, more or less, his big knuckly fighter's hands braced flat on the paper-choked table top. His eyes weren't eyes at all, just a pair of half-cooked eggs with runny whites. "The trailer. Where is it and do I need a key to get in."

There was a black metal box under all the litter, which from the looks of it wasn't any older than Mariners' Church. He flipped it open, reached in and took out a key with a green plastic tab on it that said "Vistaview Mobile Home Park," and threw it at me. I couldn't have been as drunk as I felt, because I caught it in one hand above my head. "It's on the south side. Anthony Wayne Drive. You can't miss it. The streets are all named alphabetically, starting with Algonquin, which is the first one you come to. There are some letters missing, I suppose on account of the guy that laid it out couldn't think of anyone or anything in local history that starts with Q or X or Y or X or a few others. He was kind of a history buff. Number Six."

"The Dar—the hillbillies. How long were they there?"

"Hell, for all I know they never left."

"For Christ's sake!" I started down the steps. Then I went back, tore out the bottle, and thumped it down on his table. The second time I made it.

19

O N MY WAY BACK to the car I scooped a handful of snow out of the fairly clean pile beside the jerry-built stoop and rubbed it over my face. That made me a cold drunk. The engine didn't like to start in that weather, but I climbed in and ground away until it caught, let it warm up for half a minute or so, and then got rolling. The steering wheel was a frozen eel in my hands. The vinyl on the seat felt clammy too, but not as cold as Lee Q. Story's skin. Nothing was that cold. The air had the raw dampness it always has in the low twenties. I didn't want to know what the wind chill was.

Whoever had laid out the park in its fishbone pattern, with parallel "streets" branching out horizontally from the wide main drive, had a cockeyed notion of which names from Detroit history to enshrine on the white-on-green nameplates that caught and threw back my headlights from the posts on the corners. After "Algonquin" came "John Brown," who may have had his place in the scheme of things since he picked the old William Webb home on Congress Street to lay his plans for the raid on Harpers Ferry in 1859, but it seemed to me that General Edward Braddock or Henry P. Baldwin would have made a better choice than the murderous lunatic hanged for his attempt to foment a nationwide massacre of slaveowners and their families. Daniel Boone would have been ideal, if only because he spent more time here than Brown, as a hostage of the Shawnee in 1778. By that same token, Simon Girty, that white taker of colonists' scalps in the pay of the British during the Revolution, scarcely seemed a more prudent choice to represent the seventh letter of the alphabet than Stanley Griswold, Michigan's first secretary by the appointment of Thomas Jefferson. There were other such clinkers, but it was more than likely that the people who occupied the modern, generally well-kept trailers that lined the streets had no idea of the significance of the queer names they were obliged to include in the return addresses on their correspondence. Detroiters have as much sense of history as a herd of cattle.

Number Six, Anthony Wayne Drive was a twenty-five-footer, fairly new, with two doors on the same side but on opposite ends, a striped aluminum awning over the one near the front and the usual expanse of louvered and curtained glass between them. No light showed from inside.

The little, car-length driveway in front was unoccupied. There were no tire marks in the snow to indicate that a vehicle had been pulled around behind, which meant nothing because they would have parked elsewhere and walked in. I swept past and turned into another vacant space two trailers down. No lights in this one either, but just in case someone was sleeping inside I killed my lamps and engine and coasted to a stop. I waited. No lights blinked on. No dogs started barking. Maybe they weren't allowed. I sat and waited and yearned for a cigarette but didn't light one. The engine ticked as it cooled, and then it stopped ticking and everything got quiet. The air inside the car stank sharply of hot wet metal from the heater, turned off now and silent. Damp cold wandered up to the car and sniffed and crept in through the door cracks and settled into my bones with a contented sigh.

Nothing happened in Number Six that could be seen or heard from outside.

Eight hours crawled past, although by the luminous dial of my watch it was just ten minutes. I unclipped the electronic paging device from my inside breast pocket and chucked it into the glove compartment. It would be just my luck for it to start beeping at an inopportune moment. I pocketed my keys, got out, pushed the door shut and leaned against it until it clicked, and slogged through the ankle-deep snow to the street, whose comparatively clear gray surface was more suited to efficient sneakery. Keeping to the right edge in order to avoid being silhouetted against the snow on the other side, which glowed pallidly from its own mysterious source of illumination in the absence of moon or stars, I passed the covered porch of the first door without pausing and went on to its plainer mate on the other end. There I stood and listened. No creaks or footsteps sounded from within. I hadn't expected any. The trailer was too well built for that, and it would be carpeted like all the others.

The door was raised eighteen inches off the ground with a steel step-plate beneath it. It was like a regular door in a house, with a brass knob and a keyhole, the latter at eye level when you were standing on the ground. The lock wasn't a dead bolt. Just for the hell of it I tried the knob before going for the key. It twisted and the door came open.

I didn't like that. Inside it was dark as Tut's tomb. I stepped back and waited for fireworks, but when none came I hauled out my revolver and mounted the step. Nobody was crouching on either side of the door with a sap in his hand. I stepped inside and waited for my eyes to adjust themselves to the darkness.

It wasn't as black as it had seemed at first. The white net

curtains on the small square window on the end were as good as no curtains at all, and after a while I could make out the low bulk of a double bed with its headboard just beneath the sill and an open sliding-door closet filled with plenty of nothing in the far wall. The room was seven by seven and was separated from the rest of the trailer by a walnutlike partition with a door that when opened would bump the baseboard of the bed. Right now it was closed. I changed that, but not until I had stood with my ear at the crack long enough to hear silence on the other side. I started through with my gun in my hand.

I sensed rather than felt the new weight that had entered the trailer behind me. Before I could turn, something that was not a comb or a stiffened finger dug into the fleshy part of my back just above the waist.

"I'm gonna give you a firsthand look at your own guts the second you even think about turning around," said a voice dripping with deep South at my right ear.

20

I RAISED MY HANDS, gun and all, to my shoulders. A hard dry hand raspy with calluses reached over and relieved me of the weapon, twisting it out of my grip so violently that I barely got my finger clear of the trigger guard in time to save it from being snapped off.

"Got him, Jer," he called. His calf's-bawl set my head to ringing. It still ached, thanks to the U.S. Army.

The trailer filled with light. I blinked. I was standing just inside a shallow passageway that opened onto a tiny bathroom to my left and led into a room that took up the rest of the trailer. But I couldn't see anything beyond that, because the square arch ahead of me was filled with a dark figure that stood two feet inside the room holding something in his left hand that glittered like gold.

"Well, don't just stand there, you dumb cock-sucker," he said. "Shoo him in."

He had the other's nasal twang, but his was colder, more thoughtful. The hard something prodded my back. I moved forward to spare the kidney.

The room had been a combination kitchen, living, and dining area before someone had converted it into a photographer's studio and motion picture set. Strobe lights mounted atop metal standards stood at the head and foot of a Queen Anne bed bigger than some states with a rumpled pink spread and tangled black satin bedding. A hand-held videotape camera worth a couple of G's lay on its side atop a low table with a padded top designed for that purpose, beside a smaller film-type movie camera. Another table held a good still camera and a cheap Polaroid and a number of curled black and white Polaroid shots of naked girls in every conceivable pose and a couple that would be pretty hard to conceive unless you were preoccupied with that sort of thing, and aren't we all. Test shots. Opaque black curtains, open now, had been added to the kitchen end, and there were chemical containers of glass and unbreakable plastic on the drainboards next to the double sink, turning the area into a darkroom. Negatives clothespinned to a cotton cord dangled above the sink. There were indentations in the slippery black pillows on the bed that might have been made by heads, and there were white spots on the sheet that had been made by something else. It was a nice room.

It was the room in which the picture in my pocket, the later one, had been snapped. What I had mistaken for a list of hotel checkout times was really a shooting schedule printed in neat blue-pencil characters on a child's wide-ruled composition sheet taped to the door. *September Morn*, torn from a magazine and mounted in a cheap frame, still hung to the left of it.

As with most trailers, cabinets had been built everywhere cabinets could be built. Most were open, their contents spilled out on the floor. These included dozens of flat gray metal canisters and miles of Super 8 and 16-millimeter film, exposed and unexposed to begin with, but now all exposed. They hadn't gotten around yet to tearing the bed apart and slitting the pillows.

"You shouldn't ought to call me that, Jerry," whined the

gunman behind me. "You know I don't like to be called things like that." He said *thangs*, just as the park manager had claimed.

"You'll get called a damn sight worse if you don't learn to stop using names, shithead."

Jerry was a bruiser, a college gridiron type with good shoulders growing out of his solid neck like roots from a stump, but he was carrying too much belly these days to make even semipro. His dark suit coat of no particular color wasn't buttoned at the waist and hadn't been in years. His gray topcoat needed cleaning. It was the same outfit he had been wearing when he and his brother snatched Francis Kramer on Woodward a couple of decades ago—or was it yesterday afternoon? He had a thick face with not enough chin, too much nose that threatened to pull him over onto his face, and incongruously innocent blue eyes that went as deep as the gold plate on a pair of dollar cuff links. His dishwater hair was collar-length and greased back and wasn't any cleaner than it had to be. The glittering something was behind his back.

He was working at a wad of gum and giving me a good view of his progress because he chewed with his mouth open. He studied me in silence for some moments, his gum clicking.

"You walk awful quiet for a man your size," he said at length. "We never would of knowed you was coming at all if we didn't see your car rolling slow down the main drag, like you was looking for a particular street and wasn't sure where to find it. Hubert—damn it, now I'm doing it!" He spat out his gum viciously. It made a nasty noise hitting the rug. "Well, the hell with it. I sent Hubert out behind the trailer to wait. He seen you sneaking up. Now, what's your blister?"

I said nothing.

"You ain't no Jew. Too damn good-looking. You sure as hell ain't no nigger. Kikes snoop around a lot and niggers is always looking for an easy shove-over. Only other reason I can figure you'd be on the prowl is you're a cop."

I repeated myself. In the passageway the tin furnace kicked in and began purring.

"I got to do everything for myself. Keep them hands up, you." He put whatever it was that glittered into a pocket, patted me down, and came up with my wallet and the pictures and the scrap of paper in the right side of my jacket. He left my keys and change in my pants. He didn't get my notebook with all the information I'd jotted down on this case. That was at home where I'd had the good sense to leave it.

First he opened the wallet and gave my papers a good going over in the light of the ceiling fixture. "Snooper, huh?" he said, looking up. He didn't expect an answer. The pictures interested him, particularly the bigger one, which had been taken in this room. He studied it a minute, glanced at the door that led outside, which had figured in the shooting, looked back at the picture again, and turned his attention without comment to the crumple of paper I had torn from Story's notebook. I saw his scalp move when he realized what it was. Still he didn't say anything. He gave everything one last look and then put it on the table with the Polaroids. Then he turned back to me with his blank stare.

"Shut that door and put away the piece," he told the other. "This guy ain't going nowhere."

The gun was removed from my back. I let my hands down. A second later there was a shallow rumbling noise behind me as the sliding door that separated this room from the rest of the trailer was pushed shut. Then the other man came around me, walking sideways and giving me as wide a berth as he could, considering the cramping presence of the oversized bed. Hubert was a poor carbon of his brother, not as big and even less tidy in an identically nondescript suit and shabbier topcoat. His face was badly pockmarked, and the flesh-colored nub of a hearing aid showed inside his right ear—another legacy, I supposed, of that same child-hood illness. The butt and cylinder of a Colt magnum stuck up above his big square belt buckle. My Smith & Wesson made his left coat pocket sag.

He had beady little eyes unlike his brother's that glistened unhealthily in the soft light as he directed them from me to the stuff on the table. He started to pick it up.

"Who told you to move?" snapped Jerry. "Put that down and get the hell back where you was before!"

Hubert looked at him with a hurt expression, opened his rather weak mouth, then clamped it shut and left the stuff where it was and retraced his steps around to my back, one hand gripping the magnum protectively.

"Hold him, Hube."

The older Darling gave the command as casually as a doctor calling for suction during an operation. My arms were seized and jerked behind me somewhat less casually and a variation of the *nolo contendere* hold that had led Francis Kramer to his death was applied. Any attempt on my part to escape would have cost me more than one bone.

Meanwhile, Jerry reached into his right pocket and then cupped that hand around his left, and when they came apart I saw that the glittering something I'd noted earlier was a full set of brass knuckles. I held my water with difficulty.

"You kill the coon in the pecker shop?" he asked calmly.

"No."

While I was looking at the fist with the brass knuckles he drove the other into my abdomen. I wheezed and bent, but only so far as Hubert let me. My arms creaked in their sockets.

"Let's try it again. You kill him?"

I said no again, through my teeth this time. He hit me with the same fist just below the solar plexus. I didn't have any wind left to wheeze with. That didn't stop my lungs from turning themselves inside out trying.

Jerry waited for me to recover somewhat, then repeated his question. I repeated my answer and braced myself.

He grinned, not sadistic, not friendly. It was just something he did with his mouth. " 'Course you didn't. You was there after us, not before. Otherwise you'd have the original page from the shine's book and we'd have the penciled-over one instead of the other way around. I had to know if you'd lie to save yourself a beating. Now we can get down to some serious business. Where's the film?"

"What film?"

The fist with the brass knuckles flashed around and caught me on the side of the jaw. I tried to roll with the punch. It bought me little. A hot white light burst inside my head and my jaw tore at its fastenings. I shook my head sluggishly, without any snap to it, and worked the jaw. It crunched as if there were sand in the sockets.

"Where's the film?"

"I don't—"

The right fist slammed into the other side. It was a pillow compared to the other, but I hadn't seen it coming in time to turn my head with it and caught the full force on the tender region. My vision broke into black and white checks. There was salt on my tongue and something else.

"Man, it's your face," said Jerry. "If I was wearing knucks

on that one you'd leave here in a bag. Where'd you hide it?"

He knew what the answer was going to be. He dropped his left shoulder and cocked the shining fist.

"Lay off that one, Jerry," said his brother. "What'd he be doing snooping around here if he had the film?"

"That's what I'm trying to find out." But he relaxed his stance. "The picture," he said to me. "The blow job. It was took here. Who's the bimbo and what's your interest in her?"

"She's a missing person," I replied, through a mouthful of rocks. "Her guardian hired me to find her. She disappeared from a school in Lansing last year. The picture's all I've got to go on.

"Makes sense, Jer."

"Shut up." The big man looked thoughtful. He was about my height, but he had twenty pounds on me. The knuckles gave him another hundred. "I don't like it," he snarled. "It stinks. This guardian, he got a name?"

"Ben Morningstar."

There was a moment of stunned silence. Then they both laughed out loud. They had nasty laughs.

"That's sweet, that is," said Jerry, "considering Morningstar's the money man behind this whole thing." He waved an expansive arm around the trailer.

"What whole thing?"

"Story's and about a dozen other jerk-off stands and grindhouses in town. Wasn't for him, there wouldn't be no porn traffic, for Christ's sake. At least not like we got it."

"Says who?"

"Hell, it's street dope. Right, Hube?"

"Shit, yes," said Hube.

The older Darling's doll-eyes narrowed. His face was a

tight white mask. "Which is why you're lying in your teeth, Mr. Peeper. Teeth you ain't gonna have much longer to lie in no more. Hold him good, Hubert."

Hubert held me good. Jerry set himself and stepped forward to put some weight behind his swing and I kicked him between the legs with everything I had.

Which wasn't enough, considering I'd hoped to kill him. The pain and shock had been known to do that, according to my judo instructor in the MPs. But when Jerry said, "Ga!" and went down to the floor rolling and moaning with his hands between his legs I knew I'd fallen short of the mark.

"Jer! You all right, Jer?" Hubert sounded scared. He relaxed his grip and I started to twist free, but before I could gather enough balance to wheel around he got hold again and bent my arms back and up with a violent surge that nearly forced me to my knees. I was still grunting from the pain and exertion when Jerry, pale and shaken, got up on his knees and climbed unsteadily to his feet. His top coat and right cheek were smeared with brown dust.

"You son of a bitch!" He sprayed saliva. His face wasn't a face anymore. It was a grinning skull with glazed dead eyes in the sockets. His voice was nothing more than air forced through his teeth. "Hold him, Hube," he hissed. "Hold him real good."

He positioned himself in front of me and to the left, with his right hip turned toward me as protection against another kick. "Such a good-looking boy, too," he said regretfully, and hurled a brassbound fist straight at my mouth.

21

"**B**RASS KNUCKLES ARE THE lowest, most vicious device ever concocted by man," a voice was saying. "They're almost always the property of the aggressor, and the guy too weak or scared to rely on his own fists has no right taking the offensive at all."

"But this guy was no Caspar Milquetoast," someone protested. "He was a good six-one and two hundred pounds."

"All the more reason to despise his falling back on artificial aid. Since he didn't need it, his decision to use it tells you something important about him. The man's a sadist."

I opened my eyes to yell at the two guys who were disturbing my coma. There was no one there. I was lying on a bed in a dimly lit room all alone. The voices were both mine and they were both in my head. My face didn't feel like my face. It was a numb mask. Which was merciful, because when I raised a hand from under the covers to touch it, it didn't feel as if it was all there. I ran an exploratory tongue around my teeth, some of which wobbled. There I halted my inspection. I didn't want to know any more just yet.

The light was coming from a lamp with a corrugated paper shade and a fat china base on a low square table with a single drawer in it beside the bed. On the other side was a closet with a sliding door open just far enough to show that it was empty. Aside from that the room had two doors, one on the right that looked as if it might lead outside and another just beyond the foot of the bed that opened on a shallow passage I recognized. It took me a minute to put it together. I was in the bedroom of the trailer, the one no one ever seemed to use, even for sleeping.

I was fully dressed under the top sheet and spread except for my jacket, tie, and shoes, which when I looked in that direction turned out to have been left in a heap on the floor between the bed and the right wall. That angered me for a moment, someone treating another man's clothes like that when there was a perfectly good closet standing unused nearby. I wasn't thinking straight. I hadn't been for some time.

I disregarded the ache in my arms and my own fears to feel my face again. It wasn't as bad as I'd thought. My jaw was swollen and my lower lip was puffed up and oozing fresh blood through a split near the center, but the jawbone appeared to be intact and most of my teeth were firmly in place. My nose hadn't been touched. There had been more blood but someone had sponged it off.

My watch read 2:08. Morning or afternoon? The square window on the end of the trailer above my head was black. Morning, then. Of what day?

I was turning that one over when a toilet flushed somewhere and the light in the bathroom off the passage, which I just realized had been burning all this time, blinked off under the door and the door slid open and someone came out and into the bedroom. Someone with a trim figure beneath a pale green pantsuit and who swayed as gracefully on stilt-high platform shoes as she did in clogs and nothing. Someone named Iris.

She smiled when she saw I was awake and came over and sat on the edge of the bed and put her purse on the floor. She picked up my hand and held it between her smooth palms, so pale in contrast to the deep brown, nearly purple, of the rest of her. Her eyes were bright and shiny, the pupils shrunken to pinpoints. She'd just had a fix and the world was a beautiful place again.

"This has to be Heaven," I mumbled through my cracked lips. "I've been through Purgatory."

"Close. You look like Hell." She gave my hand a squeeze.

"The gendarmes with you?"

She shook her head quickly. "I never took the time to call them. Right after you got off the line I called for a cab and headed straight here. I told Aunt Beryl a friend of mine had been in an accident and was in the hospital. The dispatcher had a hell of a time getting a cabbie that would go down John R after dark."

"You'd better tell me everything. My head hurts."

"I can't think why. You weren't lying in any more than a cup of your own blood when I found you."

"You found me where?"

"You wanted the whole story." Her dark eyes flashed. "Who are you to tell me to wait two hours to find out if you're dead or alive and then hang up? When I finally got a hack I came here and spent half an hour getting that soak in the office to tell me where you'd gone. He was two-thirds of the way through a pint of Haig & Haig and three sheets to the wind. I don't suppose you had anything to do with that."

"Tsk tsk," I said. "A member of your own race."

"Race doesn't enter into it! Anyway, he's African and I'm islander. There's a world of difference. And a soak is a soak. Stop interrupting. By the time I got here you were sprawled in a mess on the carpet. It cost me an extra ten to get the driver to help me carry you in here, and then he wouldn't stick around. Someone had been at the other bed with a knife and it made him nervous. Where do you store all that tonnage, anyway? There isn't any fat on you. Except for your head."

I took a strike on that one. "Where were the Hager twins?"

"Who? Are you delirious?"

"No more so than usual. I mean the Darlings. You know, Jerry and Hubert. The Apache dancers in the room next to yours."

"I didn't see anyone. You mean, they're the ones who did this to you?" She gripped my hand hard enough to cut off the circulation.

"Them and a hunk of brass good for a year in Jackson if the cops find it in their possession," I said. "They probably lit out the other door when you and the hackie came in the front. Two on two isn't their style, and who can tell the sex of anyone in a getup like that on a dark night?" I flitted my aching eyes over her mannish attire. "Whatever happened to skirts, or aren't I allowed to ask that anymore? A guy can't call a broad a broad these days without getting picketed."

"My, aren't we macho. And you with teeth in another room."

"Not quite." I disengaged my hand from hers with a gentle squeeze of my own and peeled back the bedspread. It was heavier than it looked. It was woven steel stuffed with cannonballs.

"What are you doing?" Her tone dripped disapproval.

"Getting up." I braced my elbows on the mattress.

"No, you're not!"

I sat up. The black and white checkerboard came back. Only it wasn't a checkerboard now, it was a net that someone had drawn over my eyeballs and was twisting behind my head. Blood boomed inside my skull. I lay back down. It was a long way to the mattress. "No, I'm not," I agreed.

Her face drifted around a bit before dropping anchor. It had I-told-you-so scribbled all over it. "You took more of a beating than you think," she said. "If I showed you the stain on the rug you'd know how much. You aren't twenty any-more; you can't expect to bounce back just like that. What are you, thirty-five, thirty-six?"

"Thirty-two."

"No kidding? You look a lot older. I was just being kind. There's gray in your hair."

"If I were half as old as I feel, I'd be ten years buried."

"What you need is a week's rest."

"What I'll take is ten minutes."

"How about an hour?"

I started to shake my head, thought better of it, and said, "I've got an appointment with the guy who runs this court. He doesn't know I've got it, but I don't want to be late."

She just stared at me. I was beginning to realize just how angry and scared she was. "You'll stay in that bed if I have to climb in there with you."

I grinned. The split in my lower lip opened some more and I tasted blood. I ignored it. "Not with those pants on," I said. "I'd feel like a fag."

She looked at me for a moment without saying anything. Then she got up. There was a metallic pop, the whine of a zipper, and then she pushed the slacks down her long slim legs and stepped out of them and her shoes in almost the same movement. If she was wearing any underwear at all there wasn't enough of it to blindfold a canary. She swept the cumbersome garment aside with a foot the way a baby bird might free itself of the egg with one last kick and slid in beside me. "Slid" was the word. She had the grace of a trained dancer. She felt warm against me, or maybe that was just me. Her expression was still mad as hell. I said something tactless. Remember, I was sick.

I said, "This isn't going to cost me anything, is it? They lifted my wallet."

"Shut up," she said, and kissed me. It hurt, but not so much I wanted her to stop.

22

I T WAS 2:45 BY my watch, which had a battery only
six weeks old and no reason to lie. Some pursuits seem
to go faster than others. I excavated my crushed pack
of cigarettes from my sodden shirt pocket and offered her
one. She accepted it.

"That certainly was restful, wasn't it?" I said.

She held the cigarette between her fingers and looked at
the imitation walnut paneling of the ceiling. She had a clean
profile and a neck like a pharaoh's erotic dream. She said,
"If that's a sample of what you can do when you've been
beat up, I'll have to catch you when you're well."

I came back with something equally flattering, but which
wasn't a lie, and let the Winston in the corner of my sore
mouth droop while I patted my pockets for matches.

"Hand me my purse," she said. "There's a lighter in it."

It was more bag than purse, an over-the-shoulder number in green leather with a strap you could use for a fan
belt on an earth mover. Times were rough for purse-
snatchers. Something rattled inside when I lifted it. I sat up
and hoisted it into my lap and opened the catch. Iris took
in her breath sharply and made a grab for it, but my
strength was returning; I held on and rooted among the keys
and cocktail napkins and wads of Kleenex and came up with
a hypodermic syringe that glittered in the soft light. She
snatched it out of my hand.

Silence stank while I mined out a slim plastic throwaway lighter—green, to match her suit and purse—and lit our cigarettes, starting with hers. She puffed at it angrily.

"How long?" I asked, when mine was a quarter-inch down.

"About two years." She dragged at hers more slowly. "Twenty-six months and three days."

"It's none of my business."

"That's right."

We smoked. Not too far away an engine started after a lot of grinding and idled, warming up. An assembly-line worker, maybe, on his way in for the early shift. Or a blind pig customer. Or both, which explained the quality of today's cars.

She took the bag from my lap, dropped in the syringe, and snapped it shut. She left the cigarette burning in her mouth and sat there with her hands clutching the bag, looking at nothing. "I wasn't forced into it, if that's what you want to know," she said. "I never did have will power. Not an ounce."

"I saw a man today who had been killed by a good stiff fix. I suppose it's as peaceful a way to go as any."

She wasn't listening. "I've thought about quitting. The turkey, not that methadone stuff. I wonder if it's the hairy trip they say."

"It's worse."

Her head jerked back as if she'd been slapped. She turned huge eyes on me. Huge and scared. "What I heard—"

"What you heard was PR put out by the drug clinics. If they told the truth they wouldn't get half the patients they get. A week to stop screaming. Ten days to two weeks before you feel like going on and can keep anything down heavier than chicken broth. Two years before you stop missing it.

That's the dangerous time. Some think they can handle it and start in all over again. I can count the people I know who kicked it twice on one finger. He died." I stopped to take a drag. She didn't say anything. Outside the idling engine took on a businesslike growl and throbbed away. "If you're serious about quitting, I can give you the name of a guy I know in Hazel Park. He runs a clinic in a private house on Woodruff. I have his card, if Jerry and Hubert didn't run off with my wallet."

"Is he a doctor?"

"Was. Even the AMA can't close ranks fast enough when the narcs move in."

"He's a doper?"

"Was again. For six years. Which is why he knows better than anyone else how to run a clinic. He has a doctor on staff, to administer glucose injections and sign death certificates for those that don't make it. I'm not trying to scare you, just telling you what to expect. People with strong hearts have nothing to worry about."

"What made you decide to become a snooper?"

I wasn't surprised by the swift change of subject. Almost anything's more fun to talk about than your own health. "It was good enough for a guy I liked," I said.

"Tell me about him."

I crushed out my cigarette in my left palm, a habit I'd picked up in the jungle when there wasn't an ashtray handy. "When I met him, I was a police trainee and he was a sergeant with twenty-six years on the force. He liked me. Some people did, back then. He put his pension on the line to try and help me out of some trouble I got into and damn near lost it when it didn't work. By the time I got out of the army he'd retired and gone private. I didn't have a job so he hired me. I didn't have a place to live so he put me up in his three-room apartment. When I decided to get married he stood up for me at the ceremony even though he'd tried to tell me she was no good. He was right. He was usually right, but he never said I told you so, not even at the divorce hearing."

I shook my head. "He wasn't much. He was fat and old and ugly and he drank too much and he wasn't much of a P.I. But there was one thing he hated, and that was a set of crooked gears that worked too smoothly. He said it was the duty of every honest man to throw sand in the works whenever the opportunity presented itself."

Iris said, "I think I'd like him too. What happened to him?"

"He's dead."

"Oh." She changed the subject again. "Why did the Darlings try to kill you?"

"They weren't trying to kill me. There are quicker ways of doing that and I imagine they know most of them. At first they thought I had something they wanted. Then they didn't think that anymore, but they wanted to know what I was doing and who I was working for. I told them, but they didn't believe me."

"Do you have what they want?"

I nodded. "Last night—the night before last, now—they put a bullet through the head of a guy I used to know because he filmed them and two of their friends executing a guy last August. The guy in the film was black and they're Klansmen and the rest you know, or ought to. This other guy they killed was working for Army Intelligence, but I figure he'd been sitting on the film all this time, bleeding the Darlings and company. He was that kind of guy, and from what the park manager here told me they're loaded. Most likely Kramer—that's the guy with the candid camera—

told them after they snatched him what he'd done with the evidence or they wouldn't have handed him his ticket. Hubert, the younger one, carries a forty-four magnum and Kramer was shot with a forty-four. And I saw the snatch.

"Only Kramer didn't have the film. He was no genius, but he wasn't so dumb he'd tell them where to find it knowing they'd kill him once he did. They knew he didn't have it because they'd been following him all over town watching him look for it. I'll come back to that. They confronted him with this knowledge and he blurted out what little he knew. Exit Kramer.

"Last night they visited a porno shop on Erskine run by a guy named Story, looking for the film, but someone had beaten them to it and tossed the place without finding it. I'd been there second and found it, never mind how. Story was dead, brained with something or other and OD'd on his own dope. Maybe he put up a fight and got slugged hard enough not to expect to come out of it and the murderer got scared and tried to make it look like an accident. It's not rational, but killers who don't do it for a living seldom are."

I paused to give her time to comment or ask questions. She didn't use it. She reached over and mashed out her butt against the closet's sliding door. It left a mark on the blond wood.

"Lee Q. Story bought and sold all or most of his merchandise locally," I continued. "Some of it came from this trailer, and some of it went to collectors and other shops in town. Kramer had just finished tearing apart the apartment of a collector who probably bought some of his stuff from Story when Jerry and Hubert picked him up. It was a last-ditch effort to find the film that could keep him alive after he'd pushed the blackmail angle too far. He'd already been to every place Story dealt with in quantity, or he wouldn't have been on his way to an appointment he'd made with another Intelligence agent for protection.

"He'd been here first, because this was where he hid the film when things started to get hot. He was seen leaving the trailer a week ago. That's why Lee Q. left this court off the list he gave me of his sources; he suspected someone here knew something and he didn't want me stumbling on it. It was the perfect cache. Who'd ever think of looking for footage of a murder in a trailer full of stag movies in identical cans? Kramer's trouble was he didn't take anyone into his confidence, and the film went out in a box or crate with maybe a dozen others to the shop on Erskine. That would have been his next stop. He wouldn't have looked as closely there as he'd have liked to, though, because Story was a mean mother with friends on the street who probably told him he'd get cut if he kept snooping around. Being something less than a hero, Kramer split with a fair idea of the places Story did business with and confined his search to them. What was wrong with that was he didn't know that Lee Q. had looked inside the box, probably screened the film, realized he had a gold mine and socked it away for future use. Blackmail, of course. Items like that carry the germs of greed like Mary Mallon carried typhoid. If he didn't know who the men in the film were, he planned to find out. Only he got burned before he could turn a profit."

She had turned onto her side and was watching me. Her body was snug against mine. She wore no perfume. Some women don't have to. Her finger traced idle circles on my unshaven cheek.

I went on. "Kramer must have told the Darlings about Story but not about this trailer, or they wouldn't have had to go to the place on Erskine to find out about it, just as I did. That's natural. He thought he was talking himself out of a jam and would want to keep his story simple and believable. Besides, he may have suspected that it was someone here who was holding out on him and not Story and planned on coming back. As for why it took the Darlings twenty-four hours to pay a call on the shop, the only thing I can think is that they wanted to check out some of the other places first. Like most bigots they'd fear blacks on their own ground, and might put off visiting the blackest part of the city until they absolutely had to. Then they would have wanted to go in after dark, because that's how they work."

"What does all this have to do with Martha?" asked Iris, still watching me. She had large eyes even when they weren't registering fright. "Aside from her entertaining the Darlings in her room that night, I mean. That could have been coincidence."

"There's only one coincidence in this case, and that's that I happened to step into the same muckhole from two directions. There is no Martha Burns, to begin with. Her name is Marla Bernstein, and that picture I showed you was taken in this trailer. You might even call *that* coincidence, except for a telephone call I made to Lansing that blows that theory all to hell. She wasn't entertaining the Darlings, not in the way you think. But the hell with that right now." I peeled aside the spread and swung my stockinged feet to the floor. A wave of nausea swept over me, but it was quickly past. I put on my shoes, bit my lip, and dipped down to scoop my jacket and tie from the floor. I nearly passed out on that one, but then I was upright again and dragging on the jacket. I balled up the necktie and thrust it into a pocket, then put on my shoes.

"Amos!" she said angrily. "I said an hour!"

But I was already up and heading for the other end of the trailer. It was like walking in a dream, with clouds shifting and crossing beneath my feet. It wasn't a dream. My jaw was starting to hurt. "No time, angel. Jerry and Hubert were thinking of rabbiting or they wouldn't have run at first sight of a car. I've got to get to a telephone."

An ugly brown stain had spoiled the nap of the carpet where my head had been lying. I tried not to think of it as my blood and rescued my overcoat from the floor where Iris and the cab driver had flung it after stripping it off me to lighten the load. My hat was where it had fallen with the first blow of Jerry Darling's brass knuckles. I got that too, and put them both on. They'd done a thorough job on the Queen Anne mattress. The cover was slashed in a ragged cross and stuffing hung out of it like entrails.

Iris came in, trying to walk and step into her slacks at the same time. She wasn't having much success. She had her bag over one shoulder and was carrying her sea-green jacket, thrown off in the heat of lovemaking, under her arm. Her white nylon blouse was milkily transparent. She wasn't wearing underwear, by the way.

"Who are you going to call?" She had stopped finally and was making progress with the slacks.

"Alderdyce. It's his case." My wallet and everything else Jerry Darling had taken from my pockets were still on the snapshot-littered table. My gun had left with them. I put the items in their respective pockets. "I guess I forgot to tell you. The guy Kramer filmed them snuffing was Freeman Shanks."

She stopped what she was doing and stared, mouthing the name without making a sound. Then, slowly and carefully, she did up her slacks, tucked in her blouse, and donned and fastened her jacket. Things were moving too fast for her. I knew how she felt.

I said, "They can post cops at both airports and alert Customs at the Ambassador Bridge and put out an APB statewide and in enemy territory. Meaning Ohio. They might pick them up in six months if the Feds stay out of it, which of course they won't. Are you coming or not?"

"I've got a hell of a lot of choice with no transportation," she said. "This is getting wild. Who killed Story?" She had slipped the bag from her shoulder to get her arm into the jacket sleeve. Now she hoisted it back into place. The syringe rattled inside.

I guess I was staring. A frightened look came over her features and she said, "Amos, what's wrong? I knew you got up too soon." She hurried over to me and put a hand on my shoulder to guide me back to bed. I left it there, but I didn't move. I was too busy looking at the bag.

"Come on," I barked, snapping out of it and grabbing her wrist. "We make a great team. I'm Nick, you're Nora." I tore open the door and towed her out into the cold and darkness. We were within ten feet of my car when we heard the shots, both of them.

23

TWO FLAT REPORTS, SPACED a second apart and brittle in the cold damp air, like a cat sneezing. They might have come from the manager's office and they might have come from Chicago. Iris and I froze in our tracks and stared at each other without seeing anything in the gloom, listening to ourselves not breathing. Then I let go of her wrist and ran to the rear of the Cutlass and fumbled out my keys and cursed as I felt for the one that opened the trunk and used it. There was no light inside. I groped along the lining on the right side until I felt a bulge and pulled the Luger out of its special pocket. It was as cold as Death's handshake. I broke out the clip, saw that it was indeed loaded, rammed it back in, and put the gun in my coat pocket.

"Stay here!" I shouted, slamming the lid. I could have saved my breath. She was already in the passenger's seat. The dome light flickered on briefly, outlining her head and shoulders in yellow, then went black again as she pulled the door shut. It was time I got that lock fixed.

There was no time to argue even if it would have worked. I climbed under the wheel, ground the engine into reluctant life, yanked on the lights, and splattered slush over the side of the trailer I'd been parked in front of as I tore off across a rectangular patch of lawn and hit Anthony Wayne Drive with a thud that did little for my front-end alignment and less for my sore jaw. Out of nervous habit I glanced up at the rearview mirror and caught a glimpse of the upper half of a determined face bathed in the eerie green glow of the dash lights. It didn't look like anybody I knew.

I was doing sixty by the time I got to the main stem and almost lost it on the turn, gouging a hunk out of a pile of plowed snow as hard as a banker's heart and raking my lights over the paralyzed figure of a dowdy matron in curlers and a housecoat who had opened the door of her trailer to see who the damned fool was who was turning her peaceful court into the last lap at Indy. She wouldn't have paid any attention to the shots. There would be deer hunting in the woods nearby, and tougher game laws had never daunted determined poachers and shiners in the past. For all I knew that might have been all there was to it, but I wouldn't have made book on the odds. Nevertheless I cooled it on the straightaway, which probably saved my life and Iris'.

A pair of blinding headlamps moving nearly as fast as mine came directly at me. I made for the right shoulder and my rear end came slueing around to block the road. The oncoming lights swept the inside of the Cutlass from right to left, blazing over Iris, who was flattened against the door on the passenger's side with her nails digging holes in the padded dash, then throwing a lone, naked tree on the left side of the road into ghastly white relief as the other vehicle, a heavy pickup, skidded to avoid striking us and slammed into the heaped snow on the shoulder. It was still rocking when the driver punched it into reverse, spraying gravel and clay from all four tires, twisted the wheel to the right, and tore off in the direction from which he'd come. A stone flying from the rear wheels struck my window with a resounding crack and sent hairline fissures forking out from the point of impact.

"Hang on!" I shouted, backed into the road, and took off in pursuit, bouncing over the ruts.

The taillights ahead blinked out as I was roaring past the manager's office, too late for me to miss that the truck was turning left onto the road that led back to Grand River. I lost a quarter-mile taking the turn, picked it up again on the first straight stretch of gravel, and could almost read the license plate number when it swung right suddenly, bounced up over the snowy bank, and cut a hundred yards off the corner on its way onto the avenue. My speedometer read eighty by this time but I was running out of road. I took my foot off the accelerator and used it to tap the brakes, on, off, on, off, rapidly, the scenery awash in my headlights and shifting wildly to right and left each time pressure was applied.

It wasn't enough. I shot past the stop sign on the corner and straight across Grand River, fighting the wheel all the way. My front wheels locked, turning the car into a two-ton iceboat. There was no traffic in the westbound lane. A taxi was crawling east, its light forming elliptical yellow pools on the glazed pavement. Iris screamed. The cab's front wheels turned to avoid us but failed to change the vehicle's course. At the last instant it looked as if I might get across its path in time. I didn't. Its right front fender struck my right rear with a bang and bounded off. The Cutlass kept rolling and fetched up against a solid bank of snow on the north shoulder with a jolt that rammed my chest into the steering column. The engine stalled. There was no sign of the four-by-four I'd been chasing.

Silence rushed in like air filling a vacuum. I wheezed to

catch my breath, remembered Iris suddenly, and darted my gaze in her direction. She was massaging a spot near her hairline with a hand that could have been steadier.

"You okay?" I snapped on the dome light.

"Bumped my head on the windshield." Her voice quavered slightly. "Didn't break the skin."

"Sure you're all right?"

She gave me a level glare. "I didn't say that."

"Any other time you couldn't find a cab on a night like this," I grumbled.

The windshield wasn't damaged. I cut the lights and clambered out. The cab driver was stalking across Grand River in my direction with a tire iron in his hand. There didn't appear to be anything wrong with his tires or mine. His hack had come to a stop off the south shoulder with its headlamps shining into the road, in which position its wrinkled fender showed in the lights of a car that was crawling past beneath an overload of curiosity. It didn't stop. They seldom do. There wasn't anyone seated in the rear of the cab.

The cabbie was an old black man whose stiff white eyebrows—the only individual feature I could make out against the glare of his lamps—bristled out beneath the shiny, broken visor of his cap, which bore a Teamsters Local 299 button on one side. His face was broad and square and dusky gray in the darkness, and the body beneath his stained Navy peacoat, with its various lumps and bulges, was anything but old. Guys like that are as easy to knock down as fire hydrants. He was barely across the turning lane when he opened his mouth.

"Where the hell'd you learn to drive, man?" he exploded in a tough, city-wise voice from which all the Alabama had been beaten out long ago. "Demolition derby?"

The wronged driver's litany. It didn't change from year to year. I flashed the sheriff's shield I'd had hidden inside a flap of my wallet. It slowed him down.

"Sergeant Duffy, County," I said, in my policeman's voice. "I was chasing a wife-beater. Lost him, thanks to you." I put up the buzzer before he could get a good look at it, walked briskly around to the other side of the Cutlass, and helped Iris out onto the shoulder. She shivered in her thin jacket. She was the first hooker I'd ever met who didn't appear to own a fur coat. I escorted her over to where the driver was standing with the tire iron dangling loosely in his grip.

"Don't waste time apologizing," I snapped. "This is the scroat's wife. Take her home while I get out an APB." I turned her over to him.

Iris' mouth fell open. "What? Amos—!"

I grinned at the cabman. "I went to school with her older sister. She calls me Amos and I call her Madeline. This should take care of the fare and that fender." I gave him one of the C-notes I'd gotten from Morningstar and supplied him with the address on John R. He stared at the money in his hand, then at me, and smiled. The night wasn't so dark when he did that.

"Man," he said, "I don't know who you are or what rules you play by, but I've knowed Iris here for a year at least, and she ain't got no husband and her name ain't never been Madeline. Sent her some of her best customers. But you can buy the right not to tell me if you give me enough to do the job proper. You can't get no fender fixed for less than two hundred these days."

"The hell with that. You can pick one up in any junkyard for twenty-five and replace it yourself. Unless of course you've been cutting your dispatcher in on your pimping action?"

The grin faded. "Man, you hoojies don't never stop screwing us poor niggers, do you?" He was gripping the iron with his old determination.

" 'Hoojies,' " I echoed, jacking my own grin back up onto my face. "Prison slang. Bet you're on parole. Whose name's on your chauffeur's ticket?"

He suggested something vile and turned back toward his rig with a hand on Iris' arm. She shook it off.

"I'm a human being, damn it!" She was glaring at me. Had been, since the exchange began. "You can't haul me around like a kid's pull-toy. I'm going with you."

"No, you're not, angel. If I find what I think I'm going to find in that office it won't be any place for a working girl. Not after I call the cops." I turned to the driver. "If you don't see her to her door I'll have you in a holding cell by first light."

He'd handled rough customers before. He pinioned her arms, kept his shins out of the way of her two-inch heels, and walked her across the avenue to the cab. She had resigned herself by the time he got her inside, which was a good thing since they don't design hacks like police cars, with no door handles in the back. The engine was still running. He got in, whined his wheels off the snow and across to the eastbound lane, and left, his right headlamp cocked a little out of line with its mate. Iris watched me through the rear window as far as I could see her, which on that night wasn't far. She looked like a little girl on her first day off the island.

Finding the Cutlass little the worse for its intimacy with the snowbank, I climbed in and started it and hit the lights. A line of four cars and a tanker with an impatient horn passed me heading into town at fifteen or twenty. I waited until they were clear, ground my way back onto the road, and swung across into the cow path that led to the trailer court.

This time I pulled around behind the office and parked. I got out quietly, fingering the Luger in my pocket. No one yelled at me. I climbed the cinderblock steps, stopped, listened for a few seconds, then manipulated the thumb latch and opened the door. My gun went in first. No one knocked it out of my hand. I followed it.

The floor lamp was still burning. Whether the manager was or not was something between him and his God. His chair had tipped over backward and was lying on its back behind the table, the X-shaped standard with its casters exposed, so that I had to walk up to the table and lean forward to see beyond the edge. He was still sitting in the chair. There were two holes in him, either one of which would have done the trick.

I figured the first bullet had struck him in the chest while he was rising to greet his visitor, something he hadn't done for me. He had sat back down then, hard enough to start the chair tipping backward. At that point the killer had fired a second time, aiming at approximately the same level, so that another wound was opened up between his eyes and an inch and a half above them. He hadn't bled much from either wound. He wouldn't have. His half-open eyes looked soft and moist and kind of sad. A thread of pink foam was drying between his lips.

The holes were far too small to have been made by a magnum of any kind, let alone a .44. It would have surprised me if they had been. I knew now who had killed this one and Story, and it wasn't the Darlings.

Nothing appeared to be missing from the table. The flat

whiskey bottle we had shared lay empty on its side atop the formidable paperwork. None of it had spilled, because he'd emptied it before it fell over. There were no new figures on the ledger sheet he'd been working on a couple of hours earlier. The butt of his Army Colt stuck out from beneath its scrawled camouflage at the same angle as before. The black metal box was still open but its contents hadn't been disturbed. I glanced around the rest of the office, but there was nothing there worth taking. Nothing but a life. I reached across the table, transferred the old-fashioned black metal telephone from the window ledge to the table, and reported two murders to the night captain at Detroit Homicide, who had told me yawningly that Lieutenant Alderdyce had gone home. I said nothing about Freeman Shanks. That would have brought them too soon. I asked him to notify Alderdyce and hung up while he was asking my name.

I left the place as boldly as someone who had a right to be leaving it at 3:30 A.M. and walked all the way to Anthony Wayne Drive. It was farther than it seemed by car, but then almost everything is. The lights in Number Six were still burning, the way Iris and I had left them. I strolled around the trailer before going in, just to make sure my quarry hadn't doubled back while I was waltzing with the cab driver, but there were no cars or trucks parked anywhere near it and no tread marks were visible in the light of my pencil flash. No one was parked in my original spot two trailers down. I entered the big trailer.

I didn't know if the Rinkers, Ed and Shirley, had turned out the lights when they vacated the place, but if they hadn't the manager would have. I did the same, after first dialing down the thermostat. Then I made myself comfortable, but not too comfortable, on the ravaged movie-set bed and got out my gun and balanced it on my thigh and waited.

I spent most of the time keeping my eyes open. I'd had two hours of sleep early in the evening, but that was a hundred years ago, and the kind of enforced nap I'd taken courtesy of Jerry and Hubert Darling is worse than no rest at all. I must have given in, because the next thing I knew there was a thrumming noise on the narrow street as of an engine approaching at a cautious rate and when I looked at my watch I found that fifteen minutes had slipped painlessly out of my life.

The Luger had slid from my leg and was a hard heaviness next to me on the mattress. I picked it up. Outside, the engine noise grew louder. I could hear the tires crunching over gravel. Something that had been nibbling at the edge of my memory took a sudden, ravenous gulp. I leaped to my feet, only to duck when a solid bar of indecent white light raped the darkness, sweeping rearward from the front of the trailer along the line of the window. It felt cold skimming the back of my neck, or maybe that was fear. The thrumming sound swelled and stopped. The light halted too, but stayed on. The silence hurt. Moving swiftly, before anyone could get out of the truck and hear me, I slunk to the front door and set the lock with a brittle snap. Then I crept back beneath the merciless shaft and straightened in the shadows beyond the curtains of the makeshift darkroom with my gun in hand.

A metal door opened flatulently outside and swung shut with a crisp thump. Then silence again, and then the scrape of a leather sole on concrete and the rattle of a doorknob being tried. I was glad I'd thought to lock it finally. Then a key turned in the lock and the door was pulled open.

At first only her profile was visible in the harsh light, all bulbous forehead and upturned nose and plump, well-shaped chin. Then she turned slowly in my direction, all of a piece as if standing on a swivel, screwing up her face in an effort to penetrate the shadows in which I stood holding my breath. She was small, not more than five-three and a hundred pounds, and her face was tiny between the wings of the worn leather collar of her jacket, and round, and might have been attractive with a little make-up. As it was, it looked like scraped bone. Add to that a great stack of frizzy hair that might be red in a kinder light, a denim bag even larger than Iris' green leather one hanging from a strap over her shoulder, and a pair of hip-hugging jeans unevenly faded and stuffed into the fringed tops of imitation buckskin boots that reached halfway up her calves, and you had what the Vistaview Mobile Home Park's late manager might consider a hippie. Her little, bare hand groped for the light switch on the wall next to the door. It was an awkward thing to do considering that the hand was curled around a gun. I stepped forward just enough to let the twin headlamps glaring through the window paint a pale stripe along the barrel of the Luger.

"No lights, Marla," I said, in as calm a tone as I could muster. "Not until you close the door and get rid of the piece."

24

S HE HISSED. I'd been prepared for her to scream, or freeze up, or try for a shot, but she did none of these things. She opened her mouth and emitted a dry, voiceless sibilant from her throat like a Gila monster gulping cool air. Tiny feet scampered down my spine at the sound of it. I raised the Luger farther into the light. She stopped hissing. Her mouth closed slowly, reminding me again of a venomous lizard.

"The door," I said again. "Then the gun. Toss it on the bed."

She closed the door and underhanded the iron. It landed on the near corner of the mattress, bounced once, and came to rest with the butt poking over the edge.

"Now the light."

She flicked the switch, bathing the trailer in yellow. I blinked, but not enough to do her any good. Outside, the truck started up again, swung around parallel to the trailer, pulled up in front of it, and started backing toward the hitch. I'd expected that. The light was the signal for all clear.

Marla's eyes did a fast tango between the discarded gun and the source of the noise. She was a good-looking girl in this light, except for the hair, of which there was too much and which was too light-colored for her eyes and complexion. It was too light-colored for almost anything. It was damn near orange.

"Would you mind ditching the wig?" I asked, not im-politely. "You don't have to, but I'd consider it a personal favor. You'll have to admit it's hard on the eyes."

She hesitated. A door slammed outside and feet crunched through snow. Metal rattled. Then she reached up and peeled off the orange Brillo pad and shook loose her black-black hair so that it tumbled over her shoulders in dishev-eled waves. That was the Marla Bernstein I knew, the stunner in the graduation photo, the sword-swallower in the porno snap. The battleworn jacket, jeans, and boots gave her a wickedly exotic look: Ilse, She-Wolf of the SS. She stood glaring at me, holding the shaggy wig down at her side.

I came out of the darkroom and crab-walked in front of her over to the bed where the gun lay. It was a long-barreled .22. I left it where it was and took up a position between it and her. I wanted her fingerprints on it when the cops came.

Someone was scraping snow away from in front of the trailer with a shovel, getting set to insert a jack beneath the steel tongue. She was listening to the miscellaneous noises.

"Don't worry, he'll join us in a little while," I said. "Then we can all have a nice talk. Is his name really Rinker, or is that as phony as 'Martha Burns'?"

"It's really Rinker." Her voice was calmer than expected. She'd had time to compose herself. It wasn't a bad voice, sultry but shallow, as when she sang. Her hiss had more depth. "I met him at Aphrodite Records. He was back-up guitarist with a group that called itself the Accelerators. For all the hits they had it could just as well have been the Brake Pedals."

"He must like money as much as you do. Musicians usu-ally have too many dreams to toss them away by throwing in with blackmailers. Unless they do drugs and lack the wherewithal. Is that his problem?"

"He does pills." Her dark eyes smoldered. "For him it was money to buy reds and angel dust. For me it was revenge.

"Revenge for your murdered boyfriend," I said, helping her out. "Freeman Shanks."

Her lips parted in surprise. They were nice lips that needed no gloss. Her teeth were even and very white. Then they closed again. "How'd you know?"

"I had no idea he was involved until I saw the film."

"You saw the film!" An animal hunger sprang into her eyes. She started forward but my gun stopped her.

"It's a long story," I said. "It's a novel, but it needs telling. Stop me when I stray too far. You met Shanks when you were both in Lansing. I called Esther Brock last night and she told me he spoke at the school while he was in town conferring with his campaign backers. That's when he was running for union office. The rest is guesswork, but somehow you and he got together alone and something happened. You fell in love with him. Maybe he reciprocated, or maybe he just liked snatch."

"He reciprocated. It was at a coffee in the students' lounge after the speech." She blushed then. It would have been adorable if I hadn't seen her other side. "We went back to my room. It didn't take long; he was a busy man. We were both back at the party before anyone missed us."

I nodded. "He was a busy man, all right. But not too busy he didn't like a little diversion now and then during a tough campaign. He was also nearing forty, and flattered to think that he could attract a pretty eighteen-year-old girl. Maybe he knew who your guardian was even then. Probably not, though, or he'd have dropped you like a rattlesnake. It didn't look good for a man who had promised to rid the union of mob influence to be carrying on with the ward of an infamous racketeer. His campaign people would have told him that eventually, but by then it was too late. He had taken you with him to Detroit."

"We were going to be married after the election." There were tears in her eyes. They glistened without falling. But her voice remained steady.

"Maybe. Maybe not. Interracial marriage is a long way from acceptance in this town. At any rate, whether he knew who you were or not, he hid you out in a brothel to keep you out of sight until the balloting was finished. Only something went wrong. Something called the Black Legion. Those good old boys don't like to see blacks doing anything but shining shoes and swamping out toilets. What a lesson it would be to the rest of the race if its greatest hero of the moment got knocked off. No doubt they tried a couple of times without success. I seem to recall reading about an attempt or two on Shanks' life that went bust. The cops hung them on the Mafia and played them that way, which explains why no one ever went up for them. They wouldn't have known about the Legion, or Klan, or whatever they prefer to be called, because the government was working that angle and Feds never talk to anyone about anything. Anyway, it was well known that Shanks had better protection than anyone except the president, and that to get to him you had to mow down twenty bodyguards who were themselves armed, which just about rendered him impervious to anything short of a kamikaze raid. You won't find many in that strutting bunch who are that ready to die for their ideals. So they had to smoke him out, and that's where you came back into the picture, Marla. You and the Darlings."

She watched me between narrowed lids. There were no tears visible now. It didn't look as if there ever had been. "Who are you?"

It seemed late in the day to be asking that question, if she really didn't know the answer. I humored her.

"Just a guy. Jerry and Hubert are the kind of dedicated bigots it takes to keep their organization from becoming an occasional rally at the VFW where they get to dress up in sheets and holler a lot about niggers and spics and kikes and Commies and taxes. Maybe they're the leaders. Anyway, they found out about you somehow. I don't think they followed Shanks when he came to visit or they could have knocked him down anywhere along the way, because he made them without his security. Most likely they spotted him by chance while they were going and he was coming. They were off-and-on customers. That's probably what gave them the idea to take him out in the first place. They could have staked out the place and ambushed him, but too many people knew them there. So they dropped in on you at Aunt Beryl's early one morning and persuaded you to help them get your boyfriend away from his private army. Probably they started by offering you money, and when you refused they got rough. One of the other girls heard it and saw your face later. You weren't very pretty right then."

"They threatened to bust me up good," she said. Her voice betrayed her finally. She covered her face with both hands. "They said they hoped I had a good picture of myself to remind me what I used to look like."

"That was just the clincher, doll. You were ready to throw in with them the minute they mentioned money. But holding out a little longer was romantic. Maybe it even drove up the price."

There must have been an edge to my tone. She lowered

her hands softly, a millimeter at a time, and looked at me with the hatred dawning in her eyes.

"You wanted to be a singing star," I went on, before she could say anything. "You wanted it so bad you could taste it. That was the one thing that everyone who knew you agreed on. But no one but you knew how far you'd go to realize that dream. You sang for Barney Zacharias at Beryl's and he told you he could make you a star if you had the money to finance the climb. Only you didn't have money. Your tuition, room, and board at the school had been paid by Morningstar directly to Esther Brock and you never even got to smell it. Shanks didn't give you any because you might get ideas about spending it, and that meant leaving the house. You couldn't go back to the old man and ask him for it because you knew he wouldn't agree, and if he found out you'd been checked into a whorehouse under a fictitious name by your lover, a *shvartze*—well, you'd be back in Arizona quicker than you can say 'Grand Canyon State.' So you took to hooking, which was nice until you had to start cutting others in on your action. Then the Brothers Darling came along and offered you big money to betray your boyfriend and it was like manna from Heaven.

"I don't think you knew they were asking you to lure him to his death. They wouldn't have told you that in any case. Maybe you thought they just wanted to get him alone so they could talk to him and maybe rough him up a little, not much, just enough to persuade him to drop out of union politics. So you agreed to it.

"Then you changed your mind. You took whatever they'd advanced you and what you'd made tricking and split. Why? It couldn't have been enough to satisfy a leech like Zacharias for long and live on besides."

She watched me a long moment before answering. Outside, the jack rattled and thumped into place under the tongue. There was a brief pause and then it began clicking. After a couple of beats it caught and I felt a slight lifting sensation beneath my feet. Soon we'd be hitched up and ready to go.

"The raid," she said finally. It wasn't a singer's voice anymore. It was just a voice, and not a very pleasant one at that. "It's impossible to sleep in jail, did you know that? Too much screaming. They have people locked up in there that belong in hospitals. I got to do a lot of thinking. About the offer the Darlings had made me. About how maybe they were paying me too much money just to get Freeman alone so they could talk to him. I was brought up in a sheltered environment, but Papa Ben couldn't keep the whole world out. Nobody can, not these days. I wasn't as naïve as they thought I was. Naïve enough to be taken by someone like Zacharias, but not by them. So after they let us out I stayed at Aunt Beryl's for a few days more, just in case Jerry and Hubert had someone watching the house. Then when I was sure it was safe I left."

"Along with Iris' money and a little gold heart she kept in a jewelry box. What happened to that, anyway?"

"Heart?" Her forehead puckered. "Oh, that. I pawned it. A place called Gershom's, over on Warren. I got twenty dollars for it, enough for the first few days' rent in the crummy little boardinghouse I fell into after I left Beryl's."

"I'll ramble some more. You loved Shanks enough to break it off with him because you thought you were poison. So you didn't tell him when you left. He nearly shouted the place down when he found out. Maybe it was love. More likely he was afraid you'd blurt out the story of your relationship to some scandal sheet or other and ruin his chances of getting into office. There's a lot of that going around these days. Anyway, he tracked you down at Aphrodite Records, probably the same way I did, but instead of pushing his luck by showing—his disguise wasn't impenetrable to anyone who followed the news—he telephoned you there. You weakened and the affair was on again.

"There's a missing piece here. Maybe you'll supply it. One night you left Zacharias' studio and didn't come back. It's my guess you ran into the Darlings." I left that hanging. She seized it, shuddering.

"They cornered me in the alley next to the studio as I was leaving," she said. "If you were a woman and that creepy Hubert stuck a pistol between your eyes and his hand up your dress and asked you which end you wanted done first, what would you do? Jerry was standing behind me. He told me I had a third choice. I took it."

"And a few nights later, during a rally to celebrate Freeman Shanks' landslide victory, you got next to him and talked him into ducking his bodyguards and meeting you somewhere. Only you weren't where you said you'd be. Jerry and Hubert were. With friends."

She nodded. The tears were back now, and rolling down her fine white cheeks.

"And the next morning he was found with three holes in him," I pressed. "And for Marla Bernstein it was time for a little vengeance."

This time she didn't move or speak. She didn't have to.

I plunged ahead. "Vengeance comes in strange packages sometimes. In this case it was in a round flat metal canister, burned into a few hundred feet of film shot by an Intelligence agent who happened to be on the scene when the execution took place. A crooked Intelligence agent, who used the evidence to blackmail the lifetakers, and who, when the situation got close and he realized he was in over his head, hid the film in a place where it would go unnoticed among a lot of similar round flat metal canisters. A place like this, which turns out two or three skin flicks a day for sale to a place like Story's After Midnight, or did until yesterday, when Story got burned and you closed up shop. Who owns the business, you or Rinker?"

"It's half and half." She didn't seem surprised to learn that I knew of Story's death. She'd have figured that out by now. "That idiot Ed thought I planned on making a career out of this filthy picture business. It was just a sideline for him to keep him in pills and see him through between gigs when I bought into it. He didn't know I was just doing it to have something to live on while I was looking for the Darlings. It's a cheap operation. Sometimes I have to pose myself when we can't afford more than one model at a time. Is that where I made my mistake?"

I got out the snapshot and tossed it to her. She glanced at it, made a face, and laid it face-down among the other pictures on the table. "That was an early shot, before I hit on the idea of the getup." She gestured with the wig she was still holding.

"Your guardian saw it and hired me to find you."

"Christ. I should have known." She didn't act ashamed. I wondered how Morningstar could have lived with her for so long without seeing this side of her. But that was easier than it seemed when you were a parent, even an unnatural one.

Ed had ceased jacking. The truck creaked through the snow, backing toward the hitch. That's hard to do when there's no one standing there to guide you. He'd be wondering what was keeping Marla. I spoke fast.

"Something I'm fuzzy about. I know Francis Kramer struck up a partnership with you on the blackmail angle when things got too hot for one man. How'd he know you even existed?"

"He used to follow Freeman when he visited me at Beryl's."

"Follow Freeman?"

"I spotted him in the shadows across the street two different times when Freeman was there, through my window. The second time Freeman got scared, thinking he was a reporter or a spy hired by the other side, and went out to find out what he was doing there. By the time he got there Kramer was gone. I never knew he was with Intelligence until you said so just now. He never said after we got to know each other."

I parked that one around the corner for the time being. "The film," I said. "How'd it get out of your hands?"

"That idiot Ed. Nobody told him about it. He shipped it off to Story's in a box with five other films. Kramer almost killed him when he found out."

"What about Story, as long as you brought him up? Of course you killed him. Shanks was a diabetic. He needed regular insulin injections to keep from going into shock. He would have shown you how to operate a hypodermic syringe in case he went into it when you were together alone. So you used that knowledge to give Story an extra dose of the heroin he'd already set up for himself when you came in to find out what he'd done with the film. Was it you that slugged him first or Rinker?"

She didn't say anything. Confessing to murder comes hard even when there's a gun on you.

"Rinker," I answered for her. "While Story was giving you a hard time, probably with that twenty-two of his there on the bed, your partner came up behind him and clobbered him. Only he did too good a job and sent him halfway to

Hell. You helped him the rest of the way. Then you searched the place.

"Which leaves the trailer court manager tonight, the only one left who could tie the whole thing together for the cops. You didn't waste any time with him. Him you just up and shot with Story's gun and then went to collect your trailer and go. Only you couldn't, because I was here waiting. Twice."

She tried to keep her eyes on me, tried hard, but they wandered beyond my right shoulder. Then I heard quiet breathing, and knew that for the second time that night there was a man standing behind me with a gun.

25

I HADN'T HEARD HIM moving toward the door at the other end of the trailer because his engine was still running outside. I'd thought he was just being extra careful about maneuvering around for the hitchup. Forgetting to lock the doors had finally caught up with me. I didn't waste time kicking myself. Without turning I hurled myself sideways toward the mutilated mattress at my left, the idea being to land on my shoulder, twist and fire, maybe hitting something worthwhile, maybe not. I hadn't a hell of a lot to lose by trying.

It didn't work, of course. Tricks like that never do, unless you wear spangled buckskins and own a horse named Trigger. While I was airborne Marla hissed again and flung her frazzled dustmop of a wig into my face. The hair seemed to envelop me. I forgot all about the gun in my hand and just fell, flailing my arms in a useless effort to regain my balance. A hand twisted the Luger out of my grasp while I was flailing. I hit the bed and bounced, but before I could turn that to my advantage Marla charged in hissing and seized the .22 from the corner of the mattress where it was about to fall and pointed it at me with both hands clasped around the butt. The muzzle looked tiny, but a bullet from it had killed one man already. I checked my momentum, allowing the tortured springs beneath me to rock me to rest.

Ed Rinker—I assumed it was him, there wasn't room for

any more characters in this Russian novel—was a skinny kid with third-degree acne bunched over his forehead and on his long chin, and hair the color of winterkilled grass sticking out in a crackling white-man's afro all over his head. His complexion was pale and his eyes were pale blue behind aviator's glasses with spidery rims and gray-tinted lenses and his hands were pale things growing out of brittle-looking wrists too long for the sleeves of a quilted combat jacket in soiled olive drab. He was too young to have served a hitch in any branch of the service. He was too young for almost anything. The Luger in his right hand aged him. His hand bent downward from the wrist under its weight, so that the muzzle was pointed at my groin instead of my chest. He didn't have any other guns. He'd never had, except in my imagination. He was shaking like a sparrow in a fist.

His partner had retreated to her original position near the door. Inflation wasn't as steady as the revolver she was holding. Her dark Jewish eyes glistened, but not with tears.

"You've asked a lot of questions," she said sharply. "Let's see if you're as good at answering them. Who are you?"

I told her. She seemed satisfied. A man doesn't lie when death is staring him in the face.

"Never heard of you. I should have, a clever detective like you. How'd you figure out Story was murdered?"

I said, "First you call me clever and then you insult my intelligence. There was a little matter of a fractured skull and a shop turned inside-out that was shipshape when I visited him yesterday morning. And three matches."

"Three matches? What are you talking about?"

I sat up on the end of the bed. The revolver jerked. I spread my hands in a gesture of peace, then began counting on my fingers. A silly thing, but it got her used to me moving. "One to sterilize the needle. Another to melt the sugar so the stuff would mix with it and be ready to shoot up. That's all anyone ever needs. There were three burned-out matches in the bathroom. Story didn't smoke; there weren't any butts or ashtrays in the joint. The explanation was that he'd just finished fixing himself when you interrupted him, and after Ed split open his head, probably with one of the joy-toys he had on display, and helped you get him into the toilet, you used a third match to melt a fresh supply. You wouldn't have bothered with heating up the needle, so there wasn't a fourth. You knew how to operate a syringe, and even if you didn't, Ed had been around the dope-rock scene long enough to show you, just as he showed you how to prepare the overdose. I didn't know that when I figured it out, but it fits. Most of it clicked home tonight when I saw another girl with a syringe."

"Maybe Ed killed him." She smirked. Her face wasn't made for smirking.

"Maybe, but I doubt it. He's not the type to commit that kind of cold, deliberate murder. Just holding that gun is giving him the screaming willies. In any case you'd be an accomplice, which in the eyes of the law is supposed to amount to the same thing."

"Only you and I know it doesn't," she said, still smirking. "But very good. You're a regular Lord Peter Wimsey."

"It works one time out of six."

"I think you're underestimating yourself. I'll bet you can even tell us what happened to Kramer after he left here, and how you ended up working with him."

"I'm not working with him."

"Prove it."

"It's difficult to strike up a working relationship with someone who refuses to climb out of the porcelain tray he's lying on in a refrigerated room. I've never had the patience for it."

"You talk funny, Mr. Private Investigator. Maybe I ought to have Ed do to your head with that gun what he did to Story's with one of his dirty souvenirs."

"I was trying not to offend your finishing school sensibilities. Kramer's dead."

She stiffened. I bored in.

"Croaked," I said. "Iced. Offed. Stiffed. Slabbed. Gone west. Knocked down. Blown away. Or, if you're poetically minded, had done what was done when 'twas best 'twere done quickly. In other words, murdered."

"Shut up! Who did it? You?"

I shook my head. "I had my chance near Hue. That was a little number of the Darlings'. They swatted him down night before last. He turned up the next morning in the parking lot at City Airport."

"Now I know you're lying!" Triumph glittered in her eye. "I haven't missed a paper or a radio broadcast since he went out to track down the film and didn't come back. Nothing's been said about any bodies turning up at City."

"Get it through your head, doll. He was a government agent. As far as the media's concerned, they don't die until the Feds say they stopped breathing. He was found jammed into the trunk of a stolen Chevy with a hole in his head and the thing that had made the hole buried in the back seat. It was a bullet from a forty-four magnum. That's Hubert's. Jerry's would be the thirty-eight used to kill Shanks. Not that Kramer would have come back in any case. He was selling you out, doll, and to the highest bidder. They don't come any higher than Uncle Sam."

"That means what?"

"I'm guessing again." I was keeping her occupied. The padded table with the videotape and movie cameras on it was just within my reach, a hundred miles away as long as she was watching me and not engrossed with what I was saying. Rinker I wasn't too worried about. The Luger's safety lever had gotten flicked down while he was wresting it out of my hand and he hadn't adjusted it. It wouldn't fire if he hit it with a hammer. "You were pushing too hard. Kramer was an opportunist—if he weren't he would never have snitched his way into the command of our outfit in Vietnam—but he wasn't aggressive. He would have been content to use the film to tap the Darlings and split. But you wanted revenge. You wanted to smoke them out and do to them what they did to your boyfriend. Kramer was the one who had approached them first, so he became the intermediary, which means exactly what it says. He was in the middle. Probably he was already thinking of cutting himself loose when the film came up missing. But he was afraid of you, doll. A guy like him would be. So he made a halfhearted search, and when it didn't look as if it would turn up the first time around he made an appointment to meet another agent and spill what he knew in return for protection. Frankly, doll, I'd have suspected you for his killing if I hadn't seen Jerry and Hubert pluck him off a public street in broad daylight."

"You seem to have all the answers." Her voice was taut, and her face wasn't pretty anymore. It had the scraped-bone look I'd blamed earlier on the harsh light of the headlamps shining through the window.

"I should," I said. "I've had plenty of time to think it out. Mostly on the wrong end of people's guns."

"Maybe you know where the film is, too. You must, or you wouldn't know what's on it. Maybe you've got it."

Her knuckles were white from gripping the .22 hard enough to crack it. I watched her hands and her eyes and tried not to look at the table to my left. Then I shook my head.

"No deal," I said. "What if I had it and I told you where it was? Killing gets easier each time you do it. You were planning on clearing out or you wouldn't have come back to pick up the trailer, which is your only means of support. Now I'm your last chance for revenge—assuming I have what you're after—and you'd have nothing to lose by offing me. I'd just be punching my own ticket."

I spread my hands on the last sentence for emphasis. That put my left within a couple of feet of the table.

"You left out one thing, Mr. Private Investigator." She raised the gun a fraction of an inch in both hands so that it was pointing at my collarbone. "I'd about given up on finding the film when you showed up. What you just said hasn't raised my hopes. I'll kill you even if you don't tell me. For Freeman, a good man. The best man this rotten town will ever see." Her voice broke on the last part. She bent her thumb over the hammer and drew it back to ease the trigger pull.

A high, thin keening noise that none of us had paid any attention to grew louder suddenly as it turned into the trailer court, where it was joined by a lower, gulping wail. It started to wind down somewhere near the manager's office, then whipped up again and grew deafening on the main stem approaching Anthony Wayne Drive. Marla swung her gaze toward the window in the door. That was enough. I didn't bother to see what Ed was doing. I reached out with my left hand and propelled the pedestal table directly at her. It was heavier than anticipated. Instead of taking flight it merely tipped over, pitching the heavy equipment toward the floor at Marla's feet. The cameras struck with an ear-splitting crash. She fired, but the shock had thrown off her aim and I was already up and charging her in a crouch. The bullet pierced the louvered window behind me at the same time as I hit her low and locked my arms around her knees in a football tackle. She grunted and slammed against the door and the gun sprang from her hands and thudded to the carpet six feet away. She lost her balance and fell sprawling with my arms still hugging her legs.

Something swished past my left ear as we were struggling and I caught a glimpse of Ed Rinker standing over me holding the Luger like a club. He couldn't figure out why it didn't shoot when he pulled the trigger. While he was still off balance from the violence of the miss I let go of Marla and brought the four stiffened fingers of my right hand up in an uppercut that caught below the arch of his ribcage. He wheezed and released the pistol and pitched forward onto his pimply face.

Outside, the scout cars—there were two or a dozen—were howling to a stop, their throbbing lights bathing the windows in blue and red and blue again. Their radios were a deafening jumble of voices half-human and half-electronic. Doors slammed, sounding like strings of firecrackers going off in uneven order.

Marla was on her hands and knees scrambling for the revolver where it had come to rest near the base of the opposite wall. Her wavy black hair was in her eyes and she was hissing constantly now, like a sidewinder coming out of its hole. Then she had the gun and was rolling over onto her elbow to fire at me and I scooped the Luger up from the floor and thumbed off the safety catch and shot her. I had a flash of her with her eyes and mouth wide open, and then the door bumped against my leg and I couldn't see her for a room full of shouting men in dark brown uniforms with guns.

26

I'D ASKED FOR JOHN Alderdyce, so of course they sent a plainclothesman with the lyrical name of Christoforo, a blocky Puerto Rican with shining black hair in which you could see the marks of the comb, delicate features, and soft, almost feminine black eyes. His jacket was a size too small around the shoulders, so that the gun he wore beneath his left arm stood out like a Swede on Twelfth Street—excuse me, Rosa Parks Boulevard. He succeeded the herd of tall, good-looking fellows in charcoal-brown uniforms and flat-brimmed hats of the Wayne County Sheriff's Department and the ambulance that had taken away Ed Rinker and his wife, Shirley, a.k.a. Martha Burns, a.k.a. Marla Bernstein, of whom Rinker was the more injured, that chop to the solar plexus having nearly killed him. Marla had a nine-millimeter hole through her right shoulder, which would probably cost her some of the use of that arm but not her life. Christoforo was a detective with the sheriff's department. The night captain at metro had kicked my report of the trailer court killing over to his bureau because it was in the county's jurisdiction.

It turned out the cops had been on their way to the manager's office when the old lady who lived across the main drive waved them down and told them something funny was going on in Number Six. She thought she'd seen someone through the window holding a gun. Which meant she'd come snooping, bless her nosy old heart.

I told Christoforo what I'd told the uniforms after they'd frisked me and read me my Miranda, and then he was gone, to be replaced by other detectives, this time from town, who didn't give a damn about the manager's murder but wanted the dope, excuse the expression, on the Story knockdown. Alderdyce wasn't with them either. I told that one a couple of times before they were satisfied for now, and then one of them handed me my hat and I was escorted out to an unmarked unit and shoved, not impolitely, into the back seat and taken to headquarters. A uniformed city officer drove my Cutlass. Alderdyce was waiting for me in his office when we got in. Proust was there too, and two others. Colonel Vespers and General Spain.

John was leaning on the edge of his desk, sipping coffee from a Styrofoam cup and looking about as disheveled as I'd seen him, meaning no necktie. He acted disgruntled and sleepy. The Inspector, in rumpled suit and overcoat and ubiquitous fedora, was standing red-faced off to one side. Army Intelligence was well represented sartorially, as trim, youthful Vespers and severe Spain sat side by side in folding chairs near the desk, their tailored suits looking fresh and white shirts crisply laundered and starched. They looked as if they'd come here straight from a night's rest and a shower. Vespers' expression was annoyed, Spain's that of a man with an ulcer acting up, which for him was normal. The electric clock on the one wall that wasn't made of yellow pebbled glass said it was ten to seven. It would be getting light soon.

"We got a copy of Christoforo's report from County," said Alderdyce after my uniformed escort had left, closing the door behind them. He was talking to the opposite wall. "That kind of cooperation we don't usually get unless the case is so screwed up one department can't handle it. It's still muck. How about letting us in on a day and a half in the life of a modern P.I.? Starting with five-thirty P.M. the day before yesterday."

So I told it again. Everything. Beginning with a cigarette I never got lit on Woodward, through a telephone call during *The Barefoot Contessa*, Ben Morningstar, Barry Stackpole, Beryl Garnet, Vespers and Spain, Barney Zacharias, three visits to Story's After Midnight, a private screening of a film of an execution that had itself led to three more murders, and finishing with the Vistaview Mobile Home Park and what had happened there. I left out one thing, a girl named Iris. She was none of their business. When I had finished, the clock on the wall read five after seven. Life always takes longer to live than talk about. The silence that came in on the heels of the last dotted i was loud and long, but Alderdyce put a stop to that.

"Why didn't the Darlings recognize Marla when they saw the picture?"

"It wasn't that great a likeness," I said. "Morningstar and his nameless associate recognized it because they knew her better than most. Just about everyone else had to be prompted, or had her on the brain enough that it clicked. And the graduation shot was retouched almost beyond recognition. The Darlings didn't even know she was the one behind the blackmail scheme. As far as they were concerned she was a dead issue."

"Damn it, Walker, you said you were working on another case entirely." He didn't yell. He was too tired for that. For some reason I found myself wishing he had.

"I was at the time. Or at least I thought I was, which

amounts to the same thing. Am I under arrest or what? Because if I am, I want a lawyer."

"Are you wearing handcuffs? We cuff prisoners. Witnesses come in of their own free will. See how neat that works? So you don't get to have your lawyer present."

"I don't see why he ain't in cuffs," snarled Proust. He was looking at me but talking to the lieutenant. "I can count five criminal offenses he's committed just in the last twenty-four hours. Withholding evidence. Failure to report a felony. Breaking and entering. Assault and battery. I bet he don't have a license for that kraut gun he shot the girl with, so let's add possession of an unregistered firearm. Reckless driving, which makes six. That's just for openers. I bet once the D.A. sits down and figures it out—"

"We'd be cutting our own throats, Inspector," Alderdyce broke in wearily. He sounded like a record winding down, and *he'd* had a few hours' sleep. I wondered what I sounded like. "We can tie the girl to the trailer court slaying through the gun, but we'll never build a case on the rest without Walker's help. There was no hard evidence at Story's to suggest anything other than accidental OD. We've got an APB out on the Darlings, but without the film—!" He turned to me. "Where is it, by the way?"

I was lighting a cigarette. I spoke between puffs. "In my mailbox, across the road from the house."

"For Christ's sake!" Proust.

Alderdyce looked dismayed. He pushed himself away from the desk, tore open the door, and relayed the information to the squad room. There was a general scraping of chairs and hasty shuffling of leather soles on linoleum, on which he closed the door and treated me to Withering Gaze Number Nine.

"Couldn't you think of anywhere else?"

"Where would you suggest?" I blew smoke and used my hand to fan it away. "My place was tossed once today already. It'll be safe in the box until the mailman comes. The neighborhood thieves must know by now I get only junk mail."

"Don't be smug. If you'd come to me earlier, that trailer court manager might still be breathing. Don't think just because of what I said I won't throw you to the wolves. I'm considering it."

"Who's being smug? I've been beaten and pistol-whipped. I've been shot at and threatened. I've been frisked and kidnapped and tailed and arrested and questioned, and in all that time I've had exactly two hours' sleep. Smug? Who's got time for smug? My jaw aches just thinking about it."

"Did you expect any better?"

"No, and I'm not complaining. Just tired. Tired as hell."

"All the same, the lieutenant's right."

I shifted my attention to the folding chairs, where Colonel Vespers sat with his legs crossed staring at the floor. General Spain was seated next to him in his customary stony silence. I'd forgotten they were there until the younger man spoke. That was undoubtedly one of the requirements of the job, a talent for being overlooked.

Vespers looked up at me. He had the most ordinary-looking face I'd ever seen on any man. There wasn't a single feature worth mentioning. "Your silence, Walker, has cost us all unnecessary time and effort, to say nothing of taxpayers' money. We had Jerry and Hubert Darling under surveillance until the afternoon rush hour, when they slipped us. If the film had been in our custody at that time we could have made a pinch and they'd be behind bars right now.

You could have broken up the Legion and saved yourself a beating in the bargain."

"Shut up," I said.

Proust glared at me as if I'd just spat on the flag. Alderdyce said, "Careful, Walker."

I ignored both of them. I was facing Vespers. "Don't talk to me about silence. There was too much before I came in or these last thirty-six hours would never have happened. You told me Intelligence was working to break up the Black Legion. I know better. I found out this morning. You never gave a damn about the Darlings or the Klan or who they killed or didn't. You said you were interested because they'd infiltrated the army, but if that's true the outfit is a hell of a lot bigger than I picture it. You weren't even watching Jerry and Hubert until they blundered into your sights. I doubt if you even knew they existed. You were watching Freeman Shanks."

Every eye in the room was on me except Spain's, which were working on the beehive pattern of the glass across the room, and he never looked at anyone. Vespers' expression hadn't changed. It belonged on an old man waiting for a bus, patient and imperturbable. Alderdyce and Proust were just watching me.

"Shanks was planning to organize the military, starting with the transport services," I went on. "He wouldn't have stopped there, but would have gone on to slap the union label on the fighting units as well. He had a chance of succeeding. Congress has made the armed forces a non-union shop, but that wouldn't have stopped him any more than Harry Bennett's bully-boys stopped Reuther and Frankensteen from banding Ford workers together more than forty years ago. Army Intelligence wouldn't stand for that. So they sent you two to watch him.

"Maybe you just wanted to get something on him good enough to make him back off for fear of exposure, or maybe you hoped to discredit him publicly. Lord knows the ammunition was there. Maybe he suspected he was being watched. Certainly he would have been smart to count on it. Anyway, he took steps to keep his relationship with Marla Bernstein hidden until well after the election, or maybe forever. They weren't good enough. They never are when you're in politics.

"Your mistake was hiring a guy like Francis Kramer to do the watching. In some ways he was the ideal choice, because he was just dimwitted enough to fall for the patriotic spiel you probably gave him about national security and the public benefit. All those hearings and investigations into the various branches of Intelligence can't have left you with many reliable agents to choose from. But dumb guys like Kramer sometimes get clever ideas that aren't always honest. He did his job all right. No doubt some secret vault in the Pentagon is full of footage on Shanks' comings and goings at Beryl Garnet's house of joy, if it wasn't burned or shredded when Shanks bellied up dead. Probably he held back some excerpts of his own for blackmail purposes. Then he stumbled onto a gold mine.

"He must have been tailing Shanks with his camera when he left the election-night rally to meet Marla, and saw the snatch. Then he followed and captured the scene of a lifetime on infrared film, a scene that could set him up for the rest of his days. Which it did, although not in the way he had figured.

"I didn't put it together until this morning, when Marla told me that Kramer had been following Shanks. It explained a lot of things that hadn't been clear to me, chief among them the hush you threw over Kramer's murder. I'd thought it was just knee-jerk cloak-and-dagger reaction to an embarrassing incident. It didn't occur to me you'd really have something to hide."

"You can't prove it!" It was Spain, his dry soldier's voice lashing out like a muleskinner's whip. He had turned halfway around in his chair and was letting me have it with the flinty grays.

"No," I sighed. "I can't. My only witness is a murderess twice over, and a gangster's ward to boot. She'd be laughed out of any Grand Jury room in the country. This is just the little guy fighting back with a popgun against cannons."

Vespers was studying me with a clinical expression. "Has it ever occurred to you, Walker, that we're not the enemy? That we're forced to do the unpleasant things we do for your protection?"

"Who protects us from the protectors?" I turned to John. "Am I free to go?"

He raised his eyebrows at Proust, who shrugged and said, "It's still your case."

Alderdyce scribbled something on a page torn from a pad on his desk and handed it to me. "Give that to the attendant at the impound for your car. I won't waste breath asking you not to leave town. You'll do as you damn well please." He gulped the rest of his coffee and flung the empty cup at the green metal wastebasket in the corner. It circled the rim and landed outside on a buckled tile.

"A word of advice," said Vespers.

I was at the door. I paused without turning.

"Stay out of espionage, Walker. You're too nice a guy for it."

"Yeah, I'm a prince."

27

T HE CITY WAS A metallic blue beneath the brightening sky as I headed east on the Edsel Ford toward Grosse Pointe. It was sort of pretty until you realized that most of it was monoxide, and that by noon it would turn to an ugly granite brown only a couple of shades lighter than the average Detroiter's lungs. Salt trucks had been out since before dawn, making the streets safe for everyone but the cars. The snow that had fallen during the night was a crusted fringe the color of dried urine along the gutters. Yesterday's heavy winds had swept away the clouds, leaving the sky a scraped blue of which the cityscape was only a tenth carbon. It was hard to believe that the sun, a swollen orb swimming in blood above the horizon, was also shining down on crisp fields so white it hurt to look at them. Here, up close, its effect on the lurid grindhouse façades was harsh and indecent, putting me in mind of hookers caught out past their time in make-up designed for soft lights and shadows. But that made me think of Iris, so I shifted my thoughts to other things.

Nothing about Morningstar's house had changed. I guess I hadn't really expected it to, but so much had since yesterday morning that I did a take when the imperturbable young German came to the gate after I had stopped and tooted my horn, looking as if he were waiting out the same shift. He appeared to recognize me, spoke into a telephone receiver taken from a call box mounted on one of the marble gateposts, hung it up, and unlocked and opened the gate, waving me in.

By day the house didn't seem quite so huge as it had under the kliegs, but it still looked as if it might seat the overflow from Tiger Stadium when the team was hot. I parked in front of the embarrassment of a porch and found the door open for me by the time I got up the steps. Wiley was holding the knob, looking funereal in a suit that couldn't decide whether to be blue or black and a soft gray necktie that looked as if it would pawn for more than my overcoat—which, by the way, he didn't offer to take. A number of suitcases and trunks messed up the clean sweep of the carpet behind him.

"You're late," he informed me grimly. "By about eight hours." He let me by and closed the door.

"My watch stopped. Going someplace?"

He cocked his head toward the library doors at the other side of the foyer. "They are. I'm not. This is my town."

While he was speaking, the doors glided open far enough to let Paul Cooke through. He saw me, drew them shut without turning, and came my way, striding like a man with too many places to go and too little time to get there. There was very little about him on this occasion that suggested the West. The checked shirt and Levi's had given way to a beige business suit of some material too rich for my blood, and a wide, woven necktie of the same color had replaced the rodeo string that had made him look like an aging country singer. The change of attire softened the lines in his face, making it look less weathered. Only his deep tan remained to lend an air of the great outdoors to his appearance, and I began to suspect that he owed that to a sun lamp. He looked sore as hell about something.

"He's waiting for you in there." He jerked his thumb toward There. "He's been waiting all night."

A muscle worked in his jaw. He didn't offer me the glad hand this time out, for which I was grateful.

I said, "He knows what I'm going to say, right?"

"What he knows or doesn't know isn't my business. I just work for him."

"What happened to the drawl? I thought you were from the Lone Star State, where the deer and the buffalo roam and the counties are dry all the day."

"That's Oklahoma. And I haven't seen Texas in thirty-seven years."

"You could have fooled me. Is Donophan with him?"

"Yeah. Why?"

"I'd rather he weren't."

He chewed on that one for a moment. Then: "Get 'em up."

I got them up. Wiley frisked me swiftly and came up empty. The Luger was in police lockup and anyway we were all friends by now, so I'd come naked. Since no one appeared eager to give me the royal escort this time around, I left them standing there and was about to knock on one of the big doors when they opened.

Merle Donophan, ugly and immovable as ever in the same too-tight black suit and strangled tie, stood to the left of the space between the doors with his right thumb hooked in his lapel. His eyes looked penciled on as before, watching me, my face and my hands, and taking them all in at once. He was a good shield. The punk with the gun in his sock must have caught him on a bad day.

"Run outside and play, Junior," I told him. "We grown-ups want to talk."

He didn't growl at me, but he might as well have. His

head sank even farther between his shoulders and the fat bands of scar tissue over his brows drew together like two sausages copulating.

"Blow, Merle," said a voice that was nothing like a voice from the other side of the room. "If I need you I'll holler."

This time he did growl, but just to get me to move. I stepped aside and he left, swiveling sideways to get through the space that was wide enough for my shoulders but not his. He left the doors open. I closed them.

He was sitting in the green Lazy Boy beneath the light of the copper standing lamp, looking as if he hadn't moved since we'd talked earlier. His shirt was probably fresh but it was the only thing that was, right down to his brown shoes, which I now noticed had no wrinkles in them, as if they had hardly been walked in. He sat with his eyes closed and head tilted back and pale hands folded like a dead man's over the place where the swell of his stomach would have been had he still had one. With his eyes sheathed, his face looked ancient and shrunken and fallen in, the face of a mummified monkey wearing a pair of man's eyeglasses. The air had a sickly sweetish smell of medication and decay. I waded through a pool of silence to his chair and looked down at him and waited for him to say something. He neither moved nor spoke.

I got impatient. "Who told you?" I asked.

"Please," he said. His eyelids sprang open, revealing the swollen, viscous puddles of black. There was a mind behind them, still alive, still struggling to free itself of its weary baggage. "I may look a hundred, but I haven't been away so long my friends don't know me."

"I'll bet one of them is named Inspector Proust."

He waved it aside, or meant to. One of his hands twitched. "I got it twice removed. I want to hear it as you

227

saw it. Before I visit the hospital. Before I go back to Phoenix to arrange things with my lawyers. Go ahead; it won't kill me. Heart trouble I don't have and isn't it a wonder."

So I told it all over again. He watched me unwaveringly as I plodded on, even when I repeated Marla's own version of what had happened to her after Shanks' death and described how she'd reacted when I put a bullet through her. He didn't close his eyes again until I had finished.

"She never said, 'I'm sorry.' " He was speaking so low now I could scarcely hear him. His artificial larynx sounded like a truck stripping its gears. "I used to beat the hell out of her for it when she was little. She'd do something wrong, like all little girls do, but she wouldn't apologize. Not even when it would save her a spanking. I used to think it was just mule-headedness. It wasn't. She really wasn't sorry. She never knew what it was like to have a conscience."

"Psychopathic, the doctors would say," I put in. "People like that can't even fall in love, although they might think they have from time to time. She thought she had, with Shanks. When he was killed she was just reacting automatically. Something was taken from her and she wanted to take something in return. She wouldn't recognize Shanks now if he walked into her hospital room."

"Did you have to shoot her?"

He was looking at me again. I returned the gaze. Finally he nodded, moving his head down and up a tenth of an inch as if he were afraid it might topple off his wasted old neck.

"Yeah, I guess you did. What's going to happen to her now?"

"That's up to you. You've probably got the pull to reduce both murder charges to second degree, or if you don't you know someone who does, which amounts to the same thing.

Maybe the judge will give her five years on each count, to run concurrently. With good behavior she could be back on the street in a couple of years. I'm hoping you care enough for her not to let that happen."

"Meaning?"

"Meaning you'll get a lawyer who'll have her examined by psychiatrists and enter a plea that she's not competent to stand trial. The court will have her examined anyway, but with both sides working toward the same thing it should happen. She'll be committed to a mental institution for however long it takes to straighten out her head. Maybe that'll take three years, maybe a lifetime. The important thing is she'll be inside where the only people she can harm are trained attendants paid to take that risk. If that isn't done she'll kill again. I won't say when. Maybe not for ten or fifteen years. But she'll kill again as sure as winter's coming. By then you may not be around to smooth things over."

That didn't cause a ripple. I hadn't expected it to. He'd been around too long and seen too much for that. He just kept watching me with those steady black eyes that I wouldn't have wanted to face twenty years ago. What the hell, I didn't want to be facing them now.

"I could have you killed, you know," he said. "For being responsible for Marla going to jail. For shooting her. I'm still not sure I shouldn't."

"I know that. I knew it when I came. But I came anyway, because I'd promised to report and because you owe me another two hundred dollars plus a hundred and fifty in expenses."

"And you risked not leaving here alive for that."

"It's what I do. I don't work gratis."

He sighed. Silently; his single lung didn't hold enough air to make much of a noise when he emptied it. His head settled wearily against the backrest. "Tell Cooke on your way out to draw you up a check for five hundred dollars. Now get out of here and leave me the hell alone."

"That's another thing I have to tell you about," I said. "Paul Cooke."

"What about him?" Testily.

"You'd better run a check of the investments he's been making for you. He's holding out."

"How do you know that? I don't doubt it's possible. I just want to know how you know."

"The Darling brothers told me."

He said nothing. I went on.

"They said the Detroit porno trade is in Ben Morningstar's pocket. They said it was common knowledge on the street. It turned out they were wrong about the trailer studio, which was all Marla's and Rinker's, but generalizations like that are easy to fall into when one man owns so much. I figure that if you'd known your money was behind that kind of traffic you'd have been able to pick up something on Marla's whereabouts without my help. Besides, I know your opinion on dirty pictures and you don't strike me as a hypocrite. You told me Cooke handles all your investments. If he didn't tell you when all this started that you had a direct pipeline into the business Marla was mixed up in, he must have had a good reason. That he was holding out on you seemed good enough."

"He could have helped find Marla." He was clenching his hands slowly into fists. "He could have prevented all this. He kept his mouth shut."

"He's an investment counselor. Pornography is a lucrative racket. It must have stung like hell to see all that dough being made by someone else while you refused to have anything to do with it. The same thing has happened to people with licenses to handle other people's money. Why not him?"

"You sure about this?"

"Jerry and Hubert had no reason to lie about it, and street dope is usually reliable. One question. Did you give orders for Wiley to follow me this morning?"

He looked startled. "No. Why?"

I nodded. "That explains it. Cooke was afraid I'd dig up his secret, so he put Wiley on my tail to see that I didn't get too close to it. I wouldn't blame Wiley, though. He slacked off after I let him know he'd been spotted. I think he's loyal to you. But Cooke hired him, so he followed his orders if only nominally. Yesterday afternoon he paid a call to my office to make sure I'd report to you as promised. I don't think he'd been told to do that."

Morningstar's fists were quivering with the effort of remaining clenched. His metallic voice grated when he spoke.

"Send Cooke in."

I did, but not until he'd handed me the check.

Outside, the blue air was clammy with late November and was already beginning to curl up and turn brown at the edges. The wind coming from the Ford plant carried the rotten-egg stink of sulfur and other chemicals with names so long they're referred to only by key letters. If it could taint the exclusive suburb it must have been especially bad in town. The taint would be in the hospital where Marla Bernstein and Ed Rinker lay still awaiting the attention of busy physicians and surgeons. It would have reached police headquarters, where cops like John Alderdyce tried to do their jobs in spite of cops like Proust and government agents like Vespers and Spain. It would be seeping through the filters on the top floors of the new Detroit Plaza, where the Colonel and the General would undoubtedly be staying on taxpayers' money while they prepared a report for their superiors at the Pentagon that the taxpayers would never see. The taint was on me now as well, deep enough so that no razor or soap would remove it. I was like the drunk in the old joke who passes out at the bar and is revived by someone rubbing garlic under his nose, and who gets up, staggers out of the joint and sniffs, and staggers back in and sniffs and wails that it's no use, the whole world stinks. The taint was part of me now.

I was right about its being worse in town. It hit me when I came out of the pawnshop on Warren with Iris' tiny gold heart in my pocket and fifty dollars less in my wallet because I had to bribe the proprietor to sell it to me without the ticket. I stood there and sniffed and thought while the sidewalk traffic flowed around me, and then I went into a stationer's shop a couple of doors down and purchased a mailer and dropped the trinket and the card of my ex-doctor friend in Hazel Park inside and scribbled Iris' name—I'd never found our her last—and the address of Beryl Garnet's place on John R on the envelope and stamped it and consigned it to the first mailbox I came to.

It didn't remove the taint, but it made me feel a little better.

28

I T WAS LATE AFTERNOON. I was fresh from four hours'
sleep, a bath, a shave, and a meal, and sitting in my car
parked illegally on Watson near the Woodward crossing
with my Nikon on the seat beside me, watching the front of
the grindhouse opposite.

I had begun to wonder if George Gibson was an honest
man. For three weeks I'd been watching his movements and
had yet to catch him without his canes or doing anything
that a man with partial paralysis shouldn't be able to do. If
he was playing it straight on this one, it was just possible
that everyone had him pegged as a crook when all he was
was accident prone. If that was the case I had some cele-
brating to do, because I'd succeeded where Diogenes had
failed.

I had both evening papers with me. The solution of the
Freeman Shanks murder made Page One in both. The *Free
Press* carried mug shots of Jerry and Hubert Darling taken
in 1972 when they were sent up for six years after the Feds
broke up an auto theft ring they were running in Georgia,
and said that a service station attendant in Kentucky had
identified them when they bought gas just below the Ohio
border this morning. They were believed to be in possession
of a couple of hundred thousand dollars that was never recovered when they were arrested on the theft charge. The
News ran a picture of Alderdyce and Proust scowling at a

gray metal canister said to contain the incriminating film in the Shanks case. It was probably a prop brought along by the photographer while the real article was in the lab. There was a late bulletin in that paper claiming that the Darlings had been picked up in Tennessee, but the radio news said that the pair turned out to be Toronto business partners motoring to Florida on vacation who were released after their stories had been verified. Kramer's killing got three paragraphs on Page Six of the *News* but missed the first section entirely in the *Free Press*, rating only a caption beneath a picture of the abandoned Nova on page Two of the second. Neither story made any connection between him and Shanks, and although both mentioned that two suspects were in custody no names were given. Lee Q. Story was identified in the *News* as the "proprietor of an East Side novelty shop" and in the *Free Press*, without the Q, as a "reputed dealer in underground literature." In each case he got a paragraph buried so far down in the Shanks piece it was jumped to another page. The trailer park manager got zilch.

The rush hour had passed its peak when Gibson came out the front door supported on his canes and started pulling himself south on Woodward. I yawned and waited for him to get out of sight so I could go home.

He had started across Watson with the light when one of his canes slipped on a ridge of ice at the curb and he fell hard on his hip. I started to get out, then forced myself back into the seat and pulled the door shut. My instincts were tingling.

No one came forward to help him. He rolled over slowly, got one cane under him and used it to support himself as he climbed painfully to his feet. He didn't appear to have suffered any serious damage. Quite the contrary, as a matter of fact.

The other cane had scooted out of his reach down the gutter. He got up, looked around, thrust its mate under his left arm, walked over, and stooped to pick up its errant mate. I used up a roll of film on him and went home to fill out my report and get drunk.

MOTOR CITY BLUE:

A WORD AFTER

by

Loren D. Estleman

MOTOR CITY BLUE HAS everything.
I say that truthfully and in all modesty; but first I must digress.

When I was a boy, one of the first generation to grow up with television, I formed a lifetime attachment to the old movies that appeared in the afternoons, evenings, and—interspersed among commercial spots for storm doors, used cars, and vegetable slicers—late at night. Creaky old horror movies and Three Stooges two-reelers caught my attention early—I was no prodigy—but soon I became attracted to crime films and detective stories of a certain type, filled with harsh male faces scowling in the shadow of wide-brimmed fedoras, feral female faces with cigarette holders protruding from between painted lips, big square automatics in fists that seemed to be made to grip their checked handles, and long cars with bug-eye headlamps squealing their tires down medieval alleys wet with rain, depositing bodies rolling into gutters like kids getting rid of their empties before returning to the parental home. Sigmund Freud may contend that these claustrophobic images represent a yearning to reverse directions up the birth canal, but if so the womb seems a pretty scary place, particularly for a youngster who was afraid of the dark.

Whatever the reasons, whatever it says about me, I liked *film noir* then and I like it even more now. At the time, that

Frenchified term was new, and had spread no more widely from the site of its coinage than the white wines of Bordeaux; indeed, I would not become familiar with it until college, long after my preference had become as much a part of me as the cowboy boots I still wear with everything. Around that same time I discovered the sources of those films and of their inspiration: the hardboiled American detective novels of Dashiell Hammett, Raymond Chandler, and their savage illegitimate children: Jim Thompson, David Goodis, and Mickey Spillane.

I had by this time decided to become a writer. Since just what kind of writer I wanted to be was still up in the air, I was willing to give everything a try. Accordingly, I wrote and sent out rip-roaring gangster yarns, science-fiction stories filled with gelatinous purple creatures and stainless-steel spaceships, cowboy potboilers, even confession stories. Had all this youthful activity taken place during the Thirties, Forties, and Fifties, when the pulp magazines that published these types of fiction flourished, I might have known a brilliant early success. As it was, I began and ended most of my submissions with *Argosy* magazine, which as the last of the pulps was still wheezing its geriatric way to dusty death through the late 1960s and early 1970s, but was by no means desperate enough to accept the purple fulminations of a teenage Michigan farm boy.

I persisted, convinced of my genius; which is the best argument in favor of starting very young. Finally, at the age of twenty-three, I placed my first novel (actually my third, but you don't count unpublished work), a rather stylish 60,000-worder based on the scarlet career of Wilbur Underhill, one of our first Public Enemies No. 1, who died in a bloody shootout with federal agents in Shawnee, Oklahoma, in 1933. Major Books, a small California paperback publisher, brought it out in April 1976, under the ex-ecrable title *The Oklahoma Punk*. I still hate that title (mine was *Twister*; and look how much money the motion picture that stole that title made), but I remain fond of the book, which launched me on my incarnadine career.

Although I tried my hand at the puzzle-type mystery of the Agatha Christie school, I had not the right-brain devel-opment necessary to keep track of such things as alibis, timetables, red herrings, and all the rest of the equipment writers require to stay ahead of the kind of reader who tracks a plot with notes and diagrams. (To this day, I'm a complete bust at figuring out the mysteries of even the sec-ond rank of artists in this school; which may be why I enjoy reading them so much.) It fell, therefore, that I should con-centrate on the kind of mystery that succeeds as a story, quite apart from whodunit and what is revealed in the final chapter.

In 1974–the year I graduated college–*Chinatown* ap-peared in theaters. Directed by Roman Polanski, written by Robert Towne, and starring Jack Nicholson, this period de-tective film singlehandedly revived the *noir* tradition that had died with the 1950s, establishing the neo-*noir* school of filmmaking that is still with us after a quarter-century, and reviving interest in the works of Hammett, Chandler, Ross Macdonald, and all the other hardboiled writers who did as much as Ernest Hemingway and F. Scott Fitzgerald to create a modern American literature independent of Eu-rope's. A raft of similar films followed *Chinatown*, some worthy, some shabby rip-offs by the same kind of hack who had ridden the leaders' coattails when the pulps were pop-ular. One of the former, in 1975, was *Farewell, My Lovely*.

This picture, written by David Zelag Goodman, was based on the novel by Raymond Chandler, set in the period of the 1940s in which it was written, and starred Robert Mitchum as the world-weary private detective Philip Marlowe. Director Dick Richards accurately and painstakingly reconstructed wartime L.A. to tell a haunting story of love, betrayal, blackmail, and murder, abetted by David Shire's bluesy, sax-heavy score. Theatergoing was a financial impossibility then, when I was struggling to make ends meet as a freelance writer, and so I did not see the film until several years later when it appeared on network television. Despite the inevitable p.c. editing and commercial interruptions (this, after all, was the format in which all the great classic films had been introduced to me), I was hooked, and determined to draw the same reaction from my readers.

Motor City Blue was the result. At the time, I was anything but certain that this first adventure for Amos Walker would not also be the last. The Eighties were beginning. Ross Macdonald was still alive, but had not published a Lew Archer private detective novel since *The Blue Hammer* in 1976. John D. MacDonald was still writing Travis McGee, but that character, who referred to himself as a "salvage consultant," had devolved from his origins as a hardboiled dick of the old school into a cartoony toxic avenger, more reminiscent of Batman than Sam Spade. True, Arthur Lyons was beginning his Marlovian series featuring Jacob Asch, and Robert B. Parker had launched Spenser, but neither writer had yet found a broad audience. The private eye of fiction appeared to be moribund. Since I had no idea whether *Motor City Blue* would have a sequel, much less find a publisher, I put everything that I liked from the movie and its literary and cinematic inspirations into the book, from the anachronistic fedora to the bottle in the desk (Scotch appeared to be the depressant of choice, from my research) to the ubiquitous cigarette to the *femme fatale* whose greed and deviant behavior put the worst in men to shame. The story is part affectionate genre send-up, part social commentary, part serious mystery; and I suppose it's my own fault, given the low-key mood lighting of its scenes and the down-and-dirty melancholy theme, that so many critics and readers continue to refer to the title as *Motor City Blues*.

From the outset it looked as if I was right to put in so much and thus get the thing out of my system, because the manuscript was met with a collective yawn on the part of the first two publishers who saw it. Cathleen Jordan, my editor at Doubleday for *Sherlock Holmes Vs. Dracula* and *Dr. Jekyll and Mr. Holmes*, asked me to set the book aside and think about doing another mystery set against the backdrop of Victorian London. (In her present incarnation as editor-in-chief of *Alfred Hitchcock's Mystery Magazine*, she has cheerfully made up for this decision by publishing several Amos Walker short stories.) An editor at another house returned the script with an apologetic note that the book would find the marketplace too tough.

What they did not recognize—and what I barely understood myself—was that the post-Vietnam, post-Watergate era of American disillusionment that was about to greet *Motor City Blue* was an almost identical match with the epoch of Prohibition and Depression that gave birth to the fictional private eye sixty years before. It's no great leap from losing faith in the cop-on-the-beat to losing trust in one's president, and there's nothing very profound in the observation that a society that has turned away from its corrupt organizations might yearn for a lone hero who represents the best of its revolutionary ideals; myth though he may be.

Motor City Blue was published in hardcover by Houghton Mifflin in the fall of 1980. It would be a lie to say the book was an immediate success. Three years would elapse before it found a publisher who would reissue it in paperback, in a typo-filled edition by Pinnacle Books, which was then Poverty Row, and there would be ten books in the series before a publisher agreed to commit to more than one title at a time, with an option on the next. But Amos Walker remains alive and well twenty years after his inception, long after series that made more money and enjoyed wider fame went to the elephant's graveyard of the "Bestsellers of Yesteryear" bin in used bookstores.

Why?

Don't know.

But nobody ever got arrested for guessing.

Walker is a dinosaur, and he knows it. There's nothing less amusing to an audience, particularly an American one, than a hero who takes himself seriously. This is why old-movie buffs like me sneer at James Cagney's self-righteous brother in *Public Enemy*, preferring the smiling bravura of gangster Cagney, and why bad girl figure skater Tonya Harding has a bigger fan club than the saccharine Nancy Kerrigan. History has shown that people who Feel Your Pain are usually less worthy of our regard than those who inflict it upon the right people. Protagonists like Walker make fun of themselves before they ridicule others and before they can be made sport of by them. Notwithstanding this relentless anti-narcissism, they are courageous and honest, and revere these virtues too deeply to parade them around or even acknowledge the fact that they exist. Code heroes who must haul out their code like a hiker consulting his compass every five minutes are suspect. The tenets of behavior should come as second nature, without need of advertisement or reminder. In fact, they perish from overexposure.

One cannot overestimate the importance of the Detroit

setting to Amos Walker's longevity. The city can certainly survive without him—it's survived worse, including twenty years of corruption at the highest level—but I am convinced that Walker would not last twenty pages without the RenCen and Ford Rouge and the auto-money palaces of Grosse Pointe and drive-by shootings on Erskine. Critics warmed to the series from the start for its "fresh" exteriors (the city will observe its tricentennial in 2001), and reader mail ran 100 percent positive on the books' non-dependence on the worn-out streets of New York, L.A., San Francisco, and Chicago. To this day, I enjoy a loyal support group consisting of editors, reviewers, and other industry-related professionals whose own Detroit origins prompted them to recommend the series to others. At the time I was researching *Motor City Blue*, some acquaintances attempted to discourage me from writing about such an unpopular place, with some justification: Elmore Leonard was then the only major writer using Detroit for his backgrounds, and even he would have to move his characters to Miami and California before he entered the national bestseller lists.

In the years since, Detroit, with its raw reputation and distinctive blue-collar personality, has become a popular and familiar setting for crime novels and action movies. I have had many opportunities to be thankful that I grew up in its shadow. Concurrently, within two years of Walker's debut, the landscape of American detective literature was crowded with half a hundred private eye series based in cities across the continent and as far away as Australia; proving out my suspicion that the social climate was ready for the revival of the homegrown phenomenon of the Hero for Hire.

For that is what Amos Walker is: a reasonably intelligent brain hooked up to a sympathetic nature, with the strength and courage necessary to maintain the right, available for a nominal day rate and modest expenses. I do not pretend he has anything in common with the private detective of reality, a practical professional who is too busy making his living to squeeze a holy crusade onto his timesheet. Would that he could; but then there would be no need for Amos Walker, or for any kind of fiction at all, for that matter. Fiction must be better than life or it has no reason to exist.

Here, then, once again and for the first time, are Walker, gangster Ben Morningstar, Lieutenant John Alderdyce, the elusive Marla Bernstein, pornographer Lee Q. Story, Barry Stackpole, Jerry and Hubert Darling, military spooks Vespers and Spain, Beryl Garnet, the huggable madam, and the enigmatic Iris; a disparate group, and only a fraction of *Motor City Blue*'s Russian novel-like cast. I hope, since you have gotten this far, that you have found that the book has everything. In my ignorance, that's what I intended.